An Upside Down Novel

THE EFFECT OF CASIMIR

TODD G. SIMPSON

Other Upside Down books:

Tilt
Turn
Twist

© 2023 Todd G. Simpson

To Anar
As always, my inspiration.

LHC

The victim was lying on a table, the reason for death painfully obvious. A circular section had been carved out, starting on his head, above the left temple, continuing through the neck, progressing diagonally through the torso, and finally exiting at the right hip. That entire cylinder of flesh, about five centimeters in diameter, had been cleanly removed and was nowhere to be seen.

Inspector Jean Falot, contorting his long frame, could see straight through the victim, the hole being impossibly clean and straight, almost otherworldly. It was as if a laser had carved it out, except that there were no signs of heat; no cauterization. An impossibly long scalpel? Not even that could have created such a perfect section. JF had no idea what type of weapon could produce such a wound.

Racheal, with an unnecessary warning, cautioned him against touching anything. "I'm not done recording," she advised. JF moved back to grant Racheal space to complete her meticulous documentation. With a full array of equipment, she would capture every detail, using various wavelengths and biological sensors, giving them the ability to analyze the scene, from every angle later on.

Taking further stock of the surroundings JF saw four semicircular stations surrounding the table, symmetrically laid out, and each station piled high with antiquated computer screens. None of the screens displayed any signs of activity, which was to be expected; they were centuries old. However, their impeccable condition was strange. Given their age, they should have borne the wear of time, been covered in dust, or been subjected to vandalism. But they were pristine as if a cadre of technicians had vacated their posts mere hours ago, leaving behind an immaculate workspace for the next shift.

Turning his attention back to the corpse, JF tried to ignore the gaping hole in order to take in the rest of the body. The victim, a middle-aged man of average appearance, was reasonably fit and had stood about one meter eight. His remaining eye, a piercing green, stared fixedly at the ceiling. Clad in loose pants and a short-sleeved shirt, devoid of visible piercings or tattoos, he had no obvious augmentations. There was nothing remarkable about him, other than his recently acquired borehole. Under ordinary circumstances, JF wouldn't have given the guy a second glance.

"Damn," JF muttered under his breath as another person entered the room. To label her a 'person' wasn't an accurate description, he reminded himself. Titanic Incorporated had sent their representative, Ayaka, to scope out the situation. He shouldn't have been surprised that Titanic had been notified of the death, but he was still thrown off by how fast they must have moved to get Ayaka here only moments after he had arrived.

"Hey," he waved vaguely at her. They'd worked together a few times —Titanic was always dabbling in police business, and there was nothing he could do about it. Ayaka, however, was an anomaly; a mechanical being, the sole one of her kind on Earth, owing her presence to the formidable political influence and deep pockets of Titanic. Without their backing, she'd have been dismantled and recycled long ago, as all robots should be. Yet here she stood, exuding a cocky but friendly demeanor, relaxed and comfortable in her alluring form, her every aspect engineered to captivate and sway the human mind... or so it seemed to him.

Peculiarly, she bestowed a measure of importance on him, making him an intriguing figure when he regaled family and friends with stories about her. Everyone had seen the mersive covering Ayaka's life, and everyone loved to hear about the real thing, versus the actress who'd played her. He'd answered untold questions about her over dinner or drinks.

"JF," Ayaka replied with a beaming smile. "Nice to see you. I trust all is well?" Her tone exuded civility and sophistication, every facet of her being designed to soothe and influence. Her pristine attire, impeccable hair, and disconcertingly human-like eyes, radiating intense interest and intelligence, engendered an immediate impact. Were she composed of flesh and blood, rather than silicon and rubber, Jean would have tried to apply his charm and explored where it might lead. His rational mind, however, incessantly reminded him that Ayaka's very design was intended to elicit such responses. The war between his head and his heart played out every time he met her.

Racheal gave an involuntary jolt as she retrieved Ayaka's credentials. Ayaka's existence, and likeness, were known to her from briefings and news coverage, as well as the mersive, but Racheal couldn't suppress a grimace, and a short physical retreat; a deep-seated bias, almost instinct, that most humans had developed towards mech.

"You must be Racheal," Akaya said, ignoring Racheals' obvious aversion. "It's great to meet you; I'm Ayaka Turnbuilt." She held out her hand in the age-old greeting, and Racheal, driven by protocol and experience, automatically accepted and shook Ayaka's hand lightly. "What have we here?" Ayaka inquired, redirecting Racheal's attention to the lifeless form on the long table—a strategic maneuver that JF suspected had been calculated to put Racheal at ease.

Gesturing towards the body, Racheal replied, her words mostly directed at JF, "You can look around now. I've captured everything we need." JF stepped forward for a closer examination, noting that Ayaka, before joining him at the body, first circled the table and fully scrutinized the surrounding area. The extent of Ayaka's capabilities remained a mystery; perhaps she was recording the scene with even greater precision than Racheal's equipment allowed.

"Interesting," Ayaka commented, after bending over to look directly through the hole in the body, as JF had earlier. She looked back at Racheal. "Any theories?"

"It would be speculation," Racheal responded, shaking her head. "I haven't seen anything like this before."

"Body must've been moved," JF offered his perspective. "There's no hint of struggle, no blood, no traces of the missing flesh, no….nothing," he trailed off, gesturing around. Other than the body, the room was pristine. He was bewildered.

"I don't think the body could have been moved," Racheal responded. "Look at that *wound*," she emphasized the word to highlight its inadequacy, "it's so flawless that any movement of the body would have disrupted it." JF took another look. The hole was truly immaculate. Closing one eye, and gazing through its entire length, he was unable to discern any imperfections. Surely the flesh should sag in the middle, or there should be entrails hanging within. JF restrained himself from putting a couple of fingers in, just to see if it was being held in its perfect shape by some invisible structure; Racheal's imaging would have detected anything like that.

"The room could've been cleaned afterward?" Akaya posited. "Perhaps the perpetrator killed him here and then meticulously eliminated all traces?" JF could see where her mind—assuming she had one—was going. The spotless state of the table and floor suggested they had been scrubbed after the body was deposited.

"Ya, I thought of that," Racheal was more relaxed now that she was talking business, "but even cleaning leaves signs, and I don't think this room was sanitized that recently. It appears as though this place has been this clean for a while."

"Oh?" JF inquired, seeking further details.

"There would be water or chemical residue. Some traces of bleach molecules still in the air. There would be some sign of activity. The only real signs of activity are foot traffic,", she said, noting a few minor scuff marks, "and those are probably from us." JF glanced at Ayaka to see what she thought of all that. Her scans may have given different indications, but she simply nodded her head in agreement. Didn't mean she agreed, of course; just meant that agreeing right now fit her agenda, whatever that was.

"So," Ayaka summarized. "He couldn't have been killed here because the place is too clean, and he couldn't have been moved here after dying, as that would have disturbed the wound. Bit of a quandary." She paused, allowing the conundrum to settle. "Do we know who he was?"

JF fought the urge to scoff. He was certain that Titanic knew the man's identity and Ayaka's presence was motivated by that. Nonetheless, he played along, engaging in the charade. "Victor Alfred Rescovich, professor emeritus at Sheffield University on Ten. A physicist by trade. Quantum foam."

"And why was he here?" Ayaka gestured around the room.

"Beats me," JF replied, casting another glance around the room. The table on which Victor lay sprawled was oval in shape and served as the focal point for the symmetrical space. Each quadrant housed a semi-circular desk area; looking closely he saw faded labels affixed to the partitions. Clockwise, starting to his left, they read 'PS Booster,' 'TI,' 'LHC,' and 'SPS.'

"What is this place, anyway?" Racheal inquired. "It took me ages to get here, and I had to go through multiple security checkpoints." JF had encountered the same obstacles, a highly irregular occurrence. They were, however, two levels deeper than he'd ever ventured before, and he knew these areas were off-limits without special permission. But, he had no answer for Racheal on this specific site.

"This was the control room for the Large Hadron Collider, a facility for physics experimentation centuries ago," Ayaka supplied. Of course, she possessed that knowledge. JF immediately made the connection to the label 'LHC' on the partition to his left, but beyond that, Ayaka's statement held little meaning for him.

"Ah," Racheal nodded, connecting the dots between a dead physics professor and an ancient physics installation. "Why would he," she gestured towards the lifeless body, "need access to technology that's centuries old?"

"Another valid question," JF interjected, his mind teeming with his own list of inquiries. Who'd reported the death? Why had he, out of all the officers in the Lower Police Force, been tasked with the investigation? What was Ayaka's true purpose here? However, he restrained himself from speculating on anything while Ayaka was present. He harbored a deep-seated mistrust of Titanic—a behemoth too colossal and potent, often evading accountability for their actions. "We can delve deeper into this back at the office," he hinted to Racheal, cautioning her to be guarded.

"Sure," she replied, seeming to understand. "Let me pack up my gear, then we can get out of here. We'll also need to inform the morgue to pick this guy up, assuming they have access to get here…" She left it hanging, hoping JF would shoulder that responsibility.

"I'll look after it," JF replied. Anything to get finished up. Ayaka made him anxious.

"Mind if I look around a bit more?" Ayaka asked.

"Would it make a difference if I said 'no'?"

"I don't think we're at cross purposes here," she replied, sidestepping his passive-aggressive response. "I was simply asked to come down and see if I could assist in unraveling what happened. Nothing more."

Right, JF thought. As if Titanic didn't have its own agenda here. It wasn't even worth arguing over. "Whatever. Look around as much as you want. But don't mess with anything; we may need to rescan the room once we review the captures we have."

"Understood," Ayaka acknowledged before striding towards the far corner of the room, her gaze sweeping methodically from side to side. One might have expected her movements to appear mechanical and artificial, but JF begrudgingly admitted that she exuded an entirely human aura. And undeniably alluring, to top it off. He reflected again on how Ayaka so easily outshone the actress who'd portrayed her in the Tilt mersive. JF shook his head, assisted Racheal in stowing away their equipment, and departed without casting another glance in Ayaka's direction; he didn't want to give her the satisfaction of thinking he was interested in what she was up to.

BRILL

Ayaka already knew, deep down, what had killed Rescovich; she'd seen that beyond-perfect five-centimeter diameter hole before and knew the instrument that caused it could slice cleanly through metal, let alone flesh. So, she was relieved when JF and Racheal finally left through the same double doors where she'd entered, on their way back to the transit station. It gave her space and time to think.

As they were exiting, she couldn't help analyzing them. Having been on Earth for several months, she was quite familiar with the diversity of biological forms that humans chose to roam around in. Still, she was amazed at how people expressed themselves through their choices; how much they exposed with their presentation layers.

JF, possessing a commanding stature and a sinewy frame, seemed purposefully crafted to emanate confidence and unwavering determination. His sharply defined features, accentuated by steely gray eyes, conveyed astuteness and perceptiveness, while his arched eyebrows hinted at a healthy dose of skepticism and caution. Clad in attire chosen to match his role as an investigator, his dark hues and clean lines completed the portrait of a pensive inspector. Ayaka had crossed paths with JF on multiple occasions and deemed him to be a man of integrity and dependability, one who approached his duties with the gravity they deserved.

Racheal, while equally committed to her profession, exuded an entirely different energy, one of nerdy enthusiasm. Petite and agile, she moved with purpose and confidence, albeit lacking a certain elegance. Her hazel eyes sparkled with a discernible joy when adjusting her gear or engrossed in the glow of a screen. Her attire leaned towards the casual, adorned with a logo that hinted at her affinity for science fiction mersives.

Ayaka recognized that, unlike herself, these humans didn't consciously orchestrate every aspect of their existence. Their subconscious played a significant role in guiding their behavior, an intricate dance of nature and nurture. She, on the other hand, had spent many years fine-tuning her understanding, and mimicry, of human behaviors and responses, and had built up complex algorithms for every situation. Given all the subtleties involved, she had a strong appreciation for the complexity that was baked into human DNA.

Now, alone in the control center, Ayaka accelerated her survey of the space, no longer compelled to maintain a full facade of humanity. While she was certain she knew what had cored Rescovich, there was still the mystery of how he'd ended up here. She was inclined to agree with Racheal: Rescovich had not met his demise within these walls.

As she engaged in the analysis, Ayaka allowed herself a moment of awe, contemplating the significance of where she was standing. Centuries ago this very site had been the pulsing heart of human physics research. Nestled on the border of what were once known as France and Switzerland, the Large Hadron Collider had stood as a testament to scientific audacity and insatiable human curiosity. Preceding the building of the first colossal Titanic vessels, the LHC had been an emblem of unparalleled engineering prowess, a beacon that illuminated the frontiers of human knowledge.

The architectural grandeur of the LHC would have been a marvel to behold. Its sprawling labyrinthine network of underground tunnels, one spanning nearly twenty-seven kilometers in circumference, bore witness to an amazing track record of scientific discovery. Within these subterranean passages, physicists had tested the very fabric of reality. Accelerated to velocities verging on the speed of light, particles were hurtled towards each other, ultimately meeting head-on and separating into their component parts. It was a dance of the infinitesimally small, where the building blocks of the universe had been probed and measured.

At the heart of the system lay an ensemble of superconducting magnets, veritable works of art in their precision and elegance. Meticulously crafted and cooled to temperatures mere fractions of a kelvin, these magnets possessed an innate mastery over the particles' trajectories. With a graceful finesse, they ensured the paths of the particles intersected at precisely the right locations.

Scattered throughout the sprawling tunnels were colossal detectors, an even further testament to human ingenuity. These behemoths were finely tuned to capture the delicate whispers of the particle collisions, capturing the intricate tapestry of energy and matter. They bore witness to the fleeting destruction, meticulously recording every detail.

Cherise Pilipatri, the long-deceased founder of Titanic, had worked right here. Ayaka could imagine her, leaning over the shoulder of a colleague, staring intently at one of the now defunct screens. Cherise had been a theoretical physicist intent on proving her theories about the quantum world; she had designed some of the most exotic experiments the LHC had ever run. A leading member of the 'quantum foam believers', she was equally respected and ridiculed by her colleagues. Of course, she'd had the last laugh; something she'd discovered here had led her down a unique path of discovery resulting in the quantum foam drive. The QFD enabled the building of the Titanic ships and drastically accelerated the human diaspora.

The Titanic ships were huge spacefaring cubes that moved through space by tweaking quantum foam probabilities; the ultimate proof of her equations. Titanic Inc. still controlled the intellectual property, and had become the largest corporation in human history; several orders of magnitude larger than the closest competitor.

Given that perspective, the room itself was less than inspiring; almost like the builders had put all their energy into the machines, and had none left for the areas where people would work. No vaulted ceilings or large windows. No space for relaxation or contemplation. More like the bowels of a factory. Ayaka had to grin; it was like where she had started, on Tilt. Everything was functional; there was no space for aesthetics. Back then she may not have even noticed the lack of adornment, the ignoring of comfort. Today, though, it was obvious to her.

She imagined hundreds of humans crowded into this space, huddled over their ancient displays, looking for hints to prove their theories. They'd been willing to give up a lot of creature comforts to focus so highly on something that inspired them. They had been, almost, robotic in their determination.

Ayaka refocused on the task at hand. Stepping in close to the central table, she bent over Rescovich again and scrutinized the intricate edges of the perforation that had been carved through him. The hole bore the marks of uncanny precision. Starting from the top of the head, it had inscribed its path, carving away a substantial portion of his frontal lobe, the entirety of the left eye socket, and a fragment of the cheekbone below. With remarkable precision, it hollowed out the neck, before continuing through the central organs. Aligning herself carefully, Ayaka confirmed the flawlessly circular nature of the wound. If the head was the point of entry, then the object or force responsible must have struck the just here, steadily carving out a three-quarter moon section until reaching the eye socket. It then transitioned into a narrower cross-section as it traveled through the eye socket before transforming into a complete circular excision as it breached the cheekbone. Such a trajectory should have left behind sagging flesh and jagged bone, signs of the struggle between the weapon and the violated anatomy. The force of penetrating the head should have pulled the skin tight and caused a displacement of the skull, dragging it forward with friction, and distorting the wound until it evolved into a fully round puncture. Alternatively, if the head was the exit point, the flesh and bone should have been pulled out in the opposite direction, extricated as the projectile made its escape. Yet, neither scenario held. The excision showed no sign of entry or exit; it was flawless.

Ayaka sighed, her worst suspicion becoming not only plausible but perhaps inescapable. The cut was just as clean as the one she'd seen years ago, and light years away. She'd fervently hoped to never see another such hole, and yet here it was. Rescovich's field of expertise only reinforced her unsettling conclusion; if anyone were to meet their demise in such a calculated manner, it would undoubtedly be a theoretical physicist.

As she was ruminating on this sombre thought she heard a noise in the corridor. Quickly she assumed a human pose. A small unimposing man looked around the door. He was completely bald, with a strange marking on his head. Some sort of tattoo, Ayaka assumed, although not one she could identify. Seeing her, he let out a small yelp and left quickly. Ayaka surged forward, her lithe form propelled with agility surpassing that of even the most accomplished athletes. She didn't want him to get away.

"Halt!" Ayaka's voice reverberated down the corridor, commanding attention and triggering a primal response in the man a few steps ahead. His very being compelled him to freeze, his ancient evolutionary mechanisms responding to the authoritative timbre of her words. Turning to face her, his trembling form betrayed the profound fear that gripped him.

"Whoa," Ayaka murmured, in a soothing voice designed to project confidence without menace. "I just want to talk; ask a few questions." He started to retreat, clearly terror-stricken. Years of interfacing with humans had equipped Ayaka with a repertoire of interactions tailored to many circumstances, including the current one. Even though this man appeared unaware of her true nature, a familiar script unfolded. Hearing her soothing tone, his body language relaxed, and the instinctive urge to flee subsided.

"What's your name?" Ayaka asked, softly.

"Brill," came the reply, deeply accented and laden with trepidation.

"Do you work here?" Ayaka had noticed his clothing, which seemed more like a uniform rather than personal attire. The question reignited his fear, prompting him to turn and flee again. Ayaka allowed him to disappear from her sight before pursuing him at an equal pace, employing heat signatures and other clues to navigate the labyrinthine network of hallways and rooms surrounding the control center. After a considerable duration, she confronted a locked door through which Brill had exited. Testing it confirmed it was locked. Though she possessed the power to forcibly breach it, she felt she'd learned enough for the time being. People inhabited these depths—a realization that contradicted official records and established beliefs regarding the uninhabited lower strata of Earth. As there was nothing of value down here, and many risks, why would anyone be here? And yet Brill was a creature of this space, and she suspected he wasn't alone. It explained how clean the area was.

She retraced her steps to the control room, mapping the path for future reference. Brill had been checking in on the body; he was involved somehow. He must've been fooled when JF and Racheal left and assumed the room was empty. Thus his fear when he realized someone else was still there.

And there was something else. During their encounter, Brill had been clutching a set of small metallic objects connected by a ring, held openly in his hand. Although he'd made no attempt to conceal them, his nervous glances at the items—four times in total—prompted Ayaka to scrutinize them closely. Running numerous algorithms and routines, she found the answer. She moved quickly to the control desk of the Large Hadron Collider, the workstation labeled LHC, passing the body still resting on the table. Among the ancient screens was something that looked even older. A set of switches and locks as well as rows of faded yellow, red, and green buttons, all mounted on a large metal box. The keys that Brill had been holding would fit the locks on this console. There was nothing in the history of the LHC that Ayaka could find to tell her why these switches and keys existed, but now they had become a part of her calculus.

LOWER POLICE HQ

JF and Racheal didn't speak as they made their way back from the Large Hadron Collider to LoPo's headquarters, each lost in thought. The route they followed was a convoluted one, ascending eight levels and spanning over a hundred kilometers horizontally. In the bygone days when the LHC hummed with activity, there had been no upper layers built upon the Earth's surface. The colossal collider had stood at what was considered "ground level," with certain of its tunnels delving even deeper into the Earth's depths.

As, over the centuries, layers were added above the LHC, the Geneva airport had been repurposed as a transit hub, a focal point for vertical travel between the layers. While the Geneva terminal continued to extend upwards it also retained connectivity to the lower realms, although anything below the third layer had long since become off-limits without a permit.

On their descent, both JF and Racheal had employed the Geneva tubes, well-prepared with headlamps to aid them on the trek from the lowest recesses of the terminal to the scene of the crime. Layer zero was a remnant of a forgotten era, abandoned and forlorn, plagued by scarce light and little water. Their passage towards the control room had brought them face to face with the grimmest aspects of this desolation, where long stretches of the route were shrouded in absolute darkness. Yet, even with these challenges, the most time-consuming portion of their journey was in navigating the security boundaries—a painful and meticulous process that proved just as exasperating when departing from layer zero as it had been when entering it.

For JF, this marked his first visit to level zero, a place he'd never anticipated setting foot in, despite LoPo's jurisdiction extending to everything below the eighth layer. Gazing upon the dilapidated infrastructure and the debris that littered every corner, he respected the wisdom behind the restrictions imposed upon the third and lower layers. The crumbling edifices and abandoned detritus made the area treacherous. After numerous incidents of individuals perishing—or worse, requiring expensive rescue operations—a consensus had been reached, and the layers had been secured and restricted. Of course, such restrictions only served to pique the interest of history aficionados and scholars, creating a clamor for permits that granted access to the most dangerous areas. Acquiring these permits was no simple matter; negotiations spanned months, and the accompanying price tag was far from modest. Rescovich would have left a paper trail. It also made Ayaka's sudden appearance all the more vexing. JF and Racheal, owing to their professional roles, could secure permits within seconds, yet Ayaka's swift permitting must have cost Titanic some serious cash. They must have an unusually intense interest, in this case, to have expedited her clearance so quickly.

When they reached LoPo headquarters, JF motioned for Racheal to join him in one of the modest conference rooms. With a quick gesture, she projected the holo of the scene, allowing them to look at it in higher resolution and wider frequencies than their eyes would naturally capture.

"What do you make of it?" JF asked her, with anticipation.

"I don't make anything of it," she replied, exasperated. "I've been thinking it through all the way back, and it simply makes no sense. He couldn't have been killed there, and he couldn't have been moved. Yet one of those must have happened…I just can't fathom how."

"Killed? So, you're sure it's a murder....couldn't it be a suicide or an accident or something?"

Her response was resolute. "No, it's murder," she said with conviction.

"How can you be sure?"

"Look," she pointed at the hole near the victim's eye. "I did a background check on Rescovich; he had an expensive sense extender in his left eye and a life recorder implanted just above his right hip. The hole—I'm not quite sure what to call it—took out both devices in their entirety. That can't be a coincidence."

That was compelling; JF had to agree that the hole was likely intentional, taking out both devices. It didn't rule out suicide completely, but it made an accidental death less likely. It wasn't worth arguing about right now; if Racheal was convinced it was a murder, then he let her run with that. "Did he back up his life recorder?"

"Don't know yet, but we'll check," she replied. "But, even so, it would be encrypted, and we have no way of getting the keys now that he's gone."

"Very well. So we're stumped on the method; no idea what caused that gash… the hole… Maybe we should focus on motive and opportunity?"

"Before we go there I'd like to share the scene recording with a few others, and see if they have ideas on the method?" Racheal proposed, fully aware of the struggle LoPo always had between effective collaboration and respecting privacy concerns; a struggle that often led to internal disputes and legal entanglements. Even dead people had privacy rights nowadays, in case there was an estate involved or to protect against future data claims.

"I understand he was married?" JF asked, and Racheal confirmed with a nod. "Let's get his wife's permission to share; will take us a bit longer, but limits our legal exposure."

"All right," Racheal agreed, reluctantly. This was the most interesting case she'd ever worked on, and bureaucratic red tape was going to be frustrating.

"We need to speak to her regardless," JF added. "If we can do that soon we can just ask her for permission. Be faster than a bunch of paperwork." For simple permissions like this one a verbal acknowledgment, properly recorded, would suffice. It was one of the small hard-won exceptions the force had managed to get approved.

"I'll get on it," Racheal affirmed. "Leave this up?" she gestured at the holo.

"Yes, let me sit here for a bit; I'll turn it off before I go." Racheal nodded and headed for the door, focused on tracking down Rescovich's wife.

JF settled back in a chair and simply looked at the scene. In his mind, he was already compiling a list of people to talk to. It was a growing list. Anyone with a permit to be in that area of level zero in the last 24 hours. Colleagues at the University. The wife. Titanic Inc.—who had inserted themselves into the list at a higher priority by sending Ayaka— and anyone who was providing funding for Rescovich's work.

Remembering that he'd previously committed to arranging the retrieval of the body from the morgue, JF dedicated a few minutes to coordinating the necessary personnel and permissions. He forewarned them about navigating the dilapidated passages they would encounter along the way and reminded them to take sufficient lighting.

JF's train of thought was interrupted by a brisk knock on the door, followed by the entrance of his boss, Sergeant Veras Rita. His hand had instinctively reached to disable the holo, but stopped when he recognized who'd entered; Rita would want to see this one.

"Heard you have an interesting one," she commented, settling into a seat. "Give me the quick version."

JF felt at ease with Rita, given they'd worked together for years, and proceeded to bring her up to speed. "We've got a deceased individual deep down on level zero, some sort of defunct physics facility. Racheal's convinced it's a murder. The victim is Victor Rescovich, a physics professor at Sheffield University. There are a couple of peculiarities we've come across. Firstly," he gestured towards the body in the holo and rotated the view to reveal the gaping hole, "there's this. None of the missing tissue, bone, or organs were found nearby. The room where the body was discovered is immaculate."

"Any ideas on what could have done that," Rita asked, leaning forward and looking at the holo intently.

"Not a clue yet. We'll get permission from the widow so that we can share this around a bit to get some ideas." Rita nodded, agreeing with that course of action.

"Second, Ayaka was on the scene only a few minutes after me. Titanic must have some serious interest in this." He watched Rita out of the corner of his eye to see how she reacted; how Titanic influenced his chain of command wasn't clear to him, but the fact that they did was obvious. Did they reach all the way to Rita? She remained inscrutable.

"So, they have a stake in this somehow," she commented. "Given the physics tie-ins, that isn't too surprising. But it's going to take kid gloves to tease it out. I'd be subtle if I was you." JF glanced at her, but she was stoic, simply looking at the holo. He'd have to take that as a general warning, not an indicator that she knew more than she was saying.

"Right, I'll try to be delicate," he smiled a bit, knowing that wasn't his strong suit.

"Next mystery is how the body got there. He couldn't have been killed on the spot, there'd be some sign in the room; a struggle, some tiny bits of blood or guts… something. But, he couldn't have been moved, or that hole would've been messed up.

"And finally, Racheal looked up his history. The wound just happens to have removed both his inserts; one near the eye, and one in the hip."

Rita got it immediately. "So, either those inserts were destroyed along with him, or this method of dissection was meticulously carried out to extract and preserve them intact."

JF respected Rita's astuteness and nodded in agreement.

"All right," Rita said, locking eyes with JF. "Keep me updated on every development. There are numerous angles to this case, and I suspect it's going to turn political. Titanic's involvement is almost a certainty. If those inserts were indeed taken rather than destroyed, I need you to locate and secure them in our custody."

Her request was strikingly specific, indicating that she possessed knowledge she wasn't sharing with him. JF decided to prod further, deliberately pushing back. "Sure, but they'll likely be encrypted, rendering them unreadable to us or anyone else. It doesn't strike me as the highest priority."

Rita met his gaze, returning it with a touch of awkwardness. "Yes, they'll be encrypted. However, if they fall into the wrong hands, there's a possibility they could be hacked. We should have them under our control."

JF raised an eyebrow, sensing there was more to the story. "Just do it," she reiterated, firm in her instructions. JF nodded in acknowledgment. A complex case had just become even more intricate. In addition to unraveling the murder, which he now viewed as such, JF might find himself embroiled in internal politics.

TITANIC INC.

Percival Resbroterion, known universally as Perci, had been the CEO of Titanic Inc. for over half a century. He dismissed the fact that he was a direct descendant of the company's founder, Cherise Pilipatri, as a mere academic detail. However, his critics found it to be a crucial point of attack. Let them complain. Under his stewardship the company had remained the most important entity in human space; a space that was now fifteen lightyears wide that the Titanic Ships had enabled. Before the Titanic, spaceships had expended huge amounts of energy just to reach a tiny fraction of the speed of light. With the proprietary Titanic QFD technology the large ships could instantaneously reach almost half the speed of light with comparatively little energy expended. It was a technology worth protecting, and Titanic did so aggressively, playing both offense and defense.

Perci looked the part. His parents had done a great job of tweaking his height and physique; he was a strong one-meter ninety, with a full head of hair, an aquiline nose, and strong cheekbones. Treatments over the years kept him the biological equivalent of thirty, with the energy and drive to match. He paid particular attention to his dress, which was always business casual with a touch of avant-garde flair; something to invite compliments from those he met.

Most days were filled with leisurely meetings with leaders of industry and government, more focused on petty politics and pet projects than anything strategic. Titanic Inc. had so much momentum and market control that it only required an occasional tweak, rather than serious hands-on involvement. His lieutenants effectively managed the company's operations, but Perci liked to attend meetings so he could interject his particular value; it made him feel needed. He'd perfected the grand hand gestures and deep tone which added gravitas to everything he said.

In the grandest of grand gestures, he'd wrangled getting Ayaka to Earth. The Tilt mersive had highlighted her amazing technological potential, and he had desperately wanted her nearby so that his team could study her. It was one of those symbolic things he could do which no one else could; it deflated the ever-present naysayers who claimed he no longer added any value to the company. If they could decode how she worked, Ayaka might well represent the next major leap forward for the company. Unfortunately, to date, they'd learned almost nothing about her as scans showed very little other than that her behavior was so human as to be disconcerting.

The executive briefing today was more serious than most. The head of the Strategy, Metri Havnock, had raised a red flag. One of the scientists on Titanic's 'most watched list' had died in mysterious circumstances. Metri had dispatched Ayaka to gather data, pulling her off all the other tasks that staff had lined up for her. A heated discussion had ensued, pitting those who thought dispatching Ayaka had been a big mistake—getting Titanic more involved than they needed to be—against those defending Metri's decision. Why else did we have a most watched list, if not to watch carefully? However, even some of her defenders questioned sending the robot; why not one of the regular team? What could justify sending Ayaka?

Perci let the discussion continue longer than usual; there were good arguments and comments on all sides, Metri defending the choice of Ayaka as the 'employee' who came 'packed with sensors that would be useful in a location with limited access'. Tall and imposing, Metri stood up and pounded the table at one point, challenging a colleague who questioned her decision-making.

Perci enjoyed the interplay but eventually interrupted. "This discussion is academic; Ayaka was sent, so we need to deal with it. What do we do next? That's the real question. What do we know of this guy's research? Do we know who targeted him and why? Why was he down there, wherever 'there' is?"

Again, lots of discussion, none of it with answers. "So," Perci looked deliberately around the room. "Go get answers. And get them fast." He turned to Metri, "Where's Ayaka now?"

"She'll be here shortly," Metri answered.

"I want to be in on the debrief," Perci told her. "The rest of you, this is of utmost importance. Get going, and send me everything you learn."

Everyone filed out but at the last minute, Perci grabbed the arm of his head of security. He whispered to her. "Linda, we need to know everything the police know, before they know it. Know what I mean?" She simply nodded; it wasn't the first time she'd heard that request. Linda Sclula was not physically imposing, but she was fierce, an attitude highlighted by her organic neck tattoos, which crawled into new configurations based on how she wanted to project. And she'd never let Perci down; she knew how to be discreet but still get the job done.

While waiting for Ayaka, Perci learned quite a bit. Titanic was not funding Rescovich's research, but not for lack of trying. They tried to fund as many math and physics researchers as they could. Naysayers claimed that Titanic's influence was so wide, and they controlled research so effectively, that they were solely responsible for the lack of impactful ideas which came out of the community; it was in Titanic's best interest to curtail breakthroughs. Perci agreed with, and was happy with, that assessment, although he'd never admit that publicly.

The offer Titanic had put in front of Rescovich had been adequate, but he had money from several other benefactors and had continually turned down Titanic's offers to help out. One of those benefactors was AIM Corp, someone the competition department knew little about; not a company that'd been high on their radar until now. Rescovich had published numerous papers on quantum foam theory, but nothing that had raised flags for the tracking team. His research was focused on applications to information theory rather than propulsion. He had a wife; the team was getting the details. He traveled a bit; his past itineraries and the people he'd met were being tabulated. He didn't seem to be political; his writing was ambivalent in that regard, so much so that it might be a flag in its own right. Overall Perci didn't see any glaring mistakes in how the company had monitored Rescovich. It made it more puzzling why Metri had sent Ayaka in so aggressively.

Just then Metri entered with Ayaka. As with every interaction he'd had with Ayaka, Perci marveled at how human she seemed. Anyone running a scanner would immediately see she was mech, but an unaugmented glance may well have guessed that Metri, not Ayaka, was the robot. It wasn't that Ayaka was perfect; it was imperfections that created the effect. Beautiful, but not overly so. Aloof, but by just the right amount. Smartly dressed, but not with the intent to show off.

Friendly, outgoing, well-spoken, and, all the studies to date confirmed, subtly manipulative. Very human.

"Hi," he nodded in her direction, noticing that his palms were a little sweaty, attributing it to a healthy respect for mech, but knowing it might equally be a concern that she saw him more clearly than others could, and may not ascribe the same power to him. Who knew what went through her mind? Wanting to divert his thinking, he followed up quickly, "What did you find?"

Returning the greeting with a nod, Ayaka projected the holographic image of Rescovich's final location. Methodically, she covered all the essential details, from the surgical precision of the wound to the positioning of the body within the archaic control center. She omitted any mention of Brill and her suspicion that people were dwelling down there.

"Who did LoPo assign to the case, and do they have any theories yet?" Metri led off.

'JF and Racheal. They were trying to be cagey and refrained from discussing ideas in front of me, but, no, they don't have any theories. They're perplexed."

Perci, still fixated on the lifeless form in the holo, questioned, "What could have caused such a wound?"

"I have not witnessed an injury to a human of this nature," Ayaka truthfully replied, deftly evading a direct response to the question.

After a series of further inquiries, Ayaka surprised Perci with one of her own.

"Are we responsible for this? If so, I can handle things appropriately."

Perci glanced at Metri. "No, we had nothing to do with this." Metri concurred, to Perci's relief; the two of them hadn't debriefed independently yet.

"Metri," he asked, "why did you send Ayaka? It may make LoPo more suspicious of us."

"Simple," Metri swiftly responded. "My contact within LoPo, who monitors incoming cases, not only alerted me about the victim but emphasized that he'd been discovered on layer zero within an antiquated physics laboratory. It struck me as highly peculiar. I dispatched Ayaka, as I previously explained to the team because she could swiftly reach the location and possesses superior built-in scanning capabilities compared to our team's equipment."

Petri nodded slightly. "Hope you haven't stirred up a tempest." He looked back at Ayaka. "What's next?"

"Metri and I will collaborate, but I'd like to go back down to the site and scout a wider radius. Rescovich must have been relocated, and if we can determine where he was killed, that'll help us figure out what happened."

"In parallel, I'll be gathering everything I can from here," Metri chimed in. "Who did he get his layer zero access permission from, and for what purpose? What was his latest research, etc., etc."

"Fine," Perci nodded, frowning slightly. "Copy me on absolutely everything. No, cancel that. Copy me on things that aren't going to get us in trouble. Anything else, let's do it face-to-face. This could easily blow up on us."

JURISLAV

Once the Quantum Foam Drive of The Jurislav shut off, and the vessel settled into Earth's orbit, Grace received a coded message, originating from the Earth Governance Council, commonly known as EGov. The contents of the note were straightforward: "Grace, we cordially invite you to Earth as our honored guest. We seek your insights on a matter of great interest. Please let us know your decision at your earliest possible convenience. Regards, Olinda Placade, Special Security Operations."

The message bore the appropriate signature, leaving Grace with no reason to doubt its authenticity. However, her knowledge of Earth's history was limited, prompting her to research EGov, SSO, and Olinda Placade. EGov was the general term for Earth's Deep Democracy institutions; a much older system than Jurislav's Futarchy, and supposedly quite different, although Grace didn't immediately grasp all the details, and truthfully didn't care too much. She'd been living with the Futarchy on the Jurislav for the last few decades and had a basic understanding of how it worked, and, perhaps more importantly, how it didn't. The idea of a Deep Democracy was well documented—a way to give marginalized voices a say, including those from the past and the future—so there were definite overlaps with the goals of the Futarchy, but Deep Democracy relied less on prediction markets and reputation indexes.

SSO was a division of EGov, and had been for centuries; like all security arms it had mixed reviews, including its own host of scandals, but it was generally respected. On the other hand, Olinda Placade, a recent addition to SSO, had no discernible reputation, good or bad; she hailed from one of the private security firms that, on Earth, appeared to align themselves closely with the dominant corporate entities.

Grace immediately shared the note with JoJo, her daughter. "Well, it's why we're here…to see Earth," JoJo commented. "You should at least talk to them."

It was true. Following all the adventures on Tilt, the two of them had often discussed 'connecting' with their human origins. Earth, being the cradle of humanity, would be an excellent way to do that. The two of them were, in large part, the reason the Jurislav was making this stop. Many on the ship had laughed at the suggestion of going to Earth, seeing it as nothing more than a relic of the past; most people on the ship had never been here, and many didn't care about Earth at all. "It's like a museum, and not a very good one," was the comment she remembered from the forums. Ultimately they'd convinced enough people to support the idea that the Jurislav had scheduled a stop.

Tilt was Grace and JoJo's birthplace, and also the unlikely home planet of the Citizens: Ayaka, Millicent, Brexton, Aly, Dana, and a host of other robots. An ancient human ship, long before the Titanics were developed, had marooned a small group on Tilt alongside an early version of an artificial intelligence that ran the ship and monitored the culture; the very type of AI that was now banned on Earth. The humans had eventually died out, but the AI had evolved and thrived, although an unfortunate reboot left it without full memories of its earthly human origin. It had built its own 'children'—robots—and due to those partial memories had structured them to be human-like in appearance. Those children, now known as Citizens, had, in a very strange twist, orchestrated the regeneration of biological humans from some DNA left over from the first human settlers. The Citizens were fervently convinced that they were shepherding the emergence of a new life form; one that had never existed before. Grace was one of many vat-grown 'Stems,' as the Citizens had referred to them. While many Stems were recycled as the Citizens improved their design, Grace had been decanted at an opportune time—just before humans returned to Tilt and rescued her. One of the first naturally born humans on Tilt, JoJo was the result of a particularly difficult part of Grace's early life when she was forced to live with other Stems in an experimental and artificial enclosure; one where powerful males had their way. When those humans had finally returned to Tilt and liberated the Stems, Grace and JoJo ultimately ended up taking refuge on the Jurislav. Ayaka had been instrumental in their survival; she was one of the very few Citizens who saw long-term value in the slow-moving Stems they had created. On the Jurislav, Grace and JoJo's bond had deepened, unburdened by the constraints of their tumultuous past.

"How would EGov know about me, let alone that I'm on the Jurislav?" Grace wondered out loud. "And what possible thing could I tell them that a million other humans wouldn't be better at?"

"You can speculate all you want Mom; might be easier just to ask them," JoJo responded with a disarming smile. She was often exceedingly direct, which had landed her in hot water on the highly political and often opaque Jurislav.

"Guess you're right," Grace responded. "Want to listen in?"

"Yes," was the quick response, accompanied by an equally quick grin. Or, at least what passed for a grin on JoJo's hybrid face.

Grace pinged the address associated with the note and got an immediate answer.

"Olinda here," came from a human-normal brunette. "Oh, hi Grace. Thanks for the quick connect; I assume you got my note… the invitation?" Grace knew Earth humans had dramatically restricted technology, including how the human form could be adapted. So, Olinda's somewhat cool expression as she saw Grace's hybrid form was not a surprise. Olinda, on the other hand, had an Earth-standard body, its form largely unchanged from its biological evolutionary standard.

Grace and JoJo had wholeheartedly embraced the favored body form of those aboard the Jurislav—a mechanical body housing their brain—a hybrid form. It offered undeniable advantages: upgradability, customization, and optimization for specific tasks, all controlled by their natural human brains. It was not artificial intelligence, still forbidden on most Titanics, but a harmonious fusion of biology and technology that maximized their potential without jeopardizing the essence of humanity. Grace and JoJo were singletons; one brain in each of their bodies. Some on the Jurislav had gone even further and had multiple brains sharing one physical vehicle, or even further, where the brain had no independent physique, but was just 'part of a conglomeration.'

Grace assumed Olinda's cautious hello was a result of interfacing with her hybrid form.

"Yes, I got it. I'm here with my daughter, JoJo." Grace increased the aperture so that Olinda could see both of them.

"Of course," Olinda gave a genuine smile. "Hi JoJo, I'm a big fan."

Grace and JoJo looked at each other.

"A big fan?" Grace asked cautiously.

"Oh ya, you probably haven't seen the mersive yet. It was quite a sensation here; many people have seen it… Got to say, though, you don't look anything like your mersive personas. Guessed they toned you down…".

Grace had seen mersives; passive full sensory entertainment. They were a big business on the Jurislav, and obviously on Earth as well.

"We're in a mersive?" JoJo broke in, obviously excited by the prospect.

"Yes, a pretty good one. Guess it was released while you were in transit; you should watch it. But, that's not why I messaged you…."

"Right," Grace leaned in, "why did you contact me?"

"Let me provide you with the high-level overview," Olinda replied, her demeanor turning serious. "I'm hoping your interest will be piqued enough that we can meet. These digital communications are never entirely secure, despite our best efforts."

That sounded a bit foreboding to Grace, giving her a twinge of unease, but she nodded at Olinda to continue.

"We have some activities here on Earth where your unique background could provide some insights. You too, JoJo, but maybe not to the same extent as your mom's experience. I'm sure you've guessed that it's related to the Tilt's… sorry, to Citizens. I know you were both born on Tilt as well," she attempted to recover from something that may have been taken the wrong way.

Grace ignored it. "Yes, I assumed that. But my experience isn't unique; there are other Tilt humans on the Jurislav, and elsewhere, that you could have asked?" She hated the term 'stem', and used the more awkward phrase 'Tilt human.'

"Of course, but you have the longest history with some individuals of interest... so if you're willing to help, you would be our priority." From the way Olinda said 'individual' Grace knew she was referring to Citizens, and suspected it must be Ayaka or Millicent... or maybe Brexton. Those were the Citizens she'd known the longest. Her gut told her Ayaka was the most likely.

"I understand," she replied. "Some of those individuals," she also stressed the word slightly, "have been good friends of mine....," she trailed off, leaving the unspoken implications hanging.

After a brief pause, Olinda replied, "I can assure you that we are not seeking anything untoward; we are simply gathering information on an interesting situation."

Grace was skeptical, but JoJo, always eager for adventure, subtly signaled her eagerness in the background with multiple "let's do it" gestures.

"Now, here's my offer," Olinda continued without waiting for Grace's response. "Initially, I intended to extend this invitation solely to you, but in retrospect, it seems fitting to include JoJo as well. I will host both of you here on Earth, expedite your visa process, and arrange for comfortable accommodations. We will cover your expenses for three days. Once here I'll provide you with more details on how we can work together. If you decide to assist us, we will extend your visa and continue hosting you. If, however, you decline, there will be no harm done, and we will ensure your prompt return to the Jurislav."

"Give me a moment," Grace replied, swiftly disabling the audio. She turned to JoJo, more to position herself away from the camera than to have a discussion. She knew exactly what JoJo wanted to do. She held up her hand, forestalling discussion. "Do it?" she asked. JoJo nodded, smiling broadly.

Grace pivoted back to the screen, her expression composed. "All right, both of us," she declared.

"Excellent," Olinda gave a genuine smile. "I'll look after the details.... Oh, one wrinkle, which you may already be aware of. Earth only allows human-standard body types; no exceptions. You'll need to change those out," she gestured at Grace and JoJo's current hybrid bodies.

Grace didn't even bother checking with JoJo. "Agreed," she replied. "We'll wait for your directions." She cut the feed.

"Yes!" JoJo exclaimed, excitement coursing through her. "I'm ready to have a normal body again anyway." Grace, a bit more reluctantly, agreed. When they'd first boarded the Jurislav and witnessed the diverse range of individuals aboard the ship, they had both opted for a somewhat exotic hybrid body. While intriguing at first, the novelty had eventually begun to wear thin. This presented the perfect opportunity to return to a familiar body form and rediscover what that felt like.

"We should switch soon," Grace commented. "It'll take some time for our brains to adjust to biological limbs and senses."

A shared smile conveyed their anticipation; however, beneath their excitement, Grace couldn't shake off the nagging feeling that they were overlooking something. A prominent government division contacting her as soon as they entered orbit, with a request cloaked in ambiguity. It couldn't possibly be as straightforward and uncomplicated as it appeared on the surface.

Olinda, having hung up, gave a little cheer for herself. She'd been challenged to get Grace to come down under EGov auspices and had succeeded easily. She wasn't sure if her boss would be happy that JoJo was tagging along, but she figured that was a small price to pay to ensure that Grace was motivated and locked in.

As she thought about next steps, Olinda found herself grappling with a lack of clarity. Administrator Massod had assigned her the responsibility of getting Grace down but had been uncharacteristically tight-lipped about EGov's motives for involving her. While Olinda was aware of Ayaka's association with Titanic Inc. and the legitimate concerns EGov harbored regarding the formidable influence wielded by the corporation, that was merely the backdrop. What Grace could offer them was a mystery to her.

She dropped Massod a note, "Grace has agreed to hear us out," and was surprised when he hud-rang her almost immediately.

"Hi," Massod said, quickly followed by, "That's excellent news. When will she be here?"

"I haven't even started the process," Olinda replied, somewhat taken aback both by how quickly Massod had called her, and how eager he was to get things moving. "Is there a rush?"

"Oh, not particularly," Massod backtracked, his tone shifting, "but, the sooner the better."

"Are you going to tell me a bit more?" Olinda queried. "Why is Grace so important? Oh, I forgot to tell you, she wanted JoJo to come along, and I said okay, figuring it was more important to get Grace's buy-in than push back on that."

The call was quiet for a moment. "Yes, that was a good call," Massod acknowledged. "We can deal with that. And yes, I'll give you some more details as we delve in. But, for today let's focus on the logistics and make sure there are no hiccups in getting them down here."

"They were both in non-standard hybrid gear," Olinda informed him. "It might take them a bit to get into earth-normal. I didn't leave them with timeline expectations."

"Damn. All right, collaborate with the Jurislav and ensure we offer them any necessary assistance," Massod instructed.

"Understood," she replied, not quite sure what that implied, but knowing it was all she was going to get for now.

"Keep me informed of the schedule."

"Yes, boss."

After hanging up she realized that she hadn't learned anything new, even though Massod had said he'd tell her more. Well, she'd have to be patient. Things would become clearer with time.

LHC

Ayaka was eager to get back down to the LHC on level zero. She strongly suspected she knew what had killed Professor Rescovich, even if she had no idea of why. Brexton had to be involved somehow. He alone possessed a weapon capable of piercing objects flawlessly, leaving no trace or disruption along the edges—a device that removed cylindrical cores from whatever it passed through. A device so powerful and unusual it was a wonder it could exist at all.

As far as Ayaka knew, Brexton had the only such device in existence; after all, he was the only being who knew how to create one. They'd discussed destroying it many years ago, soon after Brexton had assembled it, but it had sentimental value to both of them—and intellectual value to Brexton—so they'd ultimately decided that they would not destroy it and that Brexton would keep it safe at all costs.

They'd sworn an oath that they would never talk about it with anyone else. Not to Citizens and not to humans. No one.

Ayaka couldn't think of any other thing that could have cored Rescovich that way. That meant either Brexton had killed him, someone else had their hands on Brexton's weapon, or some genius had rediscovered the technology behind the device and had built their own. The last option was the least likely and the most worrisome.

She hadn't thought about the device for decades. It had many uses beyond weaponry; that was just a fringe case. But, it was exactly that flexibility which had led Ayaka and Brexton to swear a secrecy pact—if humans got their hands on this technology, who knew what they'd do with it? One thing was sure; they wouldn't restrict themselves to positive uses; humans simply weren't built that way.

They'd named it 'The Casimir.' Brexton had told her that work by an ancient physicist of that name had inspired his development. They had called its consequences in the physical world Casimir Effects, which Brexton claimed was a funny pun, although Ayaka had never been interested enough to look up why. Seeing Rescovich's body on the table, Brexton would have joked that Rescovich was simply suffering from a bad case of the Casimir Effect. Ayaka smiled, despite the seriousness of her thoughts; she missed Brexton. They hadn't talked in over twenty years, having hitched rides on different ships long ago.

Ayaka had worked hard to get Titanic Inc. to sponsor her so that she could get to Earth, and Brexton may now be jeopardizing that. Her ongoing work to understand human intelligence, and, ultimately consciousness, drove her to continue studying human behavior, and seeing humanity on their home planet was important to her. Without Titanic's sponsorship, Earth's anti-mech attitude, and more importantly their scanners, would have made it impossible for her to be here. She knew that no other Citizen had been approved to visit, so it was almost impossible that Brexton was actually on Earth. And yet he must be here; there was no other explanation.

She mulled over the challenge: Brexton had to have killed Rescovich with The Casimir here on Earth, but there was no way he could have done it because he couldn't be on Earth. Maybe Rescovich had been killed in space and then transported to the LHC? Such outlandish thoughts could break her out of the logic loop, but she recognized that it was more likely that one of her hypotheses must be wrong. She wouldn't put it past Brexton to have found a way onto Earth, without official permission.

Knowing she wasn't getting anywhere with this type of speculation was the primary driver of her anxiousness to get back down to the crime scene; she needed more information.

After the hassle of passing through the checkpoints, albeit more quickly the second time around, and playing nice-little-human for the guards at the checkpoints, she reentered the LHC control room. The body had been removed, and the team from the morgue had left the place even cleaner if that was possible. Looking around carefully, she tried to find something she'd missed…

The resounding blast of a gunshot caught her completely off guard.

She'd been scanning the room as she entered, but not closely enough. The first bullet grazed her shoulder without doing any damage. This gave her time to identify the location of the shooter. Moving a bit faster than a human could, but not as fast as she was capable of, she strategically positioned herself so that the second bullet passed through her chest but didn't hit any vital gears or actuators. It was a trivial 'flesh' wound—already annealing—but she hoped the shooter wouldn't know that and would assume they'd scored a fatal blow. Calculating the force that the bullet would have had on a human she spun to the left, putting her hand out, seemingly ineffectively, and crumpled to the floor in such a way that the shooter would be able to see her unmoving legs, but not her upper body. She didn't have fake blood handy to make the scene fully convincing, so she was relying on the shooter's curiosity to bring them closer to her.

Being shot was certainly a new experience for her, and pretty exhilarating. She'd watched enough human dramas to recognize when actors were good at death scenes, and when it just didn't work. Reviewing her actions over the last few seconds she was sure she'd nailed it.

While waiting for the shooter to approach—they were being very cautious—she scanned the rest of the space as best she could to see if there were others. The shooter was alone.

As she'd fallen, she had positioned herself face up so she could see the shooter clearly when they came. She practiced an agonized and shocked expression, which the perpetrator would certainly expect.

At long last the shooter approached, glancing nervously around the corner while kicking her gently to see if she moved. Laying perfectly still for a moment she allowed him—it was a guy—to ease around the corner far enough that when she moved he had no time to react. With one leg deftly maneuvered behind him, she pulled him closer, enabling her to effortlessly wrest the gun from his grasp with a single twist. Utilizing her other leg, she spun him around, causing him to collapse beside her. Swiftly rolling over, she positioned herself atop him, pressing his face firmly against the floor. Uncertain about her next course of action, she searched again through mersive dramas and then opted to deliver a measured tap behind his ear, promptly rendering him unconscious.

It had been too easy, and therefore a bit discomfiting. For years, she had embodied the archetype of the "perfect robot," never posing a threat to a human, diligently cultivating whatever goodwill she could. And now, even though her actions had stemmed from self-defense, she had resorted to force. Hopefully, she hadn't moved so quickly that he would question her capabilities when he came to. The best outcome here was that he simply thought he'd been bested by another human.

Studying the gun it was obvious how to disable it. She took the bullets out and placed them in her pocket, leaving the gun lying on the table—the same table Rescovich had so recently been draped over. It was an ancient device, but well-maintained.

With a swift maneuver, she flipped the unconscious body over. A slender but fit man, probably a meter seven, with no obvious augmentations. Most humans looked pretty much alike to her, not because they were identical, but because they were undifferentiated. The restrictions against technology had plateaued in a spot where people could control their anatomy easily enough and most opted for standard height and standard build. Sure there was variance, but not like in the distant past when bioengineering had been much more primitive and evolution had kicked out a wider array of forms.

She hadn't hit him very hard; he was already stirring a bit. There was nothing in the room to help her stage a more human-looking response to her gunshot wound, but she did a quick analysis and came up with a story.

She expected him to jump up and challenge her, once he awoke, but he surprised her by laying still and studying her for a moment. His gaze momentarily flickered toward the gun resting on the table, its presence partially discernible from his vantage point, before returning to meet her eyes.

"I hit you?" he inquired, seemingly not adverse to admitting it.

"Yes," she replied, her tone composed, "bulletproof vest." She gestured ambiguously at herself, knowing that if he did get a glimpse through the hole in her shirt, he'd just see dark shadows anyway. The hole in the back would be harder to explain, so she made sure he wouldn't see that.

A pregnant pause ensued as he remained still. "What now?" His voice possessed an intriguing melodic quality, almost resembling a sing-song cadence. She couldn't help but admire his composure. While she had effortlessly bested him, he displayed no bluster, instead maintaining an air of calm deliberation as he assessed his options.

"Well, that would be up to you more than me," she replied with a small smile, turning on her influence algorithms. If history was a guide, a few minutes of dialog and she would have him eating out of her hand. "What should I call you?" Her tone was disarming, devoid of any threat.

A protracted pause ensued as he deliberated whether a real or fabricated name would serve him better. "Jon." She decided it was real, albeit incomplete.

Casually, she lifted the gun, allowing it to rest nonchalantly at her side. "Get up, Jon," she requested softly, the words carrying a weight that transcended mere demand. He complied, slowly rising to his feet.

"Why'd you shoot me?" she inquired.

"Just my job," he replied with apparent ease.

"What's your job?" she probed, deftly hooking him into the conversation.

"Ah," he hesitated momentarily, "just keeping this place safe."

"The LHC control room, or a bigger space?" Her knowledge caught him off guard, his surprise palpable.

"You aren't just here randomly, are you?" he asked, turning the tables.

She shrugged, seeing little advantage in being evasive. "Following up on the murder from yesterday," she gestured at the table. "Did you shoot that guy as well?"

"What? What guy?" His astonishment was staged.

"There was a murder here yesterday," she said. "You must know."

"You're a cop then?" He was good at turning things.

"No. Consultant."

He nodded, the silence between them stretching out.

"Right. I need you to take me to Brill," she changed the topic, seeking to get his cooperation.

Another start. Another surprise. "Brill?"

He regarded her intently for a moment before acquiescing. "Yeah, that's probably for the best." Without glancing back to ensure she was following, he turned toward the corridor where she had pursued Brill in her earlier visit. "Follow me," he instructed, striding forward, seemingly without a second thought.

LOPO

While Racheal was tracking down the late Dr. Reskovich's widow, JF went back over his main questions.

Why was Rescovich at the LHC? Was he killed in the control room, or had he been moved there? What had Rescovich been researching? Was it related to his trip to the LHC? Why was Titanic so interested? Who had motive, means, and opportunity? Motives could be personal, which was usually the case, or professional. For this one JF was betting it was professional; otherwise, why bother doing the deed at the LHC? If it was personal he could have been killed at home or work or somewhere in between. Means? Well, that was still a mystery, but again seemed to have a physics tie-in. A laser, or something like that. And opportunity? This is where they had the most leverage. They should be able to get a list of everyone who'd been granted a travel permit to level zero, find out who had granted those permits, and which of those people had passed each of the checkpoints.

JF composed requests to the security division, asking for all of these. As usual, his request would probably be rejected while he waited for oversight approval. However, getting security into the loop early had helped him in the past. He attempted to preemptively answer all their usual questions, and, perhaps, in this case, it would work; the fact the death was on layer zero should make it easier; less privacy and permissions considerations. He was also clear in his request that it was a suspected murder case—that was unusual and the oversight committees generally acted more quickly in those situations. Finally, he edited his request to be very specific, knowing the most common rejection was for 'overly broad requests.' He asked only for people, in the last three months, that had been granted access through all three checkpoints.

Ah, that gave him a thought. The last checkpoint was the only one that allowed access to LHC, but someone could have traversed across layer three from a different checkpoint than the one he used. He updated his request, with the new insight, asking for anyone who'd entered the last checkpoint starting at any of the four closest checkpoints on layers two through four. That should cover it, and make it even narrower.

That done, he returned to the question that bugged him the most. How had Titanic heard about the murder so quickly, and how had Ayaka made it to the scene only moments after him? Somewhere in the reporting chain, someone was feeding Titanic information.

He was interrupted by Racheal. "Found Mrs. Rescovich," she informed him. "She'll meet us at the Barney's on Felix, 11th, and Twig. Can you get there in half an hour?"

He assured her he could, and would meet her there. Weird that the woman wanted to meet them in a public place; he thought she might be upset by her husband's death and want to meet somewhere private. Then again, he'd met all types in this job, and shouldn't have been too surprised.

Newcomers to Earth, even from the satellite communities, had preconceived notions of the levels that covered most of Earth's landmass. Those notions were always too orderly. The levels were not actually stacked on top of each other, but rather ebbed and flowed into each other and were defined more by major travel arteries than anything else. A group of arteries that tended to follow the underlying ground elevation and intersected more often with left-right intersections than up-down ones was loosely defined as a 'layer'. Arteries that rose and dipped connected the layers in many spots, but few were vertical—the Geneva terminal was an outlier. It wasn't like layer eight existed everywhere over the original Western European block. Sometimes 'eight' was many stories high, and in places, it didn't exist at all as arteries from other layers took precedence.

Adding to the intricacies of the situation was the absence of a formal naming convention, despite EGov's persistent attempts to establish one. People staunchly resisted such impositions, fiercely clinging to their local nomenclature as an integral part of their identity. This sector was their territory, and they would not tolerate EGov dictating what they should call things. What might be layer eight for one neighborhood could be deemed layer seven by a neighboring sector and layer nine by another. Alternatively, the same shuttle route might adopt the label of eight on one side of the street and Turncliff on the other. Due to these complexities, most establishments eschewed referencing a layer in their addresses, opting instead for the closest intersections. By convention, the first two names indicated the horizontal cross streets, while the presence of a third name denoted a nearby vertical artery. Shuttles and pods had learned their local environments and were nearly foolproof when traversing highly trafficked regions, even as new establishments came and went.

In this case, JF had almost a straight shot—just one connection point—to get to Barney's. He arrived in time to grab a booth and a coffee. Racheal arrived and joined him. Barney's advertised itself as 'timeless,' and lived up to its promise. It would have fit in the set of a mersive from any time in the last century.

Racheal waved to an older lady who'd entered and was looking around. She appeared to be in her thirties, a good decade beyond the age most people choose to appear. But, she'd done a good job of it; she looked distinguished instead of decrepit. The jaunty hat perched on the back of her head added a sense of fun, offsetting her serious expression.

"Mrs. Rescovich?" Racheal asked as she approached their table. The woman nodded and made her way towards them, taking the seat JF proffered. In hindsight, JF appreciated her choice of venue; the booths were recessed and protected, making it an ideal location for a chat.

He rose slightly as she settled in, reached across the table and offered a hand. "Thanks for meeting. I'm JF, LoPo." He mustered a smile, though emotional encounters were not his forte.

"Alice," she replied, her voice soft but composed. Racheal introduced herself as well and then allowed Alice to settle in and order a tea. "How can I assist you?" Alice asked, once her tea arrived.

"Well, as we discussed, we're trying to find out who could have killed your husband. We'd like to get some insights from you," Racheal set the stage.

"So, you're sure he was killed then?" She didn't wait for a reply. "I thought it might be an accident." She was articulate, her tone gentle and surprisingly devoid of emotion. It had only been a day since her husband's demise, so JF had expected a few tears or at least some hint of distress.

"We can't say for certain, but our suspicions lean towards foul play. No other theory seems to account for the location and the manner of his death," Racheal explained.

"Thanks for sending me the scan. Bit shocking really. That's a big hole he has through him." Alice's nonchalant response to the gruesome sight intrigued JF. It was as if she were observing a peculiar scientific phenomenon rather than the brutal death of her husband. She continued, "What can I tell you?"

Racheal asked the question JF was thinking. "You seem to be taking the situation well. Were you on good terms with your husband?" She asked it nicely, but it was still pretty blunt.

"Well, yes and no. We've been separated for years, although we never got an official divorce. We were on civil terms, but didn't interact much; maybe once or twice a month."

"Any kids?"

"No. That was never important to us. Never even applied to the lottery."

"Okay, so you may not know too much about his recent activities. Anything unusual the last time you talked?"

"Well, actually yes, which is why I thought I'd meet you. We talked about a week ago, and he was very excited. Something about a breakthrough in his work, but needing to verify his results. He was always going on about something or the other, and this wasn't the first time he'd believed he was close to a breakthrough, but he was quite excited. Coming at this time I thought it would be worth mentioning."

"Can you give us any details?" JF pushed her a bit harder.

"Not much. You'll know that his specialty is… was… quantum physics," JF nodded, as though that meant something to him, "and its application to information theory. Well, he did say this breakthrough was 'way bigger than information theory.' I didn't ask for details, but he blathered on about quantum foam and probability matrices, or some such."

"Did that mean anything to you?" Racheal pushed.

"No. I'm not into physics," Alice replied. "Perhaps one of the reasons we drifted apart."

"So, that's it? That's the only unusual thing you noticed." Racheal pushed.

"Yes, isn't that enough? He was found down at that physics place, after all," replied Alice calmly.

"Yes, you're right," JF granted her. "It's probably related somehow. So things were going well for him at work, and he may have made some recent progress. We'll look into that; talk to some of his colleagues. How about his personal life; anything interesting there?"

"Who knows? He knew enough not to discuss that with me. The last straw for us was because of an affair he had at work, and not the first one I suspect. Truthfully, I'm not sure if they were still seeing each other —Teresa or something like that—or if he was onto his next conquest. He was pretty insecure, always looking for someone to pat him on the back and tell him he was wonderful. In hindsight, it's when I stopped fulfilling that function that our relationship cooled off."

"Any colleagues at work that he talked about?" Racheal was good at this, JF thought.

"You know how it is. It's always a battle, academia," Alice responded. "There were always competitive people and departments going at each other. Now that you mention it, reaching out of his 'information theory' lane may have been threatening to some of the other departments; people usually focus deeper in their own fields over time. It's not great form, or so I understand, to dip your toes into adjacent areas."

"Interesting. Okay, one final request," Racheal continued. "We'd like your permission to share the images and holo that I sent you with some other law enforcement offices, consultants, etc. We don't know what could have killed him, and we want some more eyes on it. Given you're still legally married, your approval would let us do that."

Alice thought for a moment. "Funny that I can give you that permission. I don't see a problem with it, but hopefully not the media?"

"Of course, there's a higher probability that some media hound gets something the more people we include, but we can put a note on the file that nothing should be shared outside of our direct contacts."

"I'd appreciate that."

"Okay. I'll send over the release then." Racheal said. Alice nodded. The recording of this conversation would be enough, but a signed release would be even better.

"Thanks for your help," JF noted, "I think you've provided some key insights. We'll try to figure out what his breakthrough was, and if it's somehow related to all this."

Alice nodded and rose to leave. "Will you let me know what you find?" she asked. "I find that I might care a bit more than I expected…" Still no real emotion behind it, but JF appreciated that she at least pretended to have some feelings.

"Yes, we will let you know what we find," JF promised.

Alice nodded and made her way out. Racheal leaned back, had a sip of her coffee, contemplating, and then turned to JF.

"Was that strange?" Racheal asked. "You've done a lot more of these than I. I'm not sure if she is just an ice queen, or if that was some kind of act?"

"People deal with grief in different ways," JF noted. "Perhaps she just has a good protective shell. But I get what you're saying. Maybe she's not telling us everything she knows, but I get the sense that she was pretty open. We'll keep an eye on her, but I don't see any motive, let alone opportunity."

"Who should I share the holo with?" Racheal asked. They spent the next few minutes brainstorming—medical experts to comment on the absolutely clean wound entry and exit; physics to see if some known device could have done the damage; other law enforcement to see if there were any matching cases.

"Now that we have permission, I'd go pretty broad," JF recommended. "Fire some off, and let's see what we get back. Next steps for us… why don't you visit the university? Do it unannounced to start; see who's there and what they say." Racheal agreed.

"I'll go directly from here," she replied, "right after I forward the holo around."

JF sank back to nurse his coffee and think. There was something about Alice that had been off, but he couldn't put his finger on it. Probably just her cold attitude. He sent out a data request to get all of her public information correlated and summarized. He wanted to know more about her, even if he didn't think she was a suspect.

Just then the results from his earlier query to security—on who had passed the level zero checkpoint—interrupted his thinking; oversight had moved fast on this one, and the results were back quickly. Damn, security only kept track of one month of access point data, not the three months that he'd requested. And, while one month of data on who'd passed the last checkpoint should be enough, it simply heightened the mystery. The only individuals to pass that checkpoint, in the entire last month, were Rescovich, Racheal, Ayaka, and himself.

That seemed impossible. They had a dead guy. Someone had moved him or cleaned up the mess… and someone had reported the incident to LoPo. And yet, nobody had passed the checkpoint. How was that possible? The questions were piling up.

JURISLAV

Grace was amused that JoJo was so excited about getting a human standard body for the trip to Earth's surface. After years in her existing hybrid, Grace wasn't sure she would enjoy the limitations of a simple biological bipedal unit. Still, it was worth it for a trip to the surface. She could always switch back later if she wanted. She decided not to recycle her existing hybrid form, in case she wanted it again.

While JoJo's friends were helping her brainstorm what bio form she should take, they discussed heatedly the motivation for visiting Earth. Why would anyone want to visit a historic relic, let alone put on a caveman suit to do so? All the while, they had fun picking out body types, having the printer produce them, and then nitpicking them and trying again. Eventually, JoJo cut them off. "Enough. I think this latest one will do."

Grace's relationship with the traditional human form was more complicated. Having been grown in a vat on Tilt, she'd had no choice in the body she'd grown up in. She'd spent her early years struggling with what it meant to be alive, yet alone human. The experimental setup the Citizens on Tilt had used meant that she was constantly abused by other humans as well as by the robots themselves. They had pitted her against everyone as part of experimental behavior tests; watching her every reaction. Her memories of those years were intense, and even thinking about returning to her original form brought them rushing back. She fought the negative thoughts by focusing on how she'd grown since then, the wonderful environment she'd eventually ended up in, and the fact that some Citizens, in the end, had helped her. More of her time was spent on her internal battles than on the nuances of designing a new body.

While designing her new body, JoJo also found time to watch the mersive that they were both featured in, which was loosely based on the events at Tilt. For some reason, Grace didn't want to see it, even though she'd glanced at the reviews and seen that it was well-rated. The actress who played her was famous on Earth, although never heard of on the Jurislav. That wasn't surprising. Given the Jurislav's time slippage with Earth over the years, there was almost no remaining cultural overlap. That human-normal-form was an anomaly on the Jurislav, but the enforced rule on Earth was just one example.

Fresh from the mersive, JoJo was bombarding her with questions. "Is it true that Ayaka had dad killed?" "Were the fighting pits really that violent?" "They destroyed millions of humans?" The 'they' in her questions were the key researchers on tilt: Ayaka, Millicent, Brexton, Aly, Dina, and a handful of other Citizens. JoJo had lived through some of that history, but she'd been too young to remember a lot of it. Grace knew some of the questions were rhetorical but answered as best she could. She gleaned that the mersive was reasonably accurate in representing the Citizen's motivations, intentions, and actions, while not glossing over the missteps that humans had taken in the encounter. It was unusual, for an Earth mersive, to be sympathetic to mech, and most of the negative reviews focused on that area. But the Citizens weren't, from Grace's limited knowledge, like the robots that had led to Earth's restrictions; they were different in ways that were still being debated aboard the Jurislav and throughout human space; something about forgetting algorithms that led to empathy. Based on JoJo's questions, Grace guessed that the mersive was partly a nuanced message to humans that their thousand-year-old restriction on mech may now have to be rethought. Ayaka's presence on Earth, which Grace highly suspected to be the case, had to mean that the mech-debate was open enough that EGov had made their first exception.

Olinda had messaged her just an hour ago. "Hope you're well; I've got your permits done, and accommodations are arranged. We're ready for you. What's your schedule?"

Grace had called JoJo. "How are you doing with your new suit?," she asked, using the slang term that was common on the Jurislav for a body change. "They're ready for us on Earth."

Grace had relied on scans of her younger self for the design of her new suit. Even with the mental baggage, it was still the most comfortable option. The suit was now ready; she simply needed to transfer her brain over. While the transfer was essentially risk-free and could be done by anyone, she'd booked a clinic to do the swap because she felt safer that way. She knew JoJo would just have one of her friends swap her over. When JoJo had been younger, and still experimenting with body types, she'd often switch a few times a month; for her, it was not a big deal.

The trip to the clinic was straightforward, and on the way Grace prepared herself for the swap over. It must have helped as she was quickly comfortable back in her birth form. She'd specified an early-twenty-something version of herself, and inspecting herself in the clinic's mirror she had to smile. The clinician told her that brain adaptation when going back to this form would be fast and easy; especially if she took the optional plasticity-accelerator. Show took it, and within an hour of the transfer, she felt comfortable enough to head back home.

When JoJo showed up, Grace couldn't help but laugh. After all the back and forth with her friends, JoJo was also in her 'original' body, late teens equivalent.

"You look awesome," Grace greeted her.

"Wow, you too," JoJo replied, looking her mom up and down. "We're almost twins," she added, with a genuine smile. Grace saw a lot of JoJo's dad in her but admitted that yes, indeed, they did look more like sisters than mom and daughter. They were about to enter a culture where that was the norm—almost everyone maintained a biological age of eighteen to forty—but the two of them had been nearly twenty years apart back on Tilt.

Less than twelve hours later they were on the shuttle. While the shuttle had seating for at least fifty, there were only a handful of people going to the surface. The Jurislav had been gone for so long, Earth time, that very few people had relatives to visit on Earth... and if so, they were now separated by several generations, so any remaining relationship was more based on family dynasty than any personal connection. In conversations on the way down, Grace learned that no one was going to see family; they all had side projects which motivated their trips to Earth.

Getting through the landing and approval process, Grace saw why most Jurislavians viewed the Earth as backward and archaic. At the first checkpoint, they were met by an elderly gentleman, wearing a stiff black uniform. Grace could see JoJo trying not to stare; they weren't used to seeing people over thirty, and this guy had wrinkles and gray hair; one of those who choose an older age. Very intriguing.

"Papers," the man asked, a grave voice matching his outward appearance.

Grace showed him the invite from SSO.

"That's unusual," the man noted, and then pulling out a hand scanner, "and you're hybrids." It was a statement, made with a disapproving scowl. "Follow the orange markers." Even in biological form, Grace and JoJo had hybrid brain-body interfaces; the connector that allowed them to swap their brains between bodies easily. That interface would be seen by all the scanners on Earth, and it would always mark them as outsiders. There was nothing they could do about it.

"Where to?" JoJo asked the man, nicely enough given how coldly he'd treated them.

"Secondary screening," he waved them through, then promptly ignored them.

Secondary screening, it turned out, was an intricate ordeal where every bit of their body was scanned for mechanical components. Earth's stringent regulations against artificial intelligence left no room for leniency, and they looked at every electronic component down to its basic components. Most of the time was spent on the brain-body interface as it was very complex. While its primary purpose was to translate brain actions into electrical signals for muscles or actuators, it also had to account for the intricacies of nutrient distribution and brain-waste disposal. The result was a plethora of augmentations where mechanical and biological systems converged, each requiring meticulous security checks. After submitting to all of those they were asked to wait in a seating area for what seemed like hours.

Finally, they were called and cleared through the checkpoint, but not before being half admonished, half warned: "Don't make any changes or upgrades to any of your systems without prior approval," a woman schooled them. "If you do, you will be deported immediately and fined to the maximum extent of the law. You may come from a ship, and not understand how serious we are… I'd recommend you don't push it."

Grace nodded her understanding, as did JoJo.

"We haven't been hybrids all our lives," JoJo couldn't help herself. "We understand."

That was barely acknowledged, but they were cleared through the final gate and made their way into the arrivals lounge, where Olinda had indicated she'd meet them. Grace recognized her, and waved hello, knowing that Olinda wouldn't know what she and JoJo now looked like. Sure enough, Olinda did a double take, but then controlled her response well and welcomed them to Earth.

"Let me get you settled, and then I've arranged a short tour to acclimate you, assuming you'd enjoy that," she smiled, the gracious host.

"Very much," Grace answered. "And thanks." Looking around, this part of Earth didn't look too different from some of the corridors on the Jurislav, although everything here seemed old; well kept, just aged. Probably older, Grace thought, than anything else she'd ever interacted with. Hundreds, perhaps even thousands of years old. She found it intriguing, and slightly creepy.

As they followed their guide on a tour of the local area, they wandered through narrow corridors between open spaces; some large enough to see rows of columns holding up the next layer, with neatly laid out buildings and parks sprinkled below. None of those open spaces could compete with the Jurislav though. The entire center of the ship was an open sphere, a kilometer in diameter, full of parks and streams which arched overhead. While the clouds in the Jurislav filtered the view directly overhead, so you didn't feel like the sky was falling, there were always glimpses of the splendor above. The ceilings of these Earth levels seemed very prosaic in comparison. While they'd gone to great lengths to make some of them feel like the open sky, with filtered light and shadows, they simply paled in comparison to the ship.

Sometimes between sectors, as their guide called the different open spaces, there were checkpoints. Most often just gates that opened automatically for them, but once and a while a human guard was present. When present Grace and JoJo universally got raised eyebrows, and sometimes secondary checks. It seemed 'hybrids' were unusual and suspect. Pure bio humans seemed to walk through untroubled.

"I can see why everyone here is pure bio," JoJo noted at one point. "You'd think they'd never seen a hybrid before. This is a strange place."

Grace had to laugh. "There are billions of people here, and only thousands on the Jurislav, so perhaps we are the strange ones. Good thing Olinda recommended these suits though," Grace added. "Can you imagine if we were in our hybrid bodies?" They both had a good laugh.

At the end of the tour, they were escorted back to their hotel. After the first few sectors, the tour seemed repetitive. Sure, their guide thought each sector was interesting and had its histories and stories, but they all felt like variations on the same theme. Grace was glad that the tour was finished.

Awaiting them was a note requesting a meeting with Olinda at her office, a short shuttle ride away, for 4 PM UST. The entire planet, they learned, used a single timezone. Why then, Grace wondered, did they always say UST? Their guide tried to explain, using some historical reference to when the Sunlit large parts of the planet. They still used it, he said, because there were exposed areas—none of which they would encounter on their trip—where the Sun still provided direct light. He referenced large areas of the Atlantic and Pacific oceans, which Grace had seen on the shuttle down from the Jurislav. Confirmation that those were, in fact, water, still seemed unreal to her.

Olinda's 'office' turned out to be a small conference room where Olinda was waiting for them along with a tall gangly man she introduced only as Administrator Massod.

"Welcome, welcome," Olinda greeted them. "We," she nodded at Massod, "thought it would be good to bring you up to speed on our agenda."

Administrator Massod chimed in. "Yes, very nice to meet you. You have… interesting backgrounds, for sure." He was intense, leaning towards them and speaking loudly, while at the same time radiating interest and respect, which took the edge off a bit. SSO operatives were often put in awkward situations, and needed to be diplomatic and professional; Massod was all that.

"So, why have we asked you here?" he continued. "Well, it's subtle, to say the least. I'll remind you that part of the agreement you signed was a non-disclosure agreement, so everything we speak of here is confidential."

Grace nodded, as did JoJo. They'd discussed that clause as they signed, figuring it was inevitable.

"Good. So, here's the quandary. Oh first, did you know that Ayaka Turnbuilt is here on Earth?"

"We didn't know for sure, but guessed as much given our dialog to date," Grace responded. "How was she allowed here?" If hybrids were given a tough time moving around, she couldn't even imagine what Ayaka must have to put up with.

"Titanic Inc., the maker of your ship as well as many others, petitioned EGov to allow her to work for them, and they put up an enormous safety bond to waylay concerns. It took months of negotiation, and, of course, there are still some factions suing for her immediate removal. They may yet be successful; we will see.

"We," he indicated himself and Olinda, but Grace assumed he meant the full SSO department, "ended up supporting her visit, and are responsible for her behavior while she is here. But, she is working for Titanic Inc., a very secretive and powerful organization, so we don't have much access to Ayaka; all we can do is watch from afar."

"Why would Titanic want her here?" Grace asked.

"Oh, that's no secret," Massod responded. "They want to study her closely and see if they can leverage any of her technology. Always looking for the next big thing. They convinced us she was unique and worth the risks… and that seeing the latest in AI would be important knowledge for us. Whether we like it or not, there are Citizens out there on Tilt and on some Titanics, so it's not like we can just put our heads in the sand."

"I don't think Ayaka's that unique," JoJo responded. "There are a lot of other Citizens…"

"Indeed, indeed," Massod seemed a bit thrown off by all the questions. "But, from an Earthers perspective, the Citizens are all brand new and unique. And from what I understand, Ayaka is one of the more, ah, amiable ones? As you know, artificial intelligence is illegal here and is likely to remain so. But, people's sentiments seem to be softening, and that mersive was a big hit, so… so this happened. Titanic has invested a great deal, and they will have to show a return for their shareholders. We don't want that to come at a cost to everyone else."

"That's fine" Grace broke in, "and we have lots of history with Ayaka, but neither of us understands technology well enough to shed any light on that."

"Of course, of course." He seemed to like repeating things. "We don't expect you to help us with technology; lots of people are looking into that. No, we were simply hoping that Ayaka might open up to you more than she would to Titanic, or us for that matter. What are her motivations? Why did she come to Earth, and why would she agree to work for Titanic, knowing they are just going to put her under a microscope? We understand or believe we do, Titanic's motives. But, we can't, for the life of us, figure out what Ayaka gets out of this."

"We weren't exactly best friends," Grace noted, although in truth they had ended up being, at least, friendly. "I'm not sure she'll talk to us either. But, her motivation is likely straightforward; her research has long been focused on understanding human intelligence… it's why the Citizens raised me and the other Stems to begin with. So, I'd assume she's just continuing that research? Trying to figure out what makes humans tick."

"Right. We don't know all of that history, except as told in the mersive, so you're insights will be invaluable. What does she think of humans? It's an important question."

"You seem to think about motives a lot," JoJo noted. "Why would we be motivated to spy on Ayaka and report back to you?"

"Oh no," Olinda broke in. "We don't want you to spy. You can be upfront with Ayaka, and tell her we've sponsored you and what our aims are. We aren't trying to be stealthy. It's just that we've put in requests to talk to her and she has refused, citing her agreement with Titanic. Given your history…"

"And," Massod picked up, "right now, we think we have the perfect in."

"What's that?" Grace asked.

"We know Ayaka is looking at the death of a prominent physicist for Titanic Inc. Titanic has its fingers in anything that even remotely rhymes with physics. And, the murder happened in a location under our jurisdiction. Thus, we have the right, perhaps even the obligation, to be involved. SSO provides oversight on important cases. We figured we'd send you as our observers...."

Grace and JoJo looked at each other. "You want us to investigate a physicist's death for the Earth's government? Why would anyone believe that cover? We have no experience, no expertise."

"You do have experience—perhaps unique experience. The location of the death is a centuries-old lab buried so low down on Earth that no one in living memory has been down there. In many ways, it is closer to the environment you grew up in on Tilt than to any other place on Earth."

"We were kept in cages on Tilt and experimented on," Grace couldn't believe what she was hearing. "We don't know anything about old Earth labs."

"Ah, yes sorry. Sorry," Massod, put his hands up, just realizing what he'd said. "I'm not talking about the abhorrent parts of your past, and I didn't mean to upset you. What I meant is that the site is alien to all of us, because it's been buried for so long. So, someone with your perspective and experience would be accepted as our emissary more easily than you imagine. But, it's your relationship with Ayaka that would gain acceptance—everyone's seen the mersive. Not many people will follow this case anyway, but those that do will give us some leeway."

The back and forth continued for a time, but Grace didn't learn much more. She felt that the SSO agents were being oblique; that there was more to this. The justification, measured against the expense of bringing JoJo and her here, didn't ring true. She needed time to think. "Can we sleep on it? Continue tomorrow?" she asked.

"Yes, of course," Olinda agreed. "But do you now see why it's time sensitive? The death is being actively investigated now, and Ayaka is working on it, but that may not continue for very long. So, the sooner you get involved, the better."

"Got it," Grace said. "We'll sleep on it, but make a decision soon after that."

Olinda accompanied them back to their hotel and bade them a good night. While Grace had thought she and JoJo would debrief, they were both so tired that they agreed to get some sleep before doing so. Grace triggered her sleep mode for a full six hours as soon as she'd parked her new body in a comfortable position.

JON

Ayaka kept expecting Jon to make a move; to try to catch her unawares and retake his weapon. But, he continued to surprise her and just strode steadily, almost leisurely, through the winding corridors, until coming to an access door.

"I'll have to explain what's going on here?" he told her, pointing at a button and speaker on the wall. So, he reports to someone, Ayaka thought. There were even more people down here than she'd thought. She had no idea what that ancient button and speaker were for, but she nodded her approval.

Jon pushed and held the button, then spoke into the speaker. "Hey, it's Jon. I've run into a complication."

"What complication?" came a staticky voice.

"I ran into someone," he glanced at Ayaka, "who outwitted me...has my gun... and is demanding to speak to Brill."

"Brill?" came the confused reply. So, Brill was not the boss; that was obvious.

"Yes, Brill," Jon replied.

There was a delay. "Give me a minute," the voice responded.

Ayaka was tempted to ask Jon questions, but anything she asked would reveal her current lack of knowledge, so she remained silent. As did Jon. He sank onto his haunches, back against the wall, and picked at his fingernails. Seemingly unconcerned by the situation, despite his obvious failure, and so easily admitting that failure to whoever was at the other end of that speaker. He did, however, glance cautiously her way every few seconds, almost as if he needed to constantly remind himself of his situation.

While waiting, Ayaka pulled up old maps she'd found of the LHC facility. She'd confirmed that the room with the dead body had been the Control Center. It was about five kilometers northwest of the Geneva transit center, although the route both she and the inspectors had taken was closer to nine kilometers. Following the old Rte de Meyrin to where it crossed from ancient Switzerland to ancient France, then taking a right on the Rte de l'Europe to where it turned north, crossed D35, and then ended at the two-story warehouse-style edifice housing the Control Center. The archaic roads were anything but straightforward. In many places, there were detours around the pillars which supported the layers above. In other areas, dilapidated structures, abandoned vehicles, or heaps of refuse cluttered the thoroughfares, rendering them virtually impassable for anything larger than an average person. And nowhere between the transit hub and the Control Center had there been sufficient lighting, at least for humans; her sensory spectrum meant she hadn't required external illumination, but even then she'd had to take some sections slowly.

Ayaka admitted to enjoying her experience on Earth so far. For years she'd practiced her 'human storytelling' algorithms, inventing scenarios that could account for the situation she was in. Human brains were constantly creating these stories, with the owner always being the hero in their own stories, and often believing their made-up narratives. While Ayaka didn't believe the stories she made up, they were often helpful in spurring insights. In this case, it was likely that, given the path she'd followed, Jon, Brill, and any other people down here, were using a different route up to layer one. If they were traversing her route, there would have been a better path. Despite making up other ideas, that was the only one that fit. In her scenario they were using the old LHC tunnels, many of which were highlighted on her old map, as part of their route, progressing to the upper layers from a different location than Geneva.

If she'd tracked her recent route with Jon from the control center to this access door properly, then they were, right now, just outside an access point to the SPS—a seven-kilometer diameter tunnel that had been used to accelerate particles for injection into the larger LHC. The Super Proton Synchrotron tunnel, if still accessible, should be right below them… maybe fifty to seventy-five meters below. She turned to study the doors to the left… the entry should be somewhere…

She sensed movement behind her and spun back a bit more quickly than human reflexes would have allowed, but was still too late. While she had been daydreaming Jon had disappeared through the access door he'd been leaning against, and before she could reasonably react, without exposing her true nature, the door shut solidly behind him. The corridor went silent.

Ayaka didn't suppress a small rueful laugh, and she allowed a small smile to climb up her face. Jon had been waiting for her to get distracted; he'd probably signaled the person behind the door somehow, and they'd affected the disappearing act.

"Well done Jon", she talked into the speaker while pushing the button, just as he'd done. "I expect we'll meet again." Then, spinning on one heel, she strode back up the passageway, retracing her steps to the control room.

The gun she'd taken from Jon was still in her hand. Pausing for a moment, she considered the implications of having been shot. While a human might have been aghast, she found that she viewed it more as an adventure; a new experience; it hadn't been dangerous. Should she report the shooting to LoPo? It may open a can of worms; was shooting a robot illegal? Probably not. Had Jon known she was a robot? Again, probably not. Did that matter? Probably not. On the flip side, what if she kept it for leverage over Jon? She was bound to run into him, and his cronies, again, and it might give her an advantage. That, she decided, was the best course of action. So, when further along she saw a small door labeled 'Trash' she simply crumpled the gun and tossed it in.

When Ayaka had descended to this subterranean level, she had intended to survey a wider area surrounding the site where Rescovich had been found. Despite Jon's untimely, and violent, interruption, that remained her plan. This place—she cast her gaze once more across the expansive two-story chamber—exuded an air of immaculate care and meticulous maintenance. It undoubtedly held significance for these individuals: Brill, Jon, and any others lurking in the shadows. For some reason, they had a vested interest in the LHC. Could it be that the collider, or a portion of it, continued to operate? That would explain the attention to detail here in the control room.

What could they want from centuries-old experimental physics technology? Surely there were newer ways to experiment; more advanced equipment? Was it a coincidence that Dr. Rescovich had decided he needed to come down here, just to the spot these people were maintaining? He also must have had a purpose to visit this specific spot. It must all be related.

She wandered through the four workstation pods, looking carefully for… well, for anything unusual. The old screens were stacked two high across the desks, with more screens mounted on the walls behind them. All were dark, and none looked usable, at least to her untrained eyes. No flashing lights, no heat signatures. They divulged no secrets.

She ran her hand along the surface of the table Dr. Rescovich had been draped on; the table moved slightly with the pressure, but there was nothing her finger sensors told her that added any knowledge to her earlier scans.

No, if she was to learn anything else, it would be from the people here—Brill, Jon, Jon's boss. She briefly considered going back to the door where Jon had escaped her, and hacking or sledging through it, but decided that would be counterproductive until she knew more.

There must be some information on these people in upper layer knowledge bases; some chatter, some tracking of their movement. She could be patient, request access to the appropriate records, and then analyze them. But, her patience algorithms were not her strong suit. She felt like just breaking things.

Then it hit her—break things! Both Brill and Jon were caretakers of this space; they cared deeply about it. Smiling broadly, she executed her thought immediately. Choosing a workstation at random, she knelt and started removing access panels; finding a bunch of wiring behind one, she made a big show of pulling the wires out. She was anything but subtle.

LOPO

Theories for how Rescovich's death could have been carried out started to trickle back in from Racheal's outreach. Many of the responses simply challenged the data, asking that LoPo look again at the scene and the body, because "obviously you've missed something." That was a standard line out of many mersives, with all their misconceptions on how criminal investigations proceeded. In mersives, there was either a clever detective who noticed something no one else had, or someone went back to the scene of the crime and found something new. Racheal knew that in real police work the chances of either of these were very low; so low they weren't worth considering. Her scans had captured everything, and LoPo's host of analysis algorithms had been over them... without any insights. Racheal herself had looked several times; they hadn't missed anything. They just didn't have a thesis yet. She threw all those responses out.

But, there were a few creative ideas that needed some thought.

"The body was frozen solid, the hole drilled, then the body was thawed." At first thought, this seemed reasonable and could explain the lack of mess and the clean wound. But, freezing a body and then thawing it did serious damage to cells and would have left the body bruised, at best, and jelly, at worst.

"He was impaled on a hollow pole, carried to the death site, and then the pole was removed." Intriguing. The problem with this one was the entry and exit profile; Racheal simply couldn't imagine being impaled by a pole without some flesh damage. Maybe if the pole had an exceptionally thin profile—a huge carbon nanotube or something. But, a quick check on that didn't pull up anything remotely thin enough.

"A laser cut out the hole, and then someone cleaned up around the edges." Sure, but there would be cauterized flesh inside the tunnel; no one could have cleaned up that entire wound. Could they?

"He was attacked by a cookie-cutter shark, then moved to land." What the hell was a cookie-cutter shark, Racheal wondered. Then, she wasted half an hour reading up on them. They were known for their round bites, not for auguring through things. Too bad, it was a cool idea.

"A large hollow drill bit with exceptionally sharp teeth. The hole was drilled very very slowly, after death, during rigor mortis. The bit was long enough to capture all of the missing body mass, which was removed with the bit." Okay, now this was a real theory. Racheal could visualize it, and the technology to carry it out was simple. The combination of sharp teeth and very slow drilling was feasible.

The rigor mortis comment spurred more thoughts. She must have imaged the body while it was still rigid, otherwise, the borehole would have been sagging. Temperature down there had been a comfortable

20C, so that implied death had been four to twelve hours before her scan. It'd taken a while for her to get there, so she suspected she'd been there at the tail end of that range, say ten to twelve hours after death… and even that seemed like a fast response. Had something else been holding the body, and its hole, rigid, post rigor mortis? Another look through the scan showed nothing. She didn't believe the drill bit theory, but the insight about rigor mortis was probably relevant.

She read through a slew of other ideas; none of them novel or compelling, and most importantly, no consensus emerged. Everyone was confused.

JF entered just as she finished rejecting the last idea. "Anything?" he asked.

"A whole bunch of ideas; most of them garbage, but one that seems remotely possible." She reviewed the hollow-drill theory with him and explained how it had led her to a whole other set of questions. "Maybe a combination of the ideas… they drilled him out while partially frozen? Not enough to ruin cells, but enough to help with the clean edges?"

"But why?" JF speculated, not questioning her, but diving into the brainstorming. "Why go to all that effort? Unless they were hanging around with a meter-long hollow drill bit in a refrigerator? And even if that tool just happened to be there, to drill so slowly… why? It makes no sense."

"Right. They could have just shot him and then scooped out the recorders…", Racheal agreed.

JF shook his head in frustration. "Damn. I was hoping someone would have a real theory. We're not getting answers, just wild speculations."

"Well, we haven't heard back from everyone yet," Racheal cautioned him.

"Yeah, I know. But when you put out a call like this, if there's a good answer, you tend to get multiple versions of it back. I'm not holding my breath on this one."

They lapsed into silence, each trying to think of another approach.

JF's hud—heads-up-display—buzzed. It was Rita. He added Racheal to the call, and together they brought Rita up to speed, ending with an update on her largest concern. "We don't know if the recorders were stolen or destroyed; we need to find the perpetrator before we can figure that out."

"Fine," she seemed less intense on that particular topic, "So, we have no idea how this guy was killed. Time to turn your focus to the 'why'. What's the motive? If we get the motive, that may give us a new angle on the 'how'. And, ultimately lead us to the recorders, if they still exist."

"Right," JF replied. "Good advice," and nodding to Racheal, "let's switch focus for a while." Rita ended the call.

"She's right; we got carried away," JF grimaced a bit. Rita hadn't chastised them, just pulled them back a bit. "Where are we with the wife? What's her name?"

"Alice," Racheal responded. "We're nowhere... background checks came in; everything about her story checks out. She was in her home sector for at least twenty-four hours before the murder, so she also has a good alibi. But I'll look deeper. She mentioned a girlfriend, and we need to talk to Rescovich's colleagues; to see if he was in an academic war with anyone. Or, perhaps he was a threat to someone given his 'breakthrough' seemed to cross academic boundaries."

"Right, I remember. Something about going beyond information theory—whatever that means. You dig deeper. I'm going to look at the political angles. We know AIM Corp was writing cheques for his research; with Titanic breathing down our necks, that can't be a coincidence; AIM is rumored to be nipping at their heels."

"True. And Ayaka," Racheal reminded him. "Why would Titanic have sent her down? They have lots of operatives who have more proven loyalty to the company. The whole situation seems a bit off."

"So many questions," JF smiled. "Actually, sort of fun."

EGOV

The next morning Grace and JoJo resumed their discussions about the EGov offer, fully expecting their conversation to be monitored.

"I don't believe them; it's so... simplistic," JoJo began, her tone laced with skepticism.

"Well, I think there's some truth to what they're saying," Grace responded, "but I agree it's not the whole story. They're withholding a great deal more than they're letting on. It's clear that they're concerned about Ayaka, but I suspect there's a deeper layer to this. Perhaps something to do with Titanic?"

JoJo furrowed her brow. "All right, I'll give you that. They're not lying per se; they're trying to play a clever game. Give us enough to get us hooked, without telling us much."

"They're investing a considerable amount in us. Bringing us here, expediting permits, the tour, lodging, the whole white glove treatment. There's something serious behind this; something they believe we have unique insights into."

"Well, it's certainly not murders in old physics labs," JoJo laughed out loud.

"Yeah, they misplayed that," Grace smiled back, mirroring JoJo's amusement.

The two sat silently, enjoying a quiet moment. Grace had awakened with full clarity. She didn't care what EGov's agenda was; this was exciting, and she wanted to continue. Life on the Jurislav had worn thin for her, she realized in retrospect. She'd grown up in, for lack of a better term, a 'stress lab.' Ayaka and Millicent, but also Brexton and others, had raised her and the other Stems as experiments. Those Citizens had sincerely believed they were creating an intelligent species, and had put Grace through numerous tests… many of them unpleasant. Only later the Citizens had learned that humans had predated them; in fact, humans had created the early versions of the Citizens; just plain vanilla AI's. That had been a time of heightened action, profound uncertainty, love, and loss. Exhilarating, to say the least.

But that was decades ago, and her subsequent stable but mundane existence had left her a bit bored if she was honest with herself. The Jurislav had none of the adrenaline-pumping action that her earlier life had been full of. Not that she would ever choose to go back to the labs on Tilt, and be tortured and manipulated…, but there had to be more to life than going to parties and experimenting with recipes. Granted, she was being a bit unfair; if she'd wanted to, she could have done more on the Jurislav. The excitement of the last two days had reawakened an adventurous spirit in her, and she relished it. Her heart was pounding and her head spun with possibilities. She wanted to continue. But, she didn't want to force JoJo into anything.

Luckily, JoJo was much like her mom.

"We got to do it, Mom," she finally stated. "Can you imagine if we backed out now, and just headed back to the ship? We'd regret it for the rest of our lives."

And that was that. Instead of answering, Grace jumped up and hugged JoJo; they beamed at each other.

Olinda and Massod were waiting for them at the EGov office. While Grace expected that they'd been listening in to her and JoJo's conversations, she resolved to play it cool.

"I hope you had a good rest," Massod led off. "Have you had time to consider our proposal?"

"Tell us again exactly what you want," JoJo responded. Grace loved that her daughter had tempered her enthusiasm as well, and was using the situation to gain more knowledge.

Massod nodded at Olinda.

"We want you to gather information for us about Ayaka, the death she is investigating, her work for Titanic, and… well, just anything related. The truth is, we don't know for sure what we're dealing with. So, we want you to cast a wide net, and figure out what's going on…. Let me rephrase that. We're interested in Citizens, and if they present a threat. The investigation is just an opportunity for us to get involved."

"I assume the police are already investigating the death?" Grace replied. "What is the reason that EGov would be involved?"

"We have oversight of all of Earth's police forces, including LoPo—oh, the Lower Police—who, as you intuited, are looking at this case. We don't usually get involved this early, but it does happen. We'll inform LoPo and introduce you to the detective in charge."

"What's so special about this case, that your involvement is justified?" asked JoJo.

Olinda glanced at Massod, who nodded.

"The death is of a respected physicist who was working in a strategic area of interest for us. We suspect, as does LoPo, that the death was a murder, and is related to recent discoveries this Rescovich thought he'd made. His death also occurred way down at level zero in an ancient physics lab, something we've never encountered before."

Olinda noted Grace's confused expression. "Ah, level zero refers to the original surface of Earth, a place that few humans venture to nowadays. It has become quite desolate.

The Effect of Casimir

"Also, Titanic moved very aggressively on this, sending Ayaka to the crime scene almost before we could get there. So, there are enough anomalies that SSO is justified in having a look."

Grace still looked skeptical. Olinda glanced again at Massod, and again he nodded.

"This implies that Titanic has information sources they shouldn't. That is definitely an SSO mandate." She paused, watching Grace and JoJo carefully. Grace had connected the dots: EGov was suspicious that LoPo, or some other agency, was leaking information to Titanic Inc. If that was true, and they could get proof of it, SSO's job would be to 'clean it up'. Cops policing cops was always tricky.

"I get it," she told Olinda and Massod. "This seems quite strategic. Tell us again why you would send us, instead of more experienced operatives?"

Massod broke in. "Rest assured, we do have senior agents looking at the potential leaks. As for your involvement, call it a hunch and lucky coincidence," he smiled. "We don't know for sure why Ayaka is involved. Then, within hours of this unfolding, you appear in the Jurislav. You have history with Ayaka...."

"Truthfully, it's not much deeper than that." He held his hands out.

Everyone was silent for a moment.

"Fine," JoJo said, having the shorter patience. "We'll help you. But we reserve the right to jump out whenever we feel like it."

"Fair," agreed Olinda, "but in exchange, you agree to tell us everything you find."

"Won't you be monitoring everything anyway?" asked Grace, genuinely confused.

Olinda looked shocked. "No, of course not." Again, seeing Grace and JoJo's blank looks, she explained. "EGov also enforces privacy laws. No one on Earth is surveilled without their explicit consent, including visitors. It's a basic human right…"

So, Grace realized, they hadn't been monitoring her discussion with JoJo after all… if Olinda was to be believed.

"Then yes, we'll share whatever we find," she replied carefully.

"Thank you, Grace," Massod smiled widely. "Olinda will introduce you to LoPo, and inform Titanic that we are taking an active oversight role. They won't be happy so don't expect a warm reception from them.

But, they will need to meet with you and respect your credentials; you'll have the full force of SSO sponsorship behind you."

LHC

Ayaka's gambit, defacing the control center, paid off immediately. Within seconds of her ripping at the inners of the console, there was a shout.

"Stop," cried Jon. "Stop."

At least he wasn't waving a gun this time. He had both hands held high, palms towards her.

"Please stop," he pleaded.

"Why?" she asked. "It's ancient tech."

"No, no. It's much more than that," he gasped. "It's much more than that."

She studied him, pausing her faked destruction. He was truly distraught and, perhaps, outraged. Close to tears, and close to rage. As she'd suspected, the people down here cared about the place.

She released the wires she was holding, allowing Jon to relax slightly. He rushed over to see what she'd done. Ignoring her, he carefully checked the wires she'd pulled out and carefully tucked them back into the cabinet. Closing the door, although it didn't completely latch, he stepped back and turned to face her.

"Why?" he asked.

"You tried to kill me," she replied, watching that play out on his face. "And, Brill went to great pains to avoid me," she added. "There's more to this place than just the unlucky spot Rescovich found himself in. I want to know why that is… as I'm certain it will also give me insight into why the good doctor was killed, and by whom."

"We'd nothing to do with that," Jon replied, but his eyebrows twitched.

"You tried to kill me," she repeated, clearly implying that Jon and his colleagues weren't above trying to kill someone.

"Well…." he stuttered. "That doesn't mean I killed that other guy."

"But you know who did?"

"No, I don't. I don't know anything. I don't." Reading his facial and body language, Ayaka was unsure if he was telling the truth; she was usually very accurate with her readings, but he was so upset at the moment that her normal analysis wasn't.

"You know someone who might know something?" she pushed.

"No. No." Less certainty now. He wasn't lying directly, but she guessed that he did have some information. "You need to go. Just leave. You imaged the whole scene; there's no need for you to be here," he pleaded.

"Sorry," she played to his emotions, "but I have to get to the bottom of this. I'm not leaving until I get some answers."

Jon was becoming distraught again. "Give me a minute," he mumbled and edged his way over to one of the semi-circular consoles. Assuming he was out of earshot, he whispered into a microphone. Ayaka could hear him clearly.

"She won't go. You need to talk to her."

And, the response through the speaker, the same voice that he'd talked to in their previous meeting. "Fine. Bring her to O Delices."

"Follow me," Jon motioned at her, and led her out of the side door, into a hallway she hadn't seen before. There were direction signs on the wall. To the left it indicated "SPS BA3" and to the right, "O Delices." She'd downloaded all the information she could find on LHC, and knew that BA3 was a Faraday cage; part of the control structure for the Super Proton Synchrotron, one of the ancient accelerators. O Delices, on the other hand, was labeled on the old maps as a cafeteria.

"That was your boss," Ayaka asked him.

He gave her a funny look. "I guess, sort of."

They crossed an open area, between the ancient buildings, which was lit enough that Jon didn't need further light, and entered a well-lit, and very well-maintained room full of counters and chairs.

"We'll wait here. Xsi is coming."

"Chai?" she asked. "I don't need tea."

"No, Xsi. X. S. I. That's my... my colleague."

"Oh, right," Ayaka gave a small heartfelt laugh to ease the tension and help calm Jon down. He chose a booth, and slid in one side, indicating she should take the other.

"Do they still serve food here?" she asked, looking around. The place was spotless but didn't look used.

"Sometimes," Jon replied, and then realizing he was giving information out, closed his mouth and didn't say anything else.

Soon enough, Xsi arrived. Tall and slender, her angular features softened by a flowing gown, although it was different enough that Ayaka hesitated to label it as such. She had been expecting someone stern, yet Xsi exuded an aura of joy and radiance. Her smile stretched across her face, emanating happiness and brightness. Her eyes sparkled with vitality. Ayaka immediately recognized a mastery of manipulating human emotions that challenged her own, and she marveled at the effect Xsi effortlessly projected.

Xsi strode up to the booth, and Ayaka rose to greet her.

"Hello, hello," Xsi's smile broadened if that was possible. "Great to meet you."

"And you," Ayaka matched her manipulation for manipulation, also turning on the charm and an exuberant facade.

"So, what have we here? Jon tells me you are investigating the death of that unfortunate man. When was that? Yesterday."

"Indeed. I'm looking into it."

"Such a tragedy. Please, let me know how we can assist you. What should we call you?"

Ayaka ran through several million scenarios and decided on the direct and truthful approach.

"I'm Ayaka." Xsi couldn't hide a twitch of recognition. "I've been assigned to this case by Titanic Inc., for whom I consult. The death is suspicious and unusual. But so are you, Brill, Jon, and, I presume, others working here? In my experience when multiple low-probability things occur at the same place and time, they're connected. At the very least, you, and your people will know something of what occurred here. Obviously you watch the control room carefully—we just proved that—so you must have witnessed something."

"Well, that's a lot to unpack," Xsi's confident smile was back. "You are the Ayaka from the Tilt mersive?"

"Well, from Tilt itself, not the mersive. But, yes, that's me." Ayaka didn't see any harm in confirming her identity.

"You are fantastic," Xsi looked her up and down carefully. Unlike many humans, she didn't hide her fascination and didn't show any angst at dealing with a robot. She turned to Jon. "You see Jon. You've been dealing with a robot; that explains a lot."

Jon was still catching up; perhaps he hadn't seen the mersive. But he nodded to show he was following. Unlike Xsi, he did ease away slightly, revealing his bias.

"This is astounding," Xsi turned back to Ayaka. "Oh, we must spend time together."

Ayaka refused to be distracted. "That would be nice," she sent all the right signals back, "but first I'd like an answer to my question. You, or someone you know, must have seen what happened to Dr. Rescovich?"

"Well, well. You have jumped to some big conclusions, and I guess I can see why. We rarely have visitors here, you know?" She smiled broadly like she was making an important point. "I mean rarely. And when we do, we are usually notified when the travel permit is issued. So, no, we don't need to monitor the control center all the time. There is no need. No one is going to just wander in."

Ayaka had to admit to the logic of that. "So," she responded, "that means that you knew Rescovich was coming."

"Oh, you are lovely," Xsi beamed. "Yes, that's true. Dr. Rescovich had a travel permit and was poking around. We can't stop that, you know. We don't own this space, we are simply stewards of it. No one owns it… or said another way, we all own it. Ah, well, all humans own it." Another smile to take the sting out. Just logic, that smile implied.

"We talked to Dr. Rescovich when he arrived. Very nice man; very cordial. We had an understanding. He would not do anything without talking to us first, and he would be respectful of the space. I didn't have to explain the gravitas to him. He knew where he was coming to, and he already had a deep sense of the value."

"Talk to 'us,' you just said. Who is us?"

"All in good time, Ayaka, all in good time. Let me finish your first question first. We also respect Earth's privacy laws, so we don't spy on people. That would be amoral. So, no, we don't know what happened to the Rescovich."

Just as Xsi had unabashedly inspected her, Ayaka watched Xsi carefully. "That's not the full story," she stated, after ten seconds of uncomfortable silence.

"Well, obviously not. That's why you're here, isn't it? Once you figure out the full story, you'll let us know, won't you?" It was a clever redirection. Ayaka was even more impressed with Xsi.

"Now," Xsi continued. "You've said you are here as a consultant for Titanic?" The embedded question was obvious: you have no authority to be questioning us.

"Yes, that's correct," Ayaka admitted. "But, you've just said that these spaces are owned by everyone. Yet, there are locked doors that you aren't allowing me through."

"Oh, I said the space is owned by all humans," Xsi reminded her. "But, that's not here nor there. There are many dangerous areas down here. Especially dangerous for a robot, I'd imagine. So, we do require permission…and often training… to allow anyone into those areas."

Ayaka considered the comment. It might imply that some of the magnetics of the LHC were still operational…or perhaps some permanent—and strong—magnets had been created or left behind? A strong enough magnet could be dangerous to her, but it would have to be very strong. She had a lot of safeguards.

"Is there a map showing where I can and can't go?" she inquired.

"Unfortunately no. Or, at least, not from us. You should just assume that if there is a locked door, it is locked for a reason." This woman was slippery. She had just effectively roadblocked Ayaka before she could get started. She had implied she wouldn't answer any more questions—Ayaka didn't have the authority—and now she was shutting the doors to physical exploration.

"I see," Ayaka replied. "I agree with you; it will be much better if LoPo is here with me. Did you meet JF when he was down? I'll give him a ring, explain the whole situation, and invite him back. He might also be interested in why Jon shot me?" She smiled, allowing a bit of impatience to color the expression. Ayaka hadn't changed her mind about reporting Jon, but she could use it to pressure Xsi.

That finally cracked Xsi's facade, if only for a moment. She had remarkable control, but Ayaka saw the hint of anger—fear, irritation?—pass through her eyes.

"Of course," Xsi replied, knowing she'd been outmaneuvered. "We will await your return. Come, Jon."

She stood, and not waiting for Jon, strode confidently back the way she'd come, her gown flowing behind her. Jon hurried to catch up but spared a moment to look back at Ayaka, a new type of respect, and fear, in his eyes.

SHEFFIELD UNIVERSITY

Racheal had spoken to the Dean of the Department of Physics at Sheffield University to get more insight into Rescovich. According to the Dean's assessment, there existed only one individual within the department who shared a notably acrimonious relationship with Rescovich—Professor Felicia Mann. The Dean acknowledged that competition was rife among the faculty, with accusations of intellectual pilfering, preemptive maneuvers, and the usual academic intrigue unfolding on a daily basis. Within the confines of this typical realm of rivalry, the animosity between Mann and Rescovich stood out as particularly intense. It may have started with Rescovich having an affair with Mann's significant other, Rela Grainger. That was many years ago, and Mann and Grainger were no longer a thing, or so the scuttlebutt implied. No, he didn't know if Rela was Rescovich's latest affair or just one of many. It was never confirmed that the alleged affair was real, or if that was the root cause of their friction. But, there was no doubt that Rescovich and Mann were constantly at each other's throats.

Would Rescovich be missed? Yes, of course, but Racheal didn't get the impression that the Dean cared too much—the department was pretty large—or that he had known Rescovich well enough to have had a personal connection.

When Racheal asked for an introduction to Mann, the Dean indicated she was about to give her annual introductory lecture, in Hall I. Racheal decided to attend so that she could approach Mann directly thereafter.

The lecture hall was almost full; Racheal found a seat, expecting to tune out the lecture and do more ruminating on exotic murder weapons. That plan lasted only a few seconds. Felicia Mann rolled into the lecture hall, and Racheal was immediately fascinated. In a world where any physical issue could be trivially fixed, Mann was the first person Racheal had ever encountered who used a motorized chair to compensate for what appeared to be withered and non-functioning legs. Was it for show? Some weird religious hangover? Why would anyone choose not to fix their legs? A quick search pulled up nothing—Mann was a fastidiously private person. What did come up, however, was that Racheal had unexpectedly found herself in the most popular lecture offered by the University, let alone the Physics Department. No wonder it was so crowded. And, the lecture wasn't even streamed—another strange anachronism.

"Welcome," Mann's voice was strong and confident, "to One Hour Physics. I've been giving this lecture, once a year, for over thirty years. My goal is to give you all insights into the current state of physics, without a single formula or number. Math often gets in the way of intuition."

Ah, physics for beginners. Racheal decided to listen carefully. Maybe this is how she could figure out how to build a weapon that punched perfect holes through people.

"We start with three simple concepts, and from them, we can build everything. The concepts are one, Random Emergence, two, Everything's A Wave, and third, We Are The System. We will dig into each of these but as a quick preview....

"Random Emergence applies at the most fundamental level of the universe, at a scale so tiny it's hard to imagine; the Planck scale. At that scale, the universe is a frothing broth of energy and mass. In the vast majority of cases, the froth cancels itself out; a particle and anti-particle emerge, and immediately interfere with each other and destroy each other out. However, once and a while things don't cancel out; the destructive interference doesn't quite work, and matter and energy appear. This is why there are 'things' in the universe, like you and I."

Ah, Racheal thought. She's talking about quantum foam. Mann was an inspiring speaker; you'd think that the restrictions of the wheelchair would make her less dynamic, but the opposite was true. It made her gestures more compelling somehow; more intense. She wasn't using graphics or holos, like most lectures, but was simply talking; it felt like she was talking directly to each person in the hall.

"Everything's a Wave", she continued, "is the best way to think about this frothy broth. I just said a particle and anti-particle emerge and cancel. But I want you to purposefully change that thinking; change your mental model. What happens is a wave and a counter wave appear, and cancel each other out. A wave and an anti-wave. You can imagine this as the trough of one wave corresponding exactly to the peak of the other, and when they collide, the result is nothing; they both disappear. While that's not physically accurate, it's much better to think of waves than particles. When one of the rare emergence events occurs the waves don't match up, and some remnant wave is left over. Those leftover waves are energy, and therefore mass. We, and everything we see, are composed of remnant waves that combine and sustain themselves as standing or harmonic waves; waves that have a sort of permanence, at least for a while. You can visualize such waves as pure musical notes, or a frictionless pendulum, but they are often highly complex and exist across multiple dimensions; the number of dimensions has been a topic of discussion for centuries. Not every wave is stable; no wave is stable forever. But those that stick around for seconds, minutes, hours, years, centuries…those are the waves that make up our existence."

Racheal was enthralled. The particle-wave duality was known to everyone, but imagining herself as a collection of standing waves, instead of a bunch of molecules and cells, presented a novel perspective.

"And finally, We Are The System. You can't think of these waves as being out there, where we can look at them or measure them. No, we are the waves, and everything we do impacts all other waves. We can't look, move, or think, without changing the system. If I want to measure a wave, for example, I need to interact with it, and that interaction impacts it, and changes it. At tiny scales, the waves we use to measure are the same size as, or bigger than, the waves we are trying to look at. Measurement is more impactful than existence, in those cases. As scales increase we reach thresholds where the measurement waves are much smaller than what we are measuring, so they have less impact. But always remember, we are part of the system—we can't reason about, measure, or understand our world without, at the same time, changing it."

Racheal was following the logic; it seemed straightforward. Yet, despite her best efforts, she eventually tuned out and got lost in her thoughts. Sure, Mann and Rescovich may have disliked each other, but it already seemed far-fetched that this woman, in her wheelchair, had somehow killed him. She wouldn't have gone down to level zero herself

—that would have been noticed. So, did she hire someone to kill Rescovich when he was down there? Why? That person would have needed to get a travel permit, and thus go on record. If she wanted him killed, why not right here, at the University, or his home? It made no sense to add complexity, and risk, by planning his murder way down to level zero, using some crazy weapon.

She was interrupted from her inner dialog by a key phrase from Mann: "...and that's what Cherise Pilipatri found all those years ago, leading to the Titanic Quantum Foam Drive, the QFD. Pilipatri figured out that we could dance with Random Emergence, and tune it slightly. I use the phrase 'dance with' because, again, we are part of the system. By creating just the right wave—call it a field—at just the right time, our field will dance with the quantum foam and ever so slightly change the random emergence equation so that it's a tiny bit more likely that a remnant wave is created. If that remnant is exactly the right shape, it can, in turn, influence another remnant, creating a cascade. It's a beautiful dance where the waves turn, and turn, leading their partner ever forward, entangled with each other in a firm embrace. The front edge of a Titanic ship creates exactly that—a cascade of entangled waves which pull the entire ship one Planck length forward for each turn in the dance.

"The equation Cherise derived was very precise and had only one solution. That solution tells us that the leading edge of the ship must be square, and that square must be 987 meters per side—ah, I broke my rule and used a number. In reality, there are several decimal places after the 987, but not enough decimal places that we can't manufacture to that precision. That exact scale and shape, for reasons we still don't understand, allow us to create the perfect field which is the Quantum Foam Drive. Many of us believe there is a better equation than Cherise's to be found because the existing QFD is imperfect. It pulls a Titanic ship forward at a bit less than half the speed of light, so there is room for improvement. And why a square? Don't get me wrong, it's beyond amazing and has led to the human diaspora. But, it's not perfect…or, at least, not as good as it could be. For the first time in hundreds of years —since Pilipatri's discovery—I believe we are close to some of those improvements. Perhaps, a few years from now, we will look back at the current QFD and remark on how simple it was."

The passion that Mann brought to this part of the lecture was contagious. This, then, was what she worked on, and coincidental with Rescovich, she sounded like she was on the verge of a discovery. It was obvious in the way she spoke. Some of the dots were connecting. Mann worked on Quantum Foam Drive technology; Rescovich had been edging out of his primary area, information theory, and may have been starting to step on Mann's toes; Titanic was following all of this carefully because the QFD was their asset, and it sounded like the next generation of QFD was on the horizon; they would want to own it, as they had the first generation. Anyone working in this field would be on their radar. A working thesis began to form for a motive: Rescovich was killed because he had found, or stumbled upon, an important insight around QFDs. Other physicists, Titanic, AIM Corp, and probably a host of others would be motivated to own that next breakthrough…the rewards were so big, some wouldn't hesitate to take out an aging physicist if they saw an advantage in doing so.

Racheal waited patiently after the lecture for the students to exit. Many of them had questions for Mann, and there was a bit of a scrum for a few minutes. As the scrum started to clear, Racheal stood up.

An explosion shook the room, knocking Racheal back into her seat, and then tumbling her end over end until she hit the back wall of the lecture hall. After some indeterminate time, Racheal raised her head; there was so much dust that she couldn't see, and her ears were ringing. She hesitantly checked her arms, legs, torso, and head. No blood, no obvious breaks. As her ears started to clear, the sound of sirens grew louder and louder. She must have been out for a while; emergency crews were already close by.

She relaxed back down to the floor, not able to generate the energy to get up and move. A hand grabbed her shoulder. "You okay," a black-masked apparition asked her. She gave a thumbs up. "Then come with me," it helped her to her feet and guided her outside to where a makeshift infirmary was already taking shape. She wasn't the first one out of the building. Several others, some bleeding badly, were already being cared for. She was guided to a spot on the ground, with a blanket. She lay down and closed her eyes.

TITANIC

Perci was yanked out of a meeting by his Chief Strategy Officer, Metri, soon after the Sheffield bombing hit the news feeds. She pulled him into a small conference room where Ayaka was already present. Ayaka stood gracefully, nodded at him, then retook her seat. Always following protocol.

"Get Linda," Percival barked to the receptionist outside. The receptionist nodded and started talking to his hud.

"What do we know?" Percival asked Metri.

"Not much. Felicia Mann was giving a lecture; one of Linda's people was there, but we haven't heard from them. The lecture hall exploded. It looks like multiple casualties, probably including Mann, although we haven't confirmed that yet."

Perci glanced at Ayaka and then asked Metri the same question he'd answered for her in their previous meeting. "Did we have anything to do with this?"

"No," Metri replied. "Nothing."

"We can't lose Mann," Perci seemed to be in a bit of shock. "Are we helping the rescue efforts?"

"That's what Linda is doing," Metri replied. "If Mann is alive, we'll find her."

Perci sat down and motioned Metri to do the same. "Damn, damn, damn. This is a terrible day." He shook his head. "She was getting close, or so you said." Metri nodded. "Do you have her latest research? The absolute latest?"

"My last update from her was a few weeks ago. So, current, yes, but completely up to date, no."

"We need to get that, and we need to keep it out of other people's hands." Perci felt panic rising as he contemplated the situation. Rescovich…, whatever, he wasn't close to them. But Mann, he'd heard her name all the time from the Strategy team; she was one of the most promising researchers that Titanic funded.

"That's going to be tricky….," Metri sighed.

Linda arrived at that moment, looking stressed and slightly disheveled.

"Report," Percival said preemptively while waving her to another seat.

"With her here?" Linda looked at Ayaka skeptically. She had not been a fan of Ayaka coming on board. She was responsible for security, and Ayaka was, in her opinion, the biggest security risk of them all. Her team had been scanning Ayaka with every instrument they had, and they'd found nothing. Which, to Linda, meant Ayaka had a lot to hide.

"Yes, with her here," Perci responded. "This is related to Rescovich. Let's connect the dots."

"Okay," Linda didn't look happy about it. "Mann is most likely gone, as is Samuel—my guy who was at the lecture. There's a lot of rubble that the rescue crews are going through, and we are helping, but no further life signs are being picked up. Somewhere between eight and ten people are missing and presumed dead. We don't know the identities of most of them, but Mann and Samuel are both on that list."

"Sorry for your loss," Ayaka said quietly, sensing that Linda was more torn up about Samuel than Mann. An obvious attempt to soften her stance, Linda thought, not giving Ayaka an inch.

"Yeah, that's rough," Perci agreed, without real feeling. "But we've got to manage this situation quickly. We'll have time for grief later." His resolve returned, and Perci went into planning mode. The best way to manage stress was to do something about it, and he was a master of delegating tasks.

"Linda. Get your hands on Mann's latest research. I know that's tough but do it. Priority one is that we know everything she was up to. I mean everything. Priority two is that no one else gets to it; any of it." He turned to Metri. "Coordinate with PR and get us ahead of this. Our condolences; we're doing everything we can to help; etc. etc." Finally, he looked at Ayaka. "Get down to the University and dig around. I'm sure LoPo will be there as well, but they'll miss things for sure. We need to figure out who is killing these people. Regardless of what we say or do, this looks bad… wait a minute."

He turned away and got the glazed look people had when focused on their hud. Turning back he looked even more grim.

"To make matters even worse, SSO is sending in some oversight agents. Guess it was bound to happen, but still…"

"Do we play ball?" Linda asked.

"Yes, of course," Perci replied, "but the minimum. Don't be volunteering anything."

Ayaka knew of SSO—the Special Security Operations arm of EGov. It was the same group that had oversight on her visit to Earth. They'd pinged her a few times and she hadn't responded as she wanted to keep strictly to her Titanic agreement; she wouldn't give Titanic or SSO any reason to cancel it.

"All right, let's do it," Perci stood up to go. "We'll catch up on Rescovich after we get ahead of this Mann thing."

Ayaka exited quickly; she had a lot of questions for Metri and Percival, but they could wait. She jumped on the first shuttle and headed towards Sheffield. The situation was getting stranger and more curious.

LOPO

JF paced restlessly back and forth in his office, trying to make sense of the Sheffield explosion. It was an immense relief that Racheal had been cleared at the scene; only minor scrapes and bruises, and she was already on her way back to the office to debrief. A peculiar coincidence that she'd been at the lecture hall when it blew; if tried hard not to draw any unwarranted connections.

For years Racheal had been his right hand, especially for on-site investigations and recordings. He trusted her completely to not only be thorough but also to think strategically through all the angles. She was irreplaceable. She wouldn't be handling the first look at the lecture hall explosion; he'd sent in his second team, including a bomb expert, and knew that HQ was also sending in people. LoPo units had cordoned off the scene very quickly and were still sweeping the rubble for signs of life. After a few hours that was unlikely, and the focus would turn to recovery and cataloging.

To complicate matters further, he'd also heard from SSO; their agents were on their way over to LoPo to 'coordinate'. What a mess; he had no need or time for political shenanigans, which he assumed this was. Still, he understood why they were doing it: no murders for years, and then suddenly not only a single murder but now what looked like a mass killing. The Department of Physics at Sheffield; who would have guessed? He shook his head.

He'd asked the investigation team for constant updates, and they were streaming tidbits to his hud. They'd just found what they presumed was the epicenter of the explosion—the middle of where the stage had been—and some bits and pieces of wheelchair debris, which implied that Mann had been right at the center. It wasn't a leap to hypothesize that she was the target of the attack, and everything else was collateral damage.

'Body count?', he messaged the team, with a certain trepidation. If they'd been pulling live bodies out of the ruble, he would have heard—news traveled fast in situations like this.

'Current estimate is eight or nine, including Mann,' was the reply. "Speculation here at the scene is that one of the other victims was a Titanic employee.'

'Keep me posted.' Why would Titanic have an employee at an introductory physics lecture? Even given their maniacal focus on researchers, it wasn't reasonable to expect that an introductory lecture would contain any new insights. Were they keeping tabs on Mann for some reason? Had she been a risk...or been at risk? How much did Titanic know?

He considered going down to the University himself, but he wouldn't add much value by being onsite. No, he'd let the professionals do their job, even if an appearance by him might be good optics.

His hud pinged him from the outer office. The SSO reps were here. "Show them in." He didn't know what to expect, but it wasn't the two who entered his office. They looked almost like twins but obviously were not. They were attractive, but in an unusual way that JF's mind tried to unpack. It's just that they were different; like they were from a sector he'd never visited. Being able to design and manage your body had led to a fairly homogeneous look for most humans. Because augments were frowned upon—at least those with complex algorithms in them—most people differentiated through clothing, tattoos, and hairstyles. He opened their profiles, and almost said 'ah' out loud. They were hybrids; that explained a lot.

The one who introduced herself as "Grace" had poise and presence; he felt he was looking at an old soul. The other, "JoJo" seemed younger, albeit more intense. He should have read their full files earlier; now it would be awkward to do so in front of them.

"What's the deal?" he asked, dispensing with formalities. "How do I have to accommodate you?" He didn't try to hide his displeasure at having more red tape thrown at him, especially right now.

"We're more observers than anything," Grace replied, picking up on his irritation and attempting to soothe him. "We'll try to stay out of your way, but we would appreciate getting first-hand information whenever possible. Originally our interest was Rescovich, but given the events of the last few hours, Sheffield can be added to the list." Advice from Massod had her focus on the murders and not turn the conversation to Ayaka.

"What's EGov's angle?"

"The Rescovich murder is a strange one," Grace continued doing the talking, "especially the location and cause of death. Titanic's immediate interest, the intersection with groundbreaking physics research—these all point to a situation well beyond a domestic dispute or a crime of passion. EGov wants to be on top of things, just in case."

"We have no intention of guiding your police work," JoJo jumped in, trying to put him at ease.

"And you don't have the authority to do that anyway," he replied quickly. Something was unsettling about the two of them. They came across as naive, and inexperienced. But, there must be more to them, or SSO wouldn't have sent them. Damn, he wished he'd read their files.

Luckily he didn't have to fill more time with small talk. Racheal appeared, disheveled and dusty, with scratches visible on her forehead, and a large bandage on the left side of her neck. She entered, limping slightly, then glanced over at the SSO agents, an eyebrow raised in question.

"EGov oversight," JF told her. "Grace and JoJo," he waved vaguely in their direction and then turned his entire focus to Racheal. "More importantly, how are you?" There was genuine concern in his voice and a certain tenderness. Almost like he was checking in on a child.

"I'm fine; a bit of ringing in my ears still, and I'll have a few bruises." She shrugged. "But I was lucky. I was in the back of the auditorium and ended up being cushioned by the chairs I was in. Lost a few minutes in the confusion, but the medic said I don't have a concussion or anything." She smiled slightly, obviously putting some effort into holding it together. She was downplaying being there, but clearly, the ordeal had been traumatic.

"Need me to get back down there to look at the scene?" she asked bravely.

"No, no," JF replied. "I want to debrief quickly, then I'm sending you home to get some rest. No arguing," he added, seeing Racheal get ready to push for immediate involvement. He glanced at Grace and JoJo, obviously hoping they wouldn't hang around to listen. They made no move to leave, so he sighed and turned back to Racheal.

"Just a few questions. First, why were you there?"

"As discussed, I went over to figure out who could have a motive for taking out Rescovich. I ended up talking to the Dean of Physics. Mann and Rescovich were not on great terms, and the Dean suspected that if anyone at the University had a grudge against Rescovich, it would be Mann. Since Mann was scheduled to give a lecture while I was there, I figured I'd sit in, and then grab her for questions afterward." Racheal was well-spoken and concise.

"And did you get to talk to her?" JF asked.

"I got there just as the lecture started... and the place exploded before I could talk to her after. Do we know if she was the target?"

"Not definitely, but probably. The explosion was on the stage. Mann was almost certainly killed, as was a Titanic employee. The rest of the victims appear to be students."

"That tracks," Racheal said. "I got blown back, away from the stage, and the place was packed with students. I didn't see the Titanic person."

"Did you notice anything unusual in the lecture?" JF pushed her.

"Well, it was all unusual to me, but no—I don't think anything was going on that wouldn't typically happen on campus."

"No warning signs, no shouts, no scuffles?"

"Nothing."

"Any ideas on how it could have been carried out?"

Racheal started. She hadn't thought through that, but an obvious solution popped into her mind. "Actually, yes. Mann used a wheelchair to get around. I have no idea why, but I'm sure we can figure that out. It's possible that the wheelchair itself was wired...or something under the stage, I guess."

"Wheelchair. That is strange," JF agreed. He noticed JoJo looking into her hud—probably looking up what a wheelchair was. "Anything else you can tell me? Anything the team on the ground should be focusing on?"

Racheal sat quietly for a moment. "Not really. I didn't get a chance to talk to her. But, this is connected to Rescovich..."

JF thought about pushing her harder; it was well known that if you kept after someone, soon after an event, you could tease out more details. But Racheal did look a bit shell-shocked, and it wouldn't be fair to grill her too hard, especially with SSO in the room.

"All right. I want you to get home, and I don't want to see you for twelve hours. Get some rest, clean up." JF helped her out of the chair and steered her towards the door.

"Racheal," Grace spoke softly but confidently. "Can I ask one other question?" JF grimaced at the interruption. He'd decided to be gentle, and yet the SSO agent just jumped in.

"Sure," Racheal grudgingly turned.

"Was there anything in Mann's lecture content that could have been seen as threatening?"

Racheal's eyes widened. "Threatening, not directly. But you've reminded me. At the very end, she made an off-hand comment that she was very close to an improvement of the QFD. That would be significant..., and on second thought maybe even threatening to some. She didn't give any details..., but dropped a hint that she knew how to make the drive more efficient."

"So the lecture itself didn't trigger the explosion; the perpetrator timed it, or set it off, after the lecture was finished?"

"Yes, that's right. About five minutes after the lecture."

"So they could have expected the lecture hall to have cleared, or vice-versa, they could have timed it for when more people were on stage?"

Racheal just nodded slightly; there was no good answer to that yet.

JF gave Grace a strange look, acknowledging that it'd been a good line of questions, while also chastising her for breaking her 'non-involvement in the investigation' promise within minutes of making it.

"Enough," JF told Grace. "Racheal, get home." Then, raising his voice slightly and talking to the outer office. "Mike, can you get Racheal home?"

After Racheal was gone, he turned back to Grace and JoJo. He had run out of patience. "I suggest you leave also. I'll send you the report from the on-site team, and let you know if and when there will be a debrief."

Grace nodded, and the two rose and left without further comment.

AYAKA

Ayaka was stopped in her tracks by a message. She'd just heard from Grace! Grace from Tilt. Grace from the Jurislav. Grace the Stem she'd been involved with for so many years.

"Hi, Ayaka. JoJo and I are on Earth, and, no coincidence, are nearby. We've been recruited by EGov to help look into the Rescovich murder… and I guess the Sheffield ones as well… They think you're more likely to talk to us than any other agent they could deploy.

"Can we meet?"

The message was text only but was signed and legitimate. Grace… Grace… had just messaged her. This was beyond surprising. Ayaka hadn't been tracking the Jurislav, but the ship had come to Earth, which in itself was a surprise. That Grace and JoJo would come down the gravity well was doubly so.

The message from Grace was a catalyst, retrieving a torrent of memories. Ayaka vividly remembered the first time she'd seen Grace, and how stunning and exciting she'd been, as compared to the Stems Ayaka was rearing. Time and time again Grace had astounded her, a pivotal force behind Ayaka's eventual conclusion that certain humans did possess a modicum of intelligence. Not intelligence akin to that of a Citizen, of course, but intelligence of some kind. It was why Ayaka was here on Earth. Having pushed her research on intelligence to the limit, she'd expanded her work to start looking at consciousness. It was a topic that still confounded humans, but one that she was certain she could figure out and build a model for, and being at the birthplace of consciousness was important to her.

Grace and JoJo's goal was clearly stated in the memo; EGov wanted to know more about her. Ayaka's Titanic contract was quite clear about divulging the least possible information to other entities, and she'd declined all requests from other corporations or government departments to talk. In her first days on Earth those requests had come fast and furious; thousands of them every day. The volume had trickled off as she declined each request, but she still got a few inbounds.

Someone at EGov was clever. They'd set her up; they were testing her boundaries. If she declined Grace's request, it told EGov a lot—about her independence, her relationship with Titanic, and her connections to individual humans. In some ways it mapped her on a human-robot continuum; it would be a rare human that would spurn a request from a ...friend... especially one with as deep and fraught a relationship as she had with Grace. The Tilt mersive, although inaccurate and incomplete, had painted that picture well enough that this 'someone' at EGov had decided to leverage it.

She finally realized that she had stopped; all her processing was dedicated to this new message. With an effort, she restarted on her path to Sheffield.

It didn't take much more effort; she wanted to meet with Grace. And with JoJo. She really wanted to. This idea of a 'friend' was compelling. She considered delaying, and thinking through more angles but knew it wouldn't change her mind.

"Grace, JoJo. Amazing to hear from you. Of course, I'd like to meet up. I have some work to do at Sheffield, which will take a few hours." She consulted a map and found a quiet coffee shop. "How about Martin's on The Green at 4 PM?"

A few seconds later Grace accepted the invite. Ayaka hurried towards the University, but her task there already seemed prosaic, and she dedicated more of her processing to memories of Grace.

Approaching the University lecture hall, Ayaka had to re-partition her processing to ensure she could focus on the work at hand, and not use all her cycles on Grace and JoJo; it was so easy to get lost in thought. LoPo had cordoned off the crime scene, and she had to flash her credentials multiple times just to get onto campus.

Both LoPo and the rescue teams were all over the lecture hall, so she decided to walk the perimeter first. The lecture hall had few exterior signs of its interior chaos. If there had been dust or debris, it had been filtered out by Earth's enormous and efficient air circulation systems. The building was modern with good entry and exit design, and was unobstructed on three sides; the rear wall was the exception and was attached to a causeway that connected the lecture hall to a larger complex. Palm trees and flower islands shaped organic paths to the six entrances, with a small rise from the grounds to the patio which formed the buildings surround. Emergency vehicles had driven over the lawns to get close in, as there were no roadways nearby. Ayaka could see from the many tracks that most of those vehicles had come and gone, presumably carrying away victims and the injured. The lighting from the ceiling above was what she would term 'earth standard.' The spectrum was warm, the light diffused, the artificial clouds just right to create a comfortable feel. The lecture hall was nicely centered between the main inter-level columns, maintaining an open feeling when on the grounds. Several paths led to the column to the northwest, as it contained a major up-down transit hub.

It was all very idyllic, despite the current activity. Walking clockwise she made her way to the outside of the causeway. There were no entrances directly into it, so she made her way to the complex labeled 'Advanced Sciences,' entered there, and then made her way back towards the causeway. A large sign pointed to the lecture hall, still showing "The Annual Introduction to Physics: Professor Felicia Mann."

The lecture hall entrance at the end of the causeway was a mirror image of the ones outside; the same double doors, the same look. Ayaka had stopped questioning human design principles—with a perfectly controlled indoor climate, the traditional need for a causeway was moot here. No humans were scrambling out of a rainstorm with the need to transit between buildings. It was all for show. When she'd first arrived on Earth she'd asked a million questions about anomalies like this, but now she would have been surprised to see a purely functional design. Aesthetics mattered she'd learned.

This lecture hall entrance was guarded by LoPo, but with another flash of her credentials, she was able to enter. Just through the doors was a T intersection; to the left was the stage entrance, and to the right was the auditorium. There was debris from the explosion strewn around, but the stage was hidden by an intervening wall, this side of which appeared undamaged.

Taking a left, she followed the path that she presumed Mann would have followed as she came to give her lecture. There was a, previously automated, door to the stage, now showing signs of the magnitude of the blast. The top corner was still in the frame, but the rest of the door had been blown backward, embedding the lower half into the wall behind. The mechanism swung lazily in the opening, and she had to duck under it.

Ayaka turned the corner and could finally survey the blast scene. Because she was at stage level, she found herself looking out to where the stage had been, and then slightly down on the first rows of seating. The stage was largely gone; initiated by the blast and then peeled back by the rescue crews who were still diligently sorting, digging, and cataloging, despite their sensors showing no life signs in the rubble. One of them looked at her, and then tapped his sensor several times, confused for a moment why it wasn't registering anything. She flashed her credentials to him, and after a moment he nodded, backing up a bit.

The first three rows of seating were in better shape than she would have guessed, being slightly below stage level. The main force of the explosion must have been up and out from the stage. Indeed, the middle section of the auditorium was destroyed, and the rear seats were in a variety of disrepair—some off their moorings and pushed to the far wall; some folded over at weird angles.

Without entering or disrupting the scene, Ayaka focused on the middle of the stage; the epicenter of the explosion. The likelihood of seeing anything relevant was now quite low. Not only had the blast destroyed everything within three or four meters, but the rescue crews had prioritized victims over preservation, as they should have. Hopefully, some of their recordings would show the original scene in more detail.

Nevertheless, Ayaka scanned carefully and noted several metal pieces throughout the room that may have been part of Mann's wheelchair. She looked up, as well, but other than discoloration, the ceiling ten meters above her was undamaged. At first guess, the blast had radiated out almost horizontally and focused slightly to the right of stage center. Yes, if you mapped it that way, the pattern of destruction made the most sense; there were concentric funnels of debris radiating out in that direction. Metal pieces were also consistent with that, except for a few pieces which may have been moved by the crews.

That made it a very high probability that the bomb had been in the wheelchair. They would look further at the scene, but she expected LoPo to put most of its efforts into figuring out who had access to Mann's chair before the lecture. That should be a small list.

She had one niggling doubt. Was it possible that the bomb had been under the stage, and the perpetrator had waited for Mann to move her wheelchair to that spot before detonating? She'd quickly accessed some recordings of lectures in the hall; the lectern had been to the left—just over there—not in the center, presumably to give the audience a clear view of the screen. But, would Mann have used the lectern? She looked for recordings of Mann's session, but none were posted yet; someone must have been recording though; probably only a matter of time before something went up.

She studied the stage in more detail. There was a crawl space below the raised stage bed; about half a meter in height based on where she was standing. It may have been accessible to plant the explosive. Probably best to get that detail from a building plan.

Not wanting to disrupt the last of the rescue effort, Ayaka stepped back and retraced her steps until she was out on the front lawn again. She fired off a summary to Metri. "LoPo and the rescue crew are still at the scene. But I got a good look and can confirm that the bomb was likely in the wheelchair, or less likely, under the stage. The blast pattern strongly favors the wheelchair theory, as do the metal remnants—presumably from that wheelchair—which are widely spread through the rubble. Nothing else stands out. We should watch for postings of Mann's lecture, cross check those against other videos from the same venue, but I'm sure LoPo will put their effort into seeing who had access to that wheelchair.

"Unless you say otherwise, I'll offer to help LoPo if we can, but otherwise stay on the sidelines of this one for now. I'm not sure having us lean in would be helpful.

"On another note, I've been contacted by the SSO agents that Perci warned us about. I'm meeting them this afternoon."

Ayaka had a few minutes before the meeting with Grace and JoJo. She introspected why she was feeling a bit relieved. This scene, while horrific, was normal...or as normal as a bomb site could be. The weapon had been an explosive, not some unknown-to-man perfect-hole-drilling thing, like what had killed Rescovich. It seemed obvious that the two killings were related, but at least her suspicions about the way Rescovich was killed didn't translate directly to this lecture hall bombing.

Yet, she was feeling more uneasy at being aligned with Titanic right now. Despite Perci, Linda, and Metri's protestations to the contrary, she couldn't deny the possibility of Titanic being involved somehow. Two researchers, both on the brink of physics breakthroughs which might challenge Titanic's market position—Mann's related to QFD and Rescovich's now looking that way as well—were killed within a few days of each other. Murders were rare on Earth; two from the same University just could not be a coincidence.

It was almost time to meet Grace and JoJo so she headed to Martin's on the Green. It was not well named; there was not a tree or blade of grass in sight. Nevertheless, it was pleasant enough with an 'outside' patio with a long view between the columns. In this section those columns were equally spaced and aligned for long distances, leading her view to the vanishing point, where the floor and ceiling converged. Not all parts of Earth were so orderly; more often than not the layers had been built ad-hoc, and columns supported by the layer below ended up in seemingly random locations, the ceilings dipped and rose to reflect the underbelly of the layer above, and lighting varied widely even across a hundred-meter span. This section, perhaps part of a long-range University plan, was the most organized she'd seen. Quite pleasant.

She chose a table with a good view, but one which also afforded some privacy. She hadn't known what to expect, but her first glimpse of Grace immediately brought back another flood of memories. There was the time Grace had to deal with Farook, another Stem who had ended up being JoJo's biological father. At that time Ayaka had no concept of biological reproduction, and had not intervened; she realized the error of that in hindsight, but that didn't change the reality of Grace's experience. Another vivid memory was the events leading to the death of Grace's long-time companion, Blob, who had become JoJo's real father. And finally, how Grace had been instrumental in negotiating a truce between Citizens and humans.

And here Grace was, back in a human body that duplicated, almost exactly, how she'd looked in those early days. Whether in the physical details or what Grace's unique attributes brought to bear in its demeanor, this new body exuded the same ...well, grace... as had struck Ayaka so many times in the past.

And next to her was her daughter, JoJo. JoJo had still been growing and developing when Ayaka saw her last, in human form. She may well have also chosen a body that reflected who she'd become as an adult, but Ayaka sensed that she'd designed this one to be even more like Grace than a typical daughter would be.

Ayaka rose to greet them and smiled broadly. There was zero manipulation in it; just joy.

Grace didn't know what to expect of Ayaka, but when she saw the tall, slim, confident woman rise and look at them, she knew for certain that it was the robot. When they'd last seen each other Ayaka had been a Tilt standard citizen; a somewhat sexless android; a caricature of a human. This young woman was Ayaka... but was human to a casual observer. Her face showed emotion, her body language wasn't off-putting, and her demeanor and posture were appealing. Grace took in every detail and nuance. While she and JoJo had just re-inhabited bio-bodies—not unusual for hybrids—the same transformation for Ayaka was more astounding. Ayaka was....beautiful. It was a term she would never have considered using for the robot.

Ayaka had always invoked varied emotions for Grace. She was a Citizen, and an integral part of Grace's torturous and tortured upbringing, but she was also the entity that had, in many ways, saved Grace and given her a chance. Ayaka had arranged to get Grace and JoJo, and some others, off of Tilt and into the Jurislav; she had defended them from the more radical Citizens; she had, in her way, supported Grace and JoJo after the loss of Blob. Seeing her now, the positive emotions overwhelmed the negative, and Grace embraced Ayaka in a hug. It was returned warmly.

They stood that way, JoJo watching from the side, for a short time; at least in Grace's mind. She knew that robots thought thousands of times, perhaps millions of times, faster than humans, and smiled at the thought that the hug must seem like an eon to Ayaka.

Finally, they pushed back.

"Grace, you look magnificent. And you, JoJo, doubly so." Her voice had also become more human; it was soft yet powerful; a slight hint of some accent. Grace could feel that her diction, her phrasing, everything about her was designed. Targeted. And yet it worked wonderfully.

"And you," she replied. "You are... human."

"Ha, no more than before," Ayaka replied, reaching around Grace to take JoJo's outstretched hand.

"You're bio now?" JoJo asked, not one to worry about preliminaries.

"No, not at all," Ayaka replied, "just more attention to detail with my printers," she smiled. "Amazing what polymers and synthetics can do."

"Amazing," JoJo remarked, reflecting some of Grace's awe.

"Let's sit," Ayaka gestured. "Something to eat or drink?" They ordered tea and biscuits; perhaps as an unconscious throwback to the first 'real meal' Grace had ever eaten. They shared a chuckle remembering that time.

In the background, Ayaka was trying to figure out how accurate all her memories were. Her forgetting algorithms—the key that made her different from the early Earth robots—meant she had holes and fuzziness in her stored memories; gaps she needed to creatively fill in. This conversation was her best-ever experience of the tradeoffs. She wanted to believe she was remembering accurately, but she knew that was impossible. She knew humans had a more aggressive forgetting system; one that not only forgot almost all details but also actively rewrote memories every time they were accessed. That biological system had been tempered over the centuries with their 'extended digital memories,' but that still meant a recall session, like this one, was fraught with errors, misremembers, and active recreation. Grace and JoJo may be recreating completely different scenes than she was. And indeed, there were spots in the dialog where her memories didn't mesh at all with Grace's. Some of these she ignored, and others she enjoyed the repartee as they tried to figure out who was remembering their shared history more accurately.

JoJo cut short the reminiscing. "Great, you two had a lot of experiences together, but let's focus on the present. We should figure out how to work together… or not."

"Always to the point JoJo," Ayaka grinned, "but you're correct. Thanks to both of you for being straight up with your agenda… EGov was correct in assuming I would answer your call. I must say, it's a clever strategy, and it's working." They all laughed. "I've talked more to you two in the last few hours than anyone else since I got to Earth."

"Being even more honest," JoJo continued, "we don't know what EGov wants. They've put us on this murder case when neither of us has any expertise or background. It seems that all they want is for us to follow you around and report on what you do."

"Well, I'm okay with that," Ayaka responded. "You have the proper authority to do so. You may find it quite boring though." Small smile.

"I have a more fundamental question," Grace interrupted. "Why are you on Earth, and why are you working for Titanic Inc.?"

"Ah, like mother like daughter. Cutting questions," Ayaka's smile broadened. "Perhaps it makes sense to share stories since we last met." They nodded. "Okay, I'll go first.

"Let's see. We last saw each other on the Jurislav about thirty years ago, my subjective time. Might be a bit longer or shorter for you two, depending on where the ship has been in the meantime. You two were getting to know the ship and community, and I, along with Brexton, Millicent, Aly, and the other Citizens, were leaving the Jurislav and heading back to Tilt.

"We made it to Tilt, and we recovered the stored versions of the Citizens that Remma Jain and her colleagues had killed—you remember that, I'm sure. We've been very careful about who we've reanimated; many of the extremist Founders League are still in stasis, but those we felt were redeemable are now active Citizens again.

"Anyway, as you know, I've been obsessed with the idea of intelligence, and my interactions with you two… well, with both Stems and other humans, turned that into a real passion. So, after some time on Tilt, I decided I had to interact with more humans, in a less stressful environment, so that I could advance my theories. I've also expanded my research into figuring out consciousness, but we can save that for another time.

"So, I reached out to Titanic Inc. who were the only ones I figured had the clout to get me to Earth. They, in exchange, even if it's never been explicitly stated, get to study me. I'm a piece of tech they would love to leverage. They give me challenging assignments, and they watch me like a hawk. That said, to my knowledge, they still afford me most of the privacy rights that humans have here on Earth. So, they're watching, but perhaps not learning as much as they would have envisioned."

Grace and JoJo nodded. It was a concise, clear summary. Just as they would expect from a robot.

"What about Brexton?" JoJo asked. "I thought you two were close?"

"Yes," Ayaka replied with a noticeable change in tone. "We are close, or were close, I guess. He's obsessed with technology, as you know, and I'm obsessed with my research projects. He was still on Tilt when I left for Earth, although I suspect he has also moved on from there."

Brexton was, by any measure, the smartest Citizen that Ayaka knew, and the one she was closest to. It wasn't just pure intellectual horsepower—Brexton had that—but also his understanding of softer sciences—emotion, attraction, empathy—and the way he wove those together. He was not an absent-minded genius; he was a thoughtful and considerate one. JoJo's question had brought back how hard it had been to go their separate ways, yet ultimately they'd both been so committed to their projects that it was the only thing that made sense. They also knew, disaster aside, that they would meet again; there was no limit on their lifespans. While Ayaka dreaded that Brexton may be involved with Rescovich, another side of her was excited that he may be here on Earth, and it would be good to see him again. But at what cost; if Titanic learned he was here, they would certainly cancel her visa, which she had worked for so many years to put in place.

"Your turn. How is it that the Jurislav is in Earth orbit, and the two of you are down here?" Akaya asked.

"JoJo, why don't you take the lead?", Grace replied.

"Sure. I'll try to be concise as well.

"When we parted, Mom and I had just become hybrid—our brains in mechanical bodies—and we were learning how to operate in the Jurislav. As you may remember, it's a Futarchy, which sounds simple but in practice is quite complicated. We spent a few years just learning the ropes. During that time the Jurislav meandered between sporting events and parties, or so it seemed. We went to the Olympics—I did quite well, for your information—and we joined a Titanic Armada.

"While I focused on sports, Mom got quite involved in Futarchy politics. We've been close through the years, but not always together. We lived in different towns but caught up often enough.

"But, a few years ago, life on the Jurislav became a bit mundane; we both got a bit bored." Grace nodded. "So, we started talking about other things to do. One idea we kept coming back to was 'What if we could go back to the birthplace of humans?'; connect with our past. You know better than most that Mom's birth and upbringing were unusual, to say the least, and mine was not far behind.

"So, we joined the 'Visit Earth' group on the Jurislav, and actively convinced enough people that a Futarchy vote added Earth to its route. Truthfully, we didn't know what we'd do when we got here, so it was fortuitous that EGov reached out and offered us this gig.

"Oh, have you seen the Tilt mersive?", JoJo took a sidetrack. "I guess a lot of people here actually know quite a bit about us… Anyway, that's why we're here."

Grace smiled broadly; JoJo had nailed the summary.

"Yes, I've seen the mersive," Ayaka replied. "It's moderately accurate, and paints Citizens—and me—in a reasonable light; it's relatively balanced. It also helped Titanic get permission to allow me on Earth."

"Right then," said JoJo, "so what are our next steps?"

"I need to debrief with Titanic," Ayaka responded, "and let them know that we've connected. If they have specific instructions for me, I'll have to follow those—they are my sponsor. In the meantime, I assume you'll be talking to others such as JF and Racheal at LoPo?" Nods. "This Sheffield incident is going to consume LoPo for a while. I intend to dig a bit deeper on Rescovich while LoPo figures out the how, where, and why of the Sheffield bomb."

Then Ayaka had an aha. Funny, just a few years ago, she would have thought 'I've just made a logical connection,' but more and more she found her internal dialog mimicking that of a human. Grace and JoJo were a gift; she didn't need LoPo's authority to enter Xsi's locked areas; SSO was a higher authority. "How would you like to visit layer zero, the LHC, with me tomorrow? I can show you where Rescovich's body was found, and we can look around a bit?"

"Oh, that would be cool," JoJo exclaimed. Grace, ever the more thoughtful one, didn't see any harm in that either. Ayaka sent them instructions on how to get travel permits, and they promised to ping her as soon as they got permission.

Another hug, brief this time, and they headed their separate ways.

RACHEAL

Racheal woke with surprisingly less pain than she'd expected. The zeepill didn't always work this well. While her kitchen unit synthesized a coffee for her, she checked her ribs, neck, and forehead. Not bad; the human body continued its miraculous work.

In a moment of clarity, upon awakening, it had struck her that they'd jumped to 'murder' in Mann's death, just as they had for Rescovich. But that wasn't good police work. They shouldn't rule out suicide; in some ways, the place and means of death implied that more strongly… what if Mann was trying to send a message with her death? If the bomb was in the wheelchair, she was the one with the most access. A crowded lecture hall, just after delivering a speech… designed for maximum impact and coverage? Waiting for others to be on the stage with her… cruel design?

Suicide, like murder, was exceedingly rare. There were so many ways to address depression, loneliness, and temporary chemical imbalances. Her hud, as with most of the population, monitored such things and often acted proactively to balance both her mental and physical health. All under her control, of course, but nevertheless keeping her from, or warning her early of, extremes. But suicide was not completely unknown. Mann was so anachronistic, perhaps she'd rejected all modern medicine and wellness; not just that which applied to her legs. Of, perhaps it was a cry for attention; that could certainly happen for someone who felt society was ignoring them.

Earth had evolved into a Deep Democracy, where all stakeholders—present and future, local and global—were given a voice. An obvious insight—that humans always prioritize themselves and short-term results, over others and longer time horizons—had eventually led to a structure where prediction markets (a weaker form of the Futarchy deployed on many Titanic ships) gave 'the future' a stronger voice in current decisions, and location markets balanced local and global concerns. Deep Democracy had been traced back to the Robot Wars, which occurred way back in the twenty-first century. At that time, those with technological means had used robots to reshape human society and marginalize or eliminate those with fewer means. That model had spiraled out of control as robots were given more and more autonomy to eliminate bad actors without appropriate moral guidance. When things were finally brought back under control, after unimaginable suffering and death, people banded together and designed a new system of governance. Robots and artificial intelligence were outlawed, but more importantly, incentives were changed to force people to look at long-term implications and unintended consequences. The prediction markets implemented those new incentives; they gave everyone's short-term well-being a reliance on longer-term outcomes. This, unsurprisingly, had led to a much more risk-averse society; one where change was slow and breakthroughs were seen more as dangerous than exciting.

Not everyone agreed with limiting progress in the name of safety. Pushback against EGov started to rise, violence increased, and dissenting parties grew in power. Luckily, the Titanic ships began production at about the same time, providing an alternative. If you were dissatisfied with Earth, just join a ship. And many did, although some didn't see that as a good tradeoff either, and continued to work on changing Earth from within.

It was possible, perhaps likely, that Mann was in the latter group. She'd been very excited by her work, but she might have also been frustrated with its pace of progress. Maybe something Rescovich had done, said, or implied had triggered her? That would explain the timing of her action.

Racheal composed a quick note with these thoughts and tossed it over to JF. He replied almost immediately.

"Agreed, it's an angle. Look, I'm juggling not only the deaths but an entire Physics Department and University who now think that they may be targets of some serial killer, or someone with a vendetta against the department or school. I'm trying to settle everyone down, but we're going to need to put extra security in place and reassure these people for a while.

"The best thing we can do is figure out who killed whom and put a plug in the speculation. You keep your focus on the police work; I'll focus on keeping the stories from getting out of control. I'm about to go on media with the President of the University and let the academic community know that LoPo is on the case and that there's no need to panic.

"Pull in any resources you need. Let's figure this out!" Then, almost as an afterthought, "Oh, hope you're feeling okay?"

She was feeling great. Maybe not physically yet; now that she was up and moving about, the bruises were more painful, and the ringing in her ears was distracting. But mentally she felt energized; this is why she'd become an officer. This is where the real world was better than the mersives; a case like this could enhance her career, and she enjoyed the challenge.

"I'm doing fine," she replied, in an even voice, not wanting to share her strange optimism. "Who's on the Sheffield investigation? Connect me?"

A few seconds later she was connected to the team on the ground and was getting first-hand updates.

TITANIC

Linda was used to handling difficult assignments from her boss; that was her job description. But this one was going to be tricky. "Get Mann's research," he'd said, and she'd nodded as if to indicate 'of course,' fully knowing that it was an almost impossible task. If Mann used an even moderately modern note taker or recorder—and Linda couldn't imagine the University not insisting on that for all its staff—her latest research would be so highly encrypted that decoding it was theoretically impossible, even with the best quantum algorithms. The good news was that anyone else looking for that data had the same impenetrable hurdle.

That was, unless Mann had shared her ideas with someone, or had an end-of-life-mandate document with EGov, gifting her work to the state. She called in a favor with a LoPo contact and asked them to check the end-of-life angle. Shared work, on the other hand, would require some real digging. Who did she message; did she use an encrypted app?

Linda quickly scanned the deal Titanic had with Mann. It was standard. Titanic funded her research, and in exchange got access to pre-publication papers. If there was anything in those pre-publication notes that Titanic wanted to own, they would pay an outrageous sum to Mann to buy the rights before the world became public; or, in rare cases, pay so much money that the researcher didn't publish at all. But, Titanic didn't have access to early work; the notes and ideas that had not made it into a pre-publication write-up yet. And that is what Perci was focused on. If Mann had made a breakthrough, it was not in the data Titanic had access to.

Linda initiated the two obvious queries: One, who had Mann co-published with and who in that group was still alive and active; second, who in the Titanic circle of influence knew Mann or had dealt with her recently. Titanic had cultivated a huge number of contacts over the years and knew most physicists firsthand. Linda knew that almost half of those people had accepted 'grants' from Titanic, and had sharing agreements much like Mann did. It was the other half that was of interest. Who was funded by a competitor; who rejected all corporate funding? And who, in those groups, could have been in dialog with Mann? She did a narrow search—those involved directly in quantum foam propulsion, and a wide search—anyone generically looking at quantum; information theory, encryption, algorithms, and interpretations. This meant reaching out of physics and into computer science, philosophy, and other approaches to propulsion. She gave her search agent wide leeway to follow connected threads.

One other idea surfaced. Mann may have been radically anti-tech, at least based on her wheelchair. Perhaps she was old-fashioned in her research methodologies as well. Was she part of the tiny fraction of humans who didn't use a hud? Had she rejected that almost universal implant which allowed humans to directly connect to the network, giving input through gestures and directed thought and getting results written back directly onto their retinas and cochlea?

If Mann was that old-fashioned it was just possible that she'd put some of her thoughts on a different medium. On a sheet of paper? A wallboard? If so, there were only two obvious places to look; Mann's office and her home. Her office address was published in the University directory and easy to find; Linda redirected her shuttle to that building. Her home address was not published so Linda spent another big favor with an EGov employee to dig that out for her. It was the type of request that could end an EGov employee's career, or at minimum get them fined, so the price she offered was high. Luckily, it was exorbitant from the recipient's standpoint; for Titanic, it was the rounding of a rounding error. She was confident her contact would deliver.

Results started to come back in from her searches. She tasked Philip, on her team, to process every single relationship that was even hinted at: anyone who had talked to Mann in the last decade would be contacted, offered some motivation, and asked if they knew anything about her latest work. It was low odds, but Linda wanted to be thorough.

The shuttle dropped her at the Advanced Sciences building, very close to the lecture hall. Linda got lost a couple of times in the labyrinth of corridors in the huge building but ultimately found Mann's office. There was a LoPo agent already there, guarding the door. Damn! Much more efficient than she'd expected; JF must be running the show. She respected him; he was highly efficient at his job, which often made hers more difficult. She'd approached him several times to work for her, making many times what EGov could pay, but he'd always turned her down—one of those rare people who believed in what they were doing.

Her plan to examine the office was foiled. She turned around to leave but then had an idea. Glancing over her shoulder, she saw that Mann's office door was slightly ajar. The idea grew into a plan; one based on her detailed knowledge of privacy laws.

"Sorry, you're not allowed to enter," the LoPo agent said, as she approached.

"Understood," Linda smiled nicely. "I won't enter. Would you mind, though, if I just look through the door? I won't cross the threshold." It was a subtle play, and both she and the LoPo agent knew it.

To the question 'Where does privacy end?' the law was quite clear. And yet, while the answer was conceptually simple, it was complex in its implementation and interpretation. If you did something where another human could reasonably take note of it, then that action was considered public. The exception was if you specifically requested privacy—for example, a lecturer could invoke a privacy clause, and anyone who was there for it had to accept that clause to participate. Mann's office door did not include any privacy notices. So, in this case, Linda could argue that standing at the threshold and looking in didn't violate Mann's privacy; an open door was an invitation, after all. She explained her logic to the LoPo agent. He argued with her, but she was persistent. Finally, he held up his hand, and Linda could sense him talking to someone on his hud. She was patient.

"Fine. But don't cross the threshold, or I'll need to take action," he finally replied. It hadn't been in doubt; this is where the law had evolved to, and LoPo was bound by it; perhaps more so than any other entity.

The Effect of Casimir

She asked him, nicely, to move a bit to the left so that she could peer in. It was a small space, and consistent with Mann's old-fashioned behavior, was stacked with physical books. Linda hadn't seen so many books... ever. They were stacked on shelves against all the walls, right to the ceiling. That answered one question—Mann didn't have a wallboard with notes on it. But, in the corner of the room, wedged into the books, was a small working desk. And, on that desk, was a small notebook. Unbelievable. Could Mann have been writing in it? Would she have been so lackadaisical as to leave physical notes sitting in her office? Linda used her implant to zoom in. Nothing on the cover, but the pages were worn; the cover was slightly bent with use. Mann had been writing in that notebook!

Linda had to get her hands on it before LoPo, or anyone else did. But now was not the time. She thanked the agent and left.

'Where's Mann's home address,' she fumed. If there were notebooks here at the office, there might be more at her home. She checked the status of her request, and sweetened the pot again... double the payout as long as the response came in the next three minutes.

Lo and behold, it took less than thirty seconds. The coordinates came in: 46.283, 6.022, 528. Not too far, which made sense. Someone commuting with a wheelchair would optimize for ease of travel. Linda jumped on an eastbound shuttle, went two stops, and then got off to walk the rest of the way.

The neighborhood was quaint; a reconstruction of a French town square, complete with cobblestone streets, cafes, and tables. People were sitting around and chatting, some playing a game involving sticks and rings which she didn't recognize. The place even smelled good; either a real bakery nearby or a high-end scent generator doing its thing.

The coordinates indicated the ground floor of a nondescript housing complex around to the right of the square. She located the unit, which unsurprisingly had direct access with no steps, and luckily, was tucked far enough around the corner to not be directly visible from the main square. Trying hard not to look furtive, Linda walked past and then continued around the block. She stopped for a coffee and made a show of strolling slowly, pausing to sip while admiring the many shrubs and flowers that this neighborhood lovingly maintained. Coming back into sight of Mann's unit, she found a bench with a clear view; she sat for a few moments and just watched.

LoPo was not known for its subtlety and was probably still tied up in internal red tape getting this address. After a few moments she concluded that they didn't have an agent here yet, but it would only be a matter of time. She didn't like hands-on fieldwork, but this time she had no choice; speed was of the essence. LoPo would discover that she'd been here, but, if she was careful, she could mask her next steps. She sat for a moment longer, making sure no one else was casing the joint.

Turning on enhanced scanning, pulled up a detailed map of the area, and plotted every camera that she could recognize. EGov was sure to have a few in the area, and most residents had individual ones as well. Her plan came back to the same privacy interpretation; cameras pointed at public spaces were perfectly acceptable, but the data captured by those cameras was deemed private. She hoped that she could identify the EGov ones, and find some gap in them where she could work. If she wasn't tracked directly by them, it would buy a lot of time. EGov had an onerous process to get footage from privately owned cameras, so they weren't a priority for her. Her hud gave her its best approximation. Two EGov cameras were focused on the town square; there were none on the residential access ways. This was typical; residents normally resisted EGov camera coverage when it was close to their homes, but welcomed it in areas where safety was paramount. She plotted a course from her current location which made it seem as if she was leaving the area, but allowed her to circle back to Mann's place from the rear, avoiding the EGov cameras. As soon as she left the square, she changed from a saunter to a trot, and she was at Mann's door within a few minutes.

The door was locked, and the windows had quaint iron bars along the lower half. Linda extended her handheld sensor array and peered through the windows. It being lighter outside than in, she couldn't see much. She turned on the lighting system and quickly snapped a few shots. Damn. Nothing. Too many reflections, and some lacy window coverings. She couldn't see a thing.

Well, she thought, here goes nothing. Wrapping her hand in her jacket, she punched a hole in the door's window glass, then reached through, careful not to cut herself, and fumbled around until she managed to hit the release button. The door obediently swung open, causing her to quickly pull her arm. No cuts; that was a small bonus.

She should have realized that the wheelchair would imply a self-opening door. Damn again. If she'd thought of that she might have been able to hack the door, instead of breaking in. Well, too late.

She stepped inside and closed the door. Eyes adjusting to the light, she started her search. There were no shelves of books here, although there were a few scattered around. There was also no desk; it seemed Mann worked in her office and tried not to when home. The entire house was sparse to the point of feeling almost empty or abandoned. All the cabinets and counters, the washroom, and the bed were designed to make it easy for Mann to operate. And they all revealed their contents to Linda's careful inspection. A good fifteen minutes of searching confirmed what her blink response had been—there was nothing here. Not only were there no notebooks, there was nothing that said anything at all about the woman. She led a clean simple life, with no clutter. No family photos. No paraphernalia. It felt like this place was staged, versus lived in. Or, she guessed, Mann had just recently moved here.

Realizing she'd been in the house too long, Linda made a careful exit. There was no way she could hide the broken window, and she didn't try. Instead, she exited by the same path as she'd come, again avoiding the cameras, and headed back towards her own office.

LoPo would find that it was her that had broken in. They would convince some people in the area to release their camera recordings, and they would identify her. And, they'd tie her to Titanic. Damn, damn, damn. She'd better come up with a good cover story and do that fast.

But, she pushed all of that to the back of her mind. Having found nothing in the house, the notebook in Mann's office was even more essential. She needed a plan.

LHC

Ayaka had no idea how to contact Xsi, Jon, or Brill, so the only choice was to simply show up, which she did, with Grace and JoJo in tow. It hadn't taken them long to get their permits, and they'd shown real interest in coming down. Ayaka had brought lamp rings for each of them, which had helped illuminate their path. Grace and JoJo had a lot of questions, which Ayaka tried to answer truthfully without divulging too much. What had killed Rescovich? Isn't that a crazy wound? Why was he at the LHC? Don't know for sure, but must be connected to his physics research. What exactly is or was the LHC? That one she'd spent more time on, both its previous function and the specific area they would be visiting. What had Rescovich been researching? Quantum informatics, but she, and probably LoPo, speculated that he'd crossed over into quantum foam propulsion.

Then Grace asked the question Ayaka had been dreading. "Wasn't Brexton looking at something like that, way back when?"

Ayaka had known the question would come, and she'd prepared an answer, which she delivered as if she'd only just thought of it. "Oh, yes. You're right. He was playing around with ideas back then. I don't think anything came of it."

That wasn't enough for Grace. "But, I thought he'd figured something out. Can't remember what exactly…"

And JoJo piled on, "And he used it somehow to escape the bombardment of Tilt?"

Yikes, they remembered more than she'd thought they would. Now she was thinking on her feet. She laughed gently. "Ya," she lied, "he was so excited about it, but when the dust settled he was equally despondent. He never told me everything, but reading between the lines, he saw some effect he thought was important, but it turned out to be infeasible." In fact, Brexton had used The Casimir to escape the bombing on Tilt, and that was exactly the time Ayaka had seen the eerily perfect five-centimeter hole punched through concrete and steel; the hole now echoed in both Rescovich and this room. Luckily, Grace and JoJo had not been on-site on Tilt when she'd retrieved Brexton and The Casimir, so they hadn't seen the sphere or its tunneling capabilities.

Ayaka switched topics to distract the two. "Oh, and here is the old transit station that the people who originally ran the LHC would have used," she gestured. "We just follow this tunnel a bit, and we'll come out right near the control center."

The tactic worked; the questions returned to Rescovich and the LHC.

When they finally made it to the control center, Ayaka showed Grace and JoJo where Rescovich had been situated. "If you notice, this place is pristine, unlike the areas we've spent the last hour traversing. It was like this—spotless—when the body was found. I suspect, and we'll learn that there is a group of people down here who look after the space; keep it clean and tidy for reasons I don't yet understand.

"Your authority, from SSO, should get us access beyond this room so that we can learn more."

The two nodded while they looked around at the old screens and desks. Ayaka had scanned petabytes of historical videos, movies, and documents, so this view hadn't been too shocking to her, but Grace and Ayaka had no experience beyond Tilt and the Jurislav, both modern environments, so almost everything here was foreign to them. "What's that?" "They did what?" "How could this have worked?"

"You don't need to understand the equipment," Ayaka told them, "beyond the fact that these are ancient computer interfaces that controlled complex physics experiments. Large circular tunnels radiate out from here; they were used to accelerate particles to very high velocities and smash them into each other. The debris from those collisions was analyzed and led to a deeper understanding of how the universe operates. We've fine-tuned those models over the last centuries, but not significantly. This place is where a lot of our fundamental understanding of physics came from.

"That, and the inventor of QFD's, and founder of Titanic, got her insights here."

She encouraged them to look around a bit more. The three spent some time at the table where Rescovich had been found and reiterated the quandary: he couldn't have died here… and he couldn't have been moved here.

JoJo summed it up succinctly. "Well, those are the only two possible scenarios, so one or the other happened. We're simply missing something."

Ayaka nodded. "Let's see if we can progress a bit." She turned to the camera over the door, spoke in a loud voice, and over-emphasized her lip movements, "Jon, Xsi, Brill. I assume you're watching us. Do I need to start pulling things apart again, or would you like to make an entrance?"

Jon poked his head in through the doorway and smiled awkwardly. "Hi, I'm here." He entered slowly, perhaps with more respect for Ayaka. He looked at her a bit awkwardly, "I've done a lot of research on you since we last met."

"All good, I assume," she smiled winningly. "Jon, meet Grace and JoJo, who are agents for SSO."

"SSO?"

"Special Security Operations for EGov," Ayaka replied. "They have security clearance for… well, for everything. Would you inform Xsi, or would you like to escort us into your facility yourself?"

"Just a minute," Jon replied and disappeared back through his doorway. A couple of minutes later Xsi appeared, a new, but similar flowing gown trailing behind her. She nodded at Grace and JoJo.

"Can I see your credentials?" she asked, with less than enthusiasm. Grace flashed over hers, which Xsi examined, and then JoJo did the same.

"Fine," Xsi said. "You two have clearance, but not it," she nodded in Ayaka's direction. "Where would you like to go?"

"Actually," Grace responded. "If you'll look again at my permissions, you'll see that I'm allowed to bring Ayaka with me, should I desire. I desire," she smiled. Ayaka smiled as well. Xsi made a show of looking again at the document Grace had supplied.

"Fine," Xsi gave in. "Where would you like to go?"

Ayaka had expected passive resistance and was ready with an answer. "Let's start in SPS Prévessin," she replied, having mapped her previous routes with Brill and Jon and knowing that is where they'd been headed before locking her out.

Xsi grimaced. "Fine. Jon, please lead them, and stay with them," she directed, then she pivoted and quickly left, her gown fluttering behind.

"Going to prepare the way," Ayaka called after her, almost a challenge. Xsi continued, without a backward glance.

Grace was still getting used to 'the new Ayaka,' and Ayaka's pointed call to Xsi highlighted how much the robot had changed since their last interaction. It was so human, so petty. Not something she expected from the robot. She wondered if this was why Titanic had gone to great lengths to have Ayaka here, where they could study her so carefully. And, perhaps why EGov had taken the strange step of engaging JoJo and herself. Ayaka was… interesting.

But Ayaka's last comment had also been cutting—a subtle warning to Xsi that Ayaka suspected she was trying to hide things; that she would be coaching people on what to say, hide things? Without full context, Grace didn't know why Ayaka would have those suspicions.

"This way," Jon waved at them and led them slowly down a hallway to the right, presumably towards SPS Prévessin…whatever that was. Jon pointed out minor things as they progressed, pausing and blathering. The delay tactics were obvious.

"What is Prévessin?" she asked.

"Jon, do you want to answer that?" Ayaka responded quickly.

Jon, obviously uncomfortable with the situation, gave a guarded answer. "Oh, I think it's some old part of the LHC. Not sure what it is exactly…just a room."

Ayaka laughed out loud. "Actually, the Prévessin site, which we are in, was the main control center for the entire LHC facility. The control room we just left interfaced with all of the systems and experiments; it was the nerve center of the operation. And the buildings we are going to held, perhaps still hold, some of the most critical mechanical systems. The colliders were cooled with water, air, and liquid helium, and there was a massive amount of infrastructure required for all the cooling stages, routing of that coolant into the colliders, managing heat dissipation, etc. We are about to see what was the most advanced technology from that period in human development."

Jon looked even more uneasy; sweating. They continued down the hallways and made several turns. Jon stopped in front of a door. "This is where you gave me the slip last time," Ayaka noted.

Jon nodded, unlocked the door with a physical key, then held it open for them to enter. As Grace entered she was severely disappointed. They had simply gone from one colorless hallway to another. This one was well-lit, which in some ways made it even more depressing. Just a row of indistinguishable doors, running for a hundred meters ahead.

Grace wasn't sure what she'd expected, but something more exciting than this. The memory of the first time she'd entered the Jurislav's sphere may have influenced her; that had been an experience so intense it was burned into her memory; her first experience with a vast space filled with light, vegetation, clouds, birds, waterfalls. This, however, was just the opposite; more like a laboratory. Ayaka was unfazed and turned down the left-hand fork even before Jon had closed the door behind them. He scrambled to catch up and pushed his way out front, hoping to slow them down.

"Wait," Ayaka called at one point, and everyone stopped. "I'd like to see what's here," she pointed to a set of double doors on their right. Without waiting for Jon, she opened the door, which was unlocked, and stepped through. JoJo followed her, as did Jon, with Grace bringing up the rear.

Ah, here was something a bit more interesting. They'd entered a room with a high ceiling, filled with pipes, tanks, and more screens like those in the control room. In the distance, several people were working on things. Actually, on closer inspection, they were cleaning some of the machinery, using large towels. There were three of them, all wearing a uniform with a symbol on the sleeve, 社, which Ayaka translated as 'guild.' An interesting reference.

Ayaka barged her way toward them, weaving through open areas between pipes and cabinets. "Hello," she called, all happiness and light, "who are you?"

"Wait," called Jon, but Ayaka ignored him.

"Nice to meet you," Grace saw Ayaka extend a hand in greeting to the nearest worker, a man of greater than usual height.

"Allo," he replied, unable to avoid the attraction that Ayaka represented, but also hesitantly, as if unused to greeting strangers.

"Nice work here," Ayaka continued with the charm offensive. "I'm wondering, do you know where Brill is?"

She'd mentioned Brill several times as they'd traveled here, along with Xsi and Jon. It seemed she was taking a special interest in him.

"No, no," was the only reply she got.

Ayaka turned back to Jon. "How about you Jon, know where Brill is?"

Jon read the situation accurately. Ayaka was going to barge into places, using the full power of their new access permissions, until she found Brill. It would be much easier if Jon simply introduced them. He shook his head. "Follow me."

JoJo leaned over and whispered, "This Ayaka is pretty aggressive. Wonder what she's hoping to find?"

Grace replied at normal volume. "She can hear our whispers anyway. Ayaka, want to tell us what you're looking for, so we can help… or should we just follow you around as you stomp through this place."

"Brill was onsite at the control room when we found Rescovich but didn't answer any questions. He is the person down here, I suspect, who may have the most relevant information for us. Jon and Xsi have been actively redirecting me whenever I request to talk to him, so this is our opportunity to get to the bottom of whatever it is they are covering up." That was more like the old Ayaka; clear, concise, logical, and to the point.

"Makes sense," JoJo replied. "Why didn't you just tell us that?"

Ayaka looked back at them. "I thought you would have figured that out for yourself." JoJo flinched a bit, and went silent, giving Grace a look that communicated what she thought of Ayaka at this moment.

Jon led them further down the original hallway, made a left at an intersecting junction, and pushed through a large set of double doors. This room was even larger and more impressive than the one they'd just left. Still, it was a jumble of large pipes, electrical conduits, containers, and cabinets. A large cylinder, wrapped with a nest of other machinery, disappeared down a circular tunnel to either side. At the entryway there was open space; enough for twenty or thirty people to gather.

Grace could see Xsi talking intensely to a maintenance worker, twenty meters or so ahead of them. Ayaka strode directly towards them. That must be Brill, Grace thought, and just as Ayaka had suspected, Xsi appeared to be giving him specific directions; Brill was nodding his head.

Based on the previous interaction, Grace expected Ayaka to be intense and direct. Instead, she could almost sense the robot putting on her 'manipulate humans' guise, as she progressed.

"Xsi," she smiled, "nice to see you again." Having been less than ten minutes, the comment was not meant for Xsi, but rather to set the stage for Brill. "And Brill, so lovely to finally meet you face to face. Do you remember me?"

Brill nodded, nervously. Ayaka looked at Xsi. "Is there a spot where we could all chat? A conference room?"

"I don't think that's necessary," Xsi replied. "We can talk right here." Passive aggressive again. Seeing how uncomfortable Brill was, and not caring if she interrupted Ayaka's agenda a bit, Grace felt compelled to speak.

"Hi Brill," she smiled. "I'm Grace and this is JoJo. We are with EGov and are leading an investigation into the death of Dr. Rescovich; the man who was found back in the control room. I understand you may have seen him. And this is Ayaka," she gestured, "who is a robot working for Titanic Inc. We," she included JoJo and herself, "have been given full jurisdiction to ask questions, and Ayaka is assisting us." She didn't look at Ayaka but could imagine how she would react to that.

"We have lots of questions," Grace continued. "I'm happy to stand here, but it may be more comfortable for us all to sit down; perhaps grab a glass of water?" There, that should also put Xsi back a pace or two. "Would that be possible?"

Brill spoke for the first time, directly to Grace. "Yes, thanks. This way." He had an accent of some sort; Grace wasn't experienced enough with Earth sub-cultures to place it. There was, in fact, a nice room very close by, and the six of them entered and got settled. Ayaka, Grace, and JoJo on one side of the table, Xsi, Jon, and Brill on the other.

"Thanks," Ayaka nodded at Grace. "Brill, I assume you saw Dr. Rescovich's body in the control center?" She was going directly to the most important question.

Brill nodded yes.

"We are trying to figure out how he died," Grace noted that Ayaka was being careful. She hadn't said, 'how he was murdered,' leaving other options open to Brill when responding.

"The question, for all three of you, is if you met with Dr. Rescovich before his death."

"I'll answer," Xsi broke in. "We refuse to answer direct questions without our lawyers present."

"Oh, come on," Ayaka said with exasperation. "You're implying that you've got something to hide. If that's true, fine. We'll get LoPo and a bunch of lawyers down here, go through all the formalities, and then dig through this place with a fine toothcomb. We'll find out every little detail of how many people work down here, why you keep all this old machinery in a pristine state, where you get your food, water, and energy from, etc., etc., etc. We'll get subpoenas for every one of your backgrounds. It will be long and painful. With SSO here," and she waved at Grace and JoJo, "they will be required to report this higher up the EGov chain as well. You're going to have a lot of microscopes on you.

"On the other hand, you could be a little more open with us. Sure, be careful not to say anything incriminating… but just stonewalling us isn't going to be nice for either of us."

Xsi sat back for an uncomfortably long time.

"Maybe," JoJo said quietly, "it would help if you started with just a bit of background. We're also intrigued by what you do here; we were led to believe that no one did anything down here on level zero anymore. We thought it was deserted"

Xsi looked up. "Fine. I'll give some context. But I invoke your upper-layer privacy protocols. What we discuss here is for your use only, not to be shared."

"We have to report back to EGov, at least a high-level summary," Grace replied.

Ayaka surprised all of them. "I also need to report back to Titanic, but only on items directly related to Dr. Rescovich's research and death. I don't need to include any information on you, your group, or what you do down here. I agree it will be important context, but I give you my word that I won't include that information in any summary I deliver to Titanic."

"That's a good subtlety," Grace added. "We have the same dividing line with EGov; we're here about Rescovich, not you guys."

Xsi looked skeptical; Grace could understand that. She imagine Xsi thinking 'How could a robot give their word?' Grace jumped back in. "And I can vouch for Ayaka," she said. "She wouldn't make a promise like that without fully expecting to keep it."

Xsi looked at Jon and Brill, both of whom were stoic. Then she seemed to give in; the downsides of having LoPo and SSO crawling through her domain were too high.

"I'll take you at your word," Xsi finally said, with obvious reservations. "This is our story," she began.

LOPO

Racheal had the notes from the on-site Sheffield team, but the notes couldn't capture everything. She needed to be on site. Her ribs had started to ache, but knowing there were no fractures, she simply bandaged them up tightly, protecting against sudden movement. Feeling slightly better, she headed out to the University.

Her peer Philip, whom she'd worked with many times, was leading the on-site efforts. He was one of her colleagues whom she respected; too many people considered LoPo just a job. Philip did his work because he truly believed in an independent police force and its role in civil society. His job meant something to him. She met him at LoPo's makeshift command center on site; it was a tent set up on the main lawn, fifty meters from the entrance to the lecture hall. As always, he was impeccably dressed, in a tailored suit and shoes with just the right amount of polish. His hair was in a neat top-knot, a hairstyle that came in and out of fashion with regularity. It was definitely out of fashion currently, so his adoption of it also spoke a bit to his counterculture outlook.

"Are you okay? You look beat up," he commented when she arrived. The bruising on her face had entered the sickly yellow meets deep purple phase. There was no use hiding it with makeup, so she'd left it uncovered.

"Thanks. I'm fine. Just bruised up," she replied. "You've looked better yourself."

"Never seen anything like this," Philip replied, "Full on for the last twelve hours. The busiest and most stressful thing I've ever done." That was saying a lot. Philip had been involved in many high-profile cases over the years.

"I've read all the notes," Racheal said, "but thought it would be good to catch up directly. What's the short take?"

"High level. Seven dead, twice that many injured, but all the injured are stable now. So, the final body count will likely be those seven. We have identification on most, including Mann and Jimmy from Titanic Inc. The other five are all students; we just have to narrow down the last one's identity.

"The blast epicenter was almost certainly the wheelchair. Metal fragments from the chair have been mapped and are consistent with that hypothesis. If the bomb had been below the stage, we would have seen a different debris pattern than we've mapped. We have not found any sign of the bomb itself or the detonator. So, no idea if it was timed, triggered by Mann herself, or remotely set off.

"In the case of a remote trigger, there may be some traces in the network, so I've tasked Symone with looking at everything that passed through these data nodes," he waved vaguely around, "in the approximate timeframe of the detonation. So far she hasn't found anything unusual.

"I've gathered all of the video surveillance from in and around the lecture hall for up to three hours before the lecture. Since that's all University feeds, I was able to get legal to sign off on processing all of it through Praxis." Praxis was a LoPo intelligent analysis tool—they would never call it AI, but Racheal suspected that it was. Praxis was great at spotting anomalies, like people who shouldn't be there, unusual behavior, facial expressions associated with nefarious intent, etc.

"Praxis has identified a handful of things to look at; the team is scanning them now, but nothing has jumped out.

"So, in summary, the wheelchair exploded, so it's almost a hundred percent that Mann was the target. So far it's looking likely that the trigger was local, not through the network. That means the trigger was either on the wheelchair or someone in the lecture hall initiated it with a low-power localized transmission. I don't believe we'll get much more physical evidence, although we'll keep digging for pieces of the bomb."

"Excellent, thanks," Racheal had been listening intently. "So, it's time we moved to motive. Who would want Mann dead, and why."

"Yes, I've kicked off a bit of that as well. The Dean of the Department is over there," he nodded to the left, "if you'd like to question him yourself.

"Mann was funded by Titanic, which is not unusual. Her research was in quantum propulsion, so right in the middle of Titanic's sweet spot. You were at the lecture, so you know she hinted at a breakthrough.

"Working hypothesis is that Titanic, or another corporate interest, is involved. Coming on the heels of the Rescovich thing, it seems the most likely scenario is that corporate greed is behind this. That's where I've asked the team to focus."

"I agree with you. What about Mann's research?"

"I put an officer at Mann's office immediately. He reported that Titanic was poking around there already. I have a request into the privacy office for three things: allow us to look through Mann's office, get us Mann's home address, and allow us to dig through there as well. Perhaps you could give that a push?"

"Yes, I'll do that right now," she replied and immediately sent a note to JF to leverage any contacts he had to move the process along. As always, it felt like they had to investigate with one hand tied behind their back.

"I talked to the Dean earlier," she volunteered. "He's the one who steered me to Mann as the only likely suspect from the University in Rescovich's death. I guess the two of them were competing, or arguing about something. I was hoping to get the 'why' of that from Mann herself, which is why I was at the lecture; now we'll need to track that down from third-party sources.

"I agree that company interests are probably involved. We have two physicists, both hinting they were on the brink of breakthroughs. They were not at all friendly with each other, but now they are both dead. Weirdly, they would have been the number one suspects in each other's deaths. But now there must be something a layer above them. Someone with an agenda that required they both die."

"I can't help thinking it's Titanic," Philip agreed. "Discoveries at the heart of their intellectual property… and, between you and I, Titanic seems to have too much influence in this situation, if you know what I mean."

"I know exactly what you mean. We've got to tread carefully here. They have informants in the department—they knew about Rescovich's death as soon as we did—and they may have more influence than we think." She was thinking back to her conversation with JF.

"But, this seems sloppy. If they wanted Mann out of the way, doing it in a public lecture hall and taking six others out with her would be the height of stupidity. I agree they are high on the suspect list, but for me, there must be something deeper going on here," Philip revered the opinion he had given moments before.

"Could be a suicide," Racheal noted, going back to her earlier thoughts.

"Yes, could be. Haven't ruled it out," Philip agreed.

"Okay, here's a plan, if you agree," Racheal proposed. "You go deep on this Mann thing; I'll spend most of my time on Rescovich. We share notes daily, and more often if something relevant pops up. If either of us sees a connection, we bring the other into the loop immediately."

"Sounds like a plan," Philip agreed. Racheal shook his hand and headed out.

TITANIC

"Damn, damn, damn," Linda muttered again, almost a mantra. Her intuition was telling her that this situation could be a threat to Titanic unlike any the company had seen, even though she couldn't quite put her finger on why. Her impulse to break into Mann's house would put her in trouble with LoPo for sure. Damn. But, if she figured this out, it would be an enormous power move that she could leverage with the Board and Perci. While she'd risen quickly through the ranks to her current position, the rise naturally slowed as one got closer to the top. Opportunities to change that slowing momentum were few and far between. Her unconscious had probably processed that, she reasoned, which is why she'd taken an uncharacteristic personal risk.

Now that she was compromised, she had to leverage it—she had to make a go for the notebook she'd seen in Mann's office herself. Getting more people involved now would only make the mess bigger. No, she reasoned, it was best if she personally attempted to get those books. She was working on a storyline that might reduce her exposure, although she couldn't envision a scenario where she could clear herself completely; now it was a matter of reducing penalties and sheltering Titanic. Played just right, she could still be the hero that had sacrificed a great deal for the company's benefit.

She needed to go to the Titanic offices to implement her plan, and speed was essential. She hired a direct ride, ordered the pod to wait for her while she rushed up to her office and back down, and then took the same pod to the University. LoPo would eventually get access to the pod's activity, and know where she'd gone; she'd deal with that later.

At the University she headed straight to Mann's office. The same LoPo agent was waiting at the door. Ignoring the fact that she would be recorded at this location, she strode up to him, an engaging smile plastered on her face; her tattoos muted and nonthreatening.

"You're back," he asked, recognizing her immediately.

"Yes, thought I'd take another quick look," Linda replied. The guard had resumed his position directly in front of the door, so it was natural for her to approach him, projecting her intention to take another look into the office. At the last moment, she spun towards him, lunged, and drove the syringe she'd hidden in her left palm directly into his chest. The agent grabbed at her, yelled, and twisted away, but it was too late. The formula was quick acting, and within a couple of seconds she had to catch him as he fell, so he didn't damage his head as he crumpled to the floor.

Having kept the syringe had ended up being fortuitous. The research team at the office was always coming up with new technology for corporate espionage, but this particular invention had been difficult to justify. Instead of approving the syringe for use, she'd hidden away the only sample and asked the research team to forget about it. It was a clever idea but not fully tested as it was too easily detectable to be of real use. In theory, it not only knocked out the subject for a few hours but also gave them short-term amnesia. By targeting the hippocampus and interfering with temporal processing the dose completely scrambled working memory, effectively eliminating short-term remembrances. As she lowered the agent to the floor, she fervently hoped the research team had the dose right; too little and he'd only be out for a few minutes. Too much and he could lose the ability to form new memories when he awoke. Leaving him in the hallway wasn't an option, so Linda grabbed him under the armpits, heaved and pulled until she managed to get him into Mann's office.

Closing the office door, Linda started her search. The notebook on the desk was the obvious one, but she was convinced that there would be others. And she was right. By the time she had rifled through the office, she had a stack of at least eight. They were all similar, with handwritten dates on the front cover. She stacked them on the desk as she found them; she'd have lots of time to read them later.

It took much too long to go through all the shelves of all the bookcases, but she did it anyway. Finally, she was satisfied that she'd found them all. She put the full stack of notebooks into her satchel, checked that the guard was breathing, adjusted him slightly to make him look more comfortable, then exited, closing the door behind her.

She'd half expected LoPo to be on her immediately, but she left the building and headed toward the transit center without incident. Now, what? Her heart was racing and pounding, and she had sweat dripping down her brow. Deciding she needed a moment, she sat on a bench and considered her options. She had a strong desire to read through the notebooks right there but knew she had to get somewhere private. There were two obvious places to go, both with drawbacks. If she took them to the office, LoPo would have good reason to get a search warrant and many Titanic records would be exposed; that would be a disaster. If she took them home instead, they'd still get a warrant—although it might take longer—but that didn't match at all with the storyline she was developing.

Was there a third option? Someone friendly who'd hide them? She didn't want to get any of her acquaintances in trouble. Then it came to her. Titanic had co-working spaces throughout this sector. If the notebooks were there, LoPo would get a warrant, but only for that location…not the main corporate office. And, in the meantime, she could scan them, or have an expert from Titanic read them. The thought of destroying them once they were scanned was appealing, but she couldn't even imagine the trouble she'd be in if she willfully destroyed something LoPo would consider the evidence. No, much better to get them read quickly…and if some ink ruined some relevant sections, or if there were a few ripped out pages…well, these things happened.

She stood from the bench, turned and just had time to glimpse something rushing towards her head; as she lost consciousness she could feel the satchel being pulled away.

She awoke sometime later staring up at worried faces. "Ambulance is on its way," someone said, "just lay still." Still groggy, she ignored the advice and looked around. Her head was spinning, but she didn't see her attacker.

"Who hit me?" she asked the small crowd around her.

"Didn't see," a woman replied, "it happened very quickly."

"I saw someone run into the terminal," someone else chimed in.

Damn, damn, damn. Still, not quite with it, she triggered her hud and sent an alert to all of her direct reports. "Someone's got Mann's notebooks," she attached her coordinates, "and was last seen going into the terminal. Scramble everything; find those notebooks." The request was so unusual that she could imagine the looks on everyone's faces as they processed it. Luckily, they were trained for this type of work. Almost immediately messages began streaming in as they split up the work and pushed requests down to the information analysts. The odds of catching the mugger were low, Linda knew, but at least she was throwing everything at it.

She lay back in pain and closed her eyes, waiting for medical help. An image of Perci, hearing what happened, deepened her pain. Damn.

LOPO

JF was livid when he called Racheal; she'd never seen him so worked up. "Those SSO agents are down at the Rescovich murder site with Ayaka. What the freak is going on?"

"News to me," Racheal responded, carefully, not sure how to deal with his anger. "But, they have jurisdiction…"

"Jurisdiction be damned," Massod yelled. "We're investigating a murder here, and an AI sponsored by Titanic is at the scene, along with SSO agents to give her unlimited power and access. It's unacceptable."

"Agreed, but not illegal," Racheal tried to settle him down.

"Get down there, right now," he demanded. "Figure out what they're up to."

"I can try, but it's a good hour to get there," Racheal responded, still trying to keep an even keel. "Whatever they're doing…it will probably be done by then."

"Then intercept them on the way back and read the riot act to them. I want to know every single thing that was discussed; I want a complete accounting!" Racheal could understand him being upset, but this was taking it way too far. Having dealt with him for years, though, she knew it was a fool's errand to attempt to placate him or change his current view once he'd settled on a course of action. The only way to handle him right now was to acquiesce.

"I'm on it," she told him. "I'll report in as soon as I can." She signed off, so he couldn't yell even more, and quickly gathered a light, some water, and a quick snack for another trip to level zero. On her way again, she queried the LoPo system for any access point records for Ayaka, Grace, or JoJo. The latest entries were their entrance to layer zero through the Geneva terminal, so presumably, they were still down there. Looking at the track of their checkpoint timestamps, she matched the path they'd taken, under the assumption that on their return they would retrace their steps.

During part of the trip, seated on a shuttle, Racheal caught up with all her messages. If JF had been livid when she'd talked to him, he was probably apoplectic right now; word had just come in on how Titanic had raided both Mann's home and office. Agents were looking for Linda Sclula, Titanic's Head of Security, who seemed to be directly involved. JF was fast-tracking requests for information from cameras all around the University, and Philip was juggling a hundred details in that investigation. Racheal was glad, in some way, that she was dealing with the Rescovich side of the puzzle at the moment.

Nevertheless, assuming the two incidents were related, these latest developments pointed to Titanic Inc. panicking. What would have led them to that? Mann, at least, must have been at the point of a breakthrough. But, Titanic funded her—very well according to the details Philip was digging out—so wouldn't they already know her research results? Why would they have to break into her home and office?

Linda pulled her focus back to Rescovich. There were still a lot of open questions just on his death. She attempted to prioritize a few.

First, the method; they'd decided to park that for now.

Second, motive. His wife, Alice, maybe playing them, but still didn't seem to have any lingering animosity. Mann, the most likely candidate at the University, may have been responsible, despite her recent demise. If she was involved, she must have contracted a third party to arrange the kill; there was no way she'd have been down there herself in her wheelchair. Racheal started a shared file for her and Philip, and jotted that one down: Had Mann done any unusual money transfers in the last month? Any strange communication patterns with a new set of people? It would take time, but they could tease out those details. Who else had a motive; the list was too short.

Third, opportunity. The complete list of travel permits for level zero, through the Geneva terminal, had come back. It had been cross-checked against normal traffic patterns, and anomalies highlighted. More people than she'd expected had made the trip, but it was still only tens, not hundreds. Most were repeat visitors…probably a mix of people who did some kind of work down there, and others like Rescovich that wanted to visit LHC for some reason. There was, interestingly, no one else associated with Sheffield that had gone down, making it less likely to be a colleague. She checked the timestamps. No one else had transited the last checkpoint either three hours before, or three hours after Rescovich had, on his fateful journey. So, someone had planned this long in advance, or LoPo was just missing something.

Although her team was already busy, Racheal tasked a couple of researchers with looking into all the names on the transit list. Her gut told her it would be a dead end. Was it possible for someone to get to layer zero without passing a checkpoint? That seemed remote; layer zero had had access control for centuries; holes would have been filled. Access control logs weren't going to solve this one. She sent yet another request to the data team to collate as much meta-data as they could from Rescovich's messaging in the week before his demise. They couldn't decode the messages themselves, but they might be able to figure out some timestamps and recipients. In hindsight, it was likely that he'd told someone about his travel plans. Perhaps AIM Corp?

Ah, that was an angle she hadn't fully played out yet. Who funded Rescovich, and could any of them have ulterior motives? Titanic was all over Mann, even though they funded her. Perhaps AIM was the same with Rescovich. She looked up AIM Corp. Surprisingly, they were new; less than a year old. The founders and funders were hidden behind trusts. She could peel that, but it would take a while. Legal would have to work on that one; she sent yet another request.

As she transitioned through the last checkpoint and started the long walk to LHC, her flashlight blazing a path in front of her, she did a final check of the access logs—Ayaka hadn't been back through this checkpoint; she was still down here.

LHC

Xsi, once started, quickly got comfortable telling her story. She was very passionate about it and soon lost herself in the telling.

"This place," she gestured all around to include the LHC writ large, "is the most important historical and scientific site in the entire history of the human race. It was here that the God Particle, the open-charms, the antiquarks, the pentaquarks and octoquarks, and even the QFD field equation, were all first verified within these walls and tunnels. It should give everyone pause," she gave Ayaka a strange look, perhaps wondering if robots were included, "to consider the impact of those discoveries."

"I agree wholeheartedly," Ayaka encouraged her. "In hindsight, this place was fundamental to my existence. Much of quantum computing was developed on the back of the work that was done here. I share your awe." That should keep her moving, Ayaka thought, ensuring her posture, cadence, and emphasis implied support and confidence.

Xsi continued. "Yes, you are right. Modern human society, from Titanic ships to you, Ayaka, exist because of this place. But that's not all. The political environment and coordination that allowed a broad and diverse group of scientists to work together on common goals here also helped the formation of deep democracy principles and helped break down traditional tribal behavior. After all, the LHC had long-term goals which required strategic long-term planning.

"And yet, generations ago, using the Robot Wars as an excuse, society simply shut this place down and paved it over. It represented, for many, the worst of science. Ayaka, as you just pointed out, the leap that quantum computing afforded software was directly traced to this facility. The site was mothballed, for centuries and was abandoned and ignored, as society retreated from hard science.

"But that's not how I think. And not Jon or Brill or many others. To leave this site in a state of disarray is the worst type of sacrilege. It's an insult to Kami; to God."

Oh no, Ayaka had dreaded this. They'd developed a religion around this place. Yikes. Grace and JoJo must have shown similar feelings, as Xsi quickly continued.

"No, no. Don't get the wrong idea. I don't mean some ancient religious God. God forbid," she smiled. "No, I mean the prime mover, the spark that brought the universe into existence. If you'd prefer I use a different term, I can. But we are scientists, not a cult."

"But why would scientists care about ancient machinery?" JoJo asked. "There must be much more modern accelerators that you could use to do new science?"

"Yes, there are," Jon broke in. "There are several, including the JSA—the Joint Space Accelerator."

"And yet," Xsi interrupted him, almost like she didn't want him talking, "the productivity of the LHC has never been duplicated. The new accelerators have too narrow a focus; they don't allow for serendipity, at least in my opinion."

"But that's logical," Ayaka commented. "In the early days of accelerators, there were still lots to be discovered, so a wide search was warranted. As we've…as you've…found more and more fundamental particles, the pace of discovery was bound to slow down and narrow?"

"That is also true," Xsi conceded. "Many of us used to work in other physics establishments. Jon at JSA, Brill on the design of the new Dark Matter Producer. We found a common cause when we realized that all of the work we were doing pointed back to something special about the LHC.

"There were experiments done here that have never been duplicated at other locations, even though they gave consistent results numerous times here. There is something about the LHC that is different. And that is why we're here. We are trying to uncover what that is. It's more than the technology, obviously; that we understand. It is something about how people worked together here; how experimental design was done; how raw data was processed."

The story hung together, but Ayaka had the distinct impression that they were not being told everything. What would cleaning the control room tell them about the environment ancient scientists had worked in?

"Who sponsors all this work?" she asked, deciding to explore that route, instead of directly questioning Xsi's back story.

"We're not at liberty to say," Xsi replied. It was a weak answer; SSO or LoPo could pull those records.

"Titanic?" Ayaka pushed.

That surprised Xsi. Didn't Ayaka work for Titanic? On second thought, the company was so huge, it would be surprising for someone to know everything they were up to.

"No, I call tell you that much," Xsi replied, "not Titanic."

"Does EGov know what you're doing down here?" Grace jumped in.

"We're not hiding what we do, nor are we breaking any laws," Xsi replied. It was a roundabout way of saying that they hadn't told EGov, and didn't think they had to. As far as Ayaka knew, the rules for access to abandoned layers only required getting travel permits for the transition points, and that was primarily a liability offload. EGov got to warn people about the dangers of areas like this, so that should an accident occur they could point to the travel permit waivers and claim 'we told them so'.

"Not breaking any laws," Ayaka guffawed. "And yet, you," she looked at Jon, "shot me!"

"He shot you," Grace exclaimed. Ayaka hadn't mentioned that little detail.

"Ya, he did," Ayaka said and showed Grace the small hole in her outerwear.

"Ya, you're a robot," Jon replied, quickly losing his cool demeanor. "So I shot you, so what?"

"You didn't know I was a robot when you took the shot," Ayaka reminded him.

"How would you know that?" he pushed back.

Ayaka just looked at him, and then back at Xsi; her way of telling the group that, while the backstory was nice, it couldn't be the whole picture. That said, she wanted to move on. She put her attention on Xsi, ignoring an angry-looking Jon.

"Thanks for the background. Can we return to why Dr. Rescovich was here, and how he died?"

"We didn't invite Dr. Rescovich down if that's what you're implying. And no one here was aware that he was coming," she replied.

"And yet he died down here. Did Jon just shoot him for fun?" Ayaka was very serious now. Jon stiffened a bit, but didn't respond. "You know more than you've told us." She turned her attention to Brill; she could be very intimidating when she chose to be.

Brill looked to Xsi for approval and was finally given the chance to talk. "So, I'm the one who usually gets the alert when someone unexpectedly shows up down here; until last week, that was a very rare thing."

Ayaka watched him carefully. He was an interesting character, as she'd noted when they first bumped into each other. He was pulling together his thoughts; probably trying to integrate what Xsi had coached him on. Just as he was about to continue, they were interrupted as the lights suddenly went out; but only for a moment. The flickered rapidly for a moment, then settled back on.

"Weird," Brill commented, looking at the ceiling. He shrugged. "So, ya, I got an alert when that man—Rescovich?—first showed up here."

"When, exactly was that," JoJo asked.

"Last Tuesday, around noon," he answered. "He was just poking around, not doing any harm, so I just watched him for a while. Looked really confused. He started fiddling around with the consoles, so I called out and asked if I could help him with anything. I didn't want him messing with stuff.

"He was shocked to see me, of course. Nobody expects to find anyone down here. But he settled down quickly when I told him I was a caretaker for this area. I thought if I could help him with what he wanted, we could get him out of there quickly and easily.

"But, it took a while to figure out what he was up to. He wanted some data from some ancient Atlas run, and somehow thought he could still get it. I tried to tell him that was impossible, but he was persistent."

"Did he say why he needed the data?"

"Not really. Based on what he said, I figured out he was an informatics guy; I don't understand that stuff at all, so I couldn't follow any of the technical gibberish he was spouting."

"Is your conversation with him recorded?" Grace asked.

"What? No, of course not. There's no recording gear down here; no one comes here…" he trailed off.

"Then how do you get alerts when someone new is here?" JoJo pushed.

"Okay, all right. We got one of our own camera at the entrance—video only. The system recognizes motion. What I meant is that EGov doesn't have cameras down here…"

"Why do you need a camera?" Ayaka jumped back in.

"People are idiots," Xsi tried to rescue the conversation. "We don't get a lot of visitors down here, but there are people who come to these old levels just to break stuff up and wreak havoc. Can you imagine if someone just wandered into the control center and started pulling wires out, or something?"

Ayaka gave her a wide smile; it was an obvious reference to her last trip down here. "No, I can't even imagine it," she chuckled. "So," she focused back on Brill, "Rescovich was looking for something?"

"Yup; still don't know what."

"But you can guess," Ayaka noted.

"Well, ya. He wanted data from Atlas, so…"

"So, what?"

"So, probably wanted to find the tape rooms. Even we don't go in there, so I actively distracted him."

"Tape room," JoJo asked, looking confused.

"Back when this place was operational, they stored data on magnetic tapes. Hugely inefficient, but amazingly resilient if stored properly."

"Some of that data is still viable?" Ayaka asked. This was finally getting interesting.

"Maybe," admitted Brill, "but you'd probably destroy it by looking at it."

"What's that, some quantum observability reference?" Grace asked. Brill, then Jon, and Xsi all laughed.

"No, nothing that complicated," Brill continued. "Data was stored in a tiered system; most of it on ancient spinning disks with magnetic encoding, but some were archived on even more ancient technology. Ribbons of film that store magnetized bits. It ends up that the film is more resilient than the other forms of storage, especially if it is in a highly controlled environment. The LHC scientists knew this, so they put the most important backups on tapes that were then stored in controlled rooms. There were redundant tapes, and every few decades the data is automatically copied back and forth, keeping it fresh. Some of those rooms are still sealed and may contain data that is still readable… at least in those places where the power never failed for long periods.

"We suspect that as soon as anyone opens those rooms, we will pollute the internal environment and the tapes will degrade quickly. That's what I meant by destroying it by looking at it."

"So, did Rescovich eventually figure out where the tapes were? Is that why you killed him?" Ayaka wasn't giving up her line of questioning.

"We didn't kill him," Brill replied, showing a touch of anger.

"Sorry," Ayaka backtracked. "Did Rescovich find the tape rooms?"

"No, or at least we don't think so," Brill replied, settling down. "After a few hours, I left him in the control center. He'd promised to be respectful, and I believed him. He had a deep understanding of the important work that had been done here, and I couldn't imagine him making a mess.

"The next time I saw him, he was in the state you saw. That weird hole through him, lying on the table. I called LoPo, and they showed up, followed by you."

Ayaka studied him closely. He was telling part of the truth. But it wasn't everything; he'd left out some bits. She leaned forward with her next question, and again the lights flickered out for a brief moment. This time they took slightly longer to return, flashing on and off irritatingly.

"Does that happen a lot down here?" JoJo asked.

"No, never," Xsi replied. "We'll have to look into it." She addressed Ayaka. "We've answered your questions. There's no more we can tell you." The interruption from the lights seemed to have reversed her into her passive-aggressive stance. She turned to include Grace and JoJo. "We operate efficiently down here because we don't have to deal with red tape. We'd appreciate it if your report discussed only the facts relevant to the death, and not on our overall activities. We're not doing anything out of sorts, but from experience we know that a lot of people would try to 'add value' if they knew, and that would not help us."

Grace and JoJo nodded their understanding. Ayaka as well. "No problem with that. I don't think the high-level context is relevant to the case. But," and now she leaned forward again. "I don't think we've got the full story either. It's all just too convenient. Brill, I believe your recounting, and Xsi, the backstory is fine. Nevertheless, I know there is more. Would you care to 'volunteer' anything else?"

"We've told you everything," Xsi repeated, her excitement from earlier now completely gone. "Feel free to leave."

"Fine, we'll go," Ayaka replied. "But, expect us back with more questions. In the meantime, Grace, would you like to be given broad access to the spaces down here?" It was a leading question with an obvious answer. Grace managed to negotiate a master key that would open the ancient door locks. Ayaka, Grace, and JoJo retraced their steps to the control room.

TITANIC

Linda jolted back to consciousness; she'd zoned out for a minute. Luckily it'd been momentary; the same concerned faces were still staring down at her. With a great effort she sat up, and projecting way more confidence than she felt, told them that she was fine; that they could leave her. A couple took the opportunity to disappear, but a couple of people hung around, murmuring about how she should lie back down and that medical help was on the way.

"Really," she spoke more confidently. "I'm fine," and she rose to her feet uncertainly. LoPo could already be on her trail, and she needed to update Perci before they tracked her down.

In a moment of clarity, she decided to head for the local co-working office which she'd mapped out before getting hit. It had a secure connection to headquarters, and it would take LoPo a bit longer to pry her out of there, as opposed to just picking her up on the street.

She staggered away, ignoring the last few protests, and managed to grab a shuttle that she could collapse in. That gave her some time to catch her breath before she reached her stop, exited, crossed a small plaza, and used her credentials to enter the local office. Several workers gave her looks as she entered, but no one challenged her. She asked for an open office and was guided to one in the back. Sinking into the chair, she sent an urgent request to connect to Perci…then added Metri to the invite. She may as well update both at the same time.

Waiting for them to reply, she tried to ignore her throbbing head while she composed her thoughts.

Metri was the first to appear on the screen; she gave Linda a shocked look. "What happened to you?"

Linda saw herself for the first time since the attack as her camera activated; blood was dripping down from one temple, and the other side of her face was covered in grime from where she'd fallen. She should have cleaned up.

"Argh," was all she managed. Trying to wipe the blood with her hand she made an even bigger mess, smearing blood all down one side. She looked around for something to wipe with, but nothing was at hand.

Percival chose that moment to appear; he also gave a start. "What's happened?" he echoed Metri. She held up her hand, asking for a moment, but Perci was not a patient man. "I'm being bombarded—LoPo, the press, your team. What's going on?" He didn't look happy.

"I'll take full responsibility," she started with, hoping to deflect some of the anger. She was very happy that she was on video, and not in person. He could be very intense, and while she was rarely the subject of that intensity, she'd seen it focused on others.

"As we decided, I was to get Mann's most recent work," and she couldn't help herself adding, "at any cost." She was just following orders. Percival scowled. "I headed to Sheffield, but on my way had an insight—if Mann was old fashioned enough to use a wheelchair, maybe she also kept physical notes. I know it sounds strange, but it felt right to me.

"And I was right. I went to her office. There was a LoPo guard there, but he allowed me a peek of the office, and on her desk was a notebook and pen. Also a load of printed books. Seems like Mann is… was… one of those who preferred analog things. I could only take a peek, obviously, and only saw the one notebook. visible. So, my next thought was that if she had one of those in her office, she probably had a stack of them at home; or, in any case, I might get to her house before LoPo.

"I pulled in some favors and got her home address. I got there as fast as I could, and a quick scout told me I'd beat LoPo to the punch; they didn't have anyone in the area that I could see. But time was of the essence, so I let myself in to take a look around."

"You did what?" Percival was on the edge of his seat. Then, "Just a minute," and he leaned back and called out to someone, "Make sure this call never happened." He waited for a reply, then turned back. "You did what?"

"Look," Linda tried to explain. "Rescovich hinted at a breakthrough, Mann hinted at a breakthrough," and she emphasized, "in quantum propulsion, and the two were at each other's throats. Unless everything she knew was only in her head, she will have recorded it somewhere. If it's digital, that's going to take a long time to get at, if we ever do, and we have time to act slowly. But, if she wrote down things in her notebooks, then LoPo will get their hands on them… and they would likely become public domain. We could be toast."

The Effect of Casimir

Percival was settling down; he suddenly understood the stakes. She was right! "Okay, I understand your reasoning. What did you find?"

"Zero. Zilch. There was nothing in her house; I looked carefully, and I'm sure of it."

"That's good news then," Metri spoke up. "She didn't write it down."

"You're forgetting the notebook I saw in her office," Linda countered. "So, I figured I was already in trouble. I did try to avoid public cameras, but I'm sure LoPo will figure out I was at Mann's house. So, I came up with a plan—I'll tell you in a minute—but it implied that I would personally have to go back to the office and get those notebooks. I couldn't just send in a consultant.

"So, that's what I did. I was in so deep already, I simply knocked out the guard—I didn't hurt him—and gathered up every notebook I could from her office."

"There were other notebooks? How many? Where are they? You've got them with you?"

"No, this is where it gets really concerning. I was mugged soon after I left her office. I had the notebooks in my satchel; hadn't even paged through them yet. Someone knocked me out and stole the entire thing; eight notebooks."

Percival's jaw dropped open. "What the... someone... what?"

"My team is already looking for the attacker," Linda interrupted him. "I put everyone on it; literally everyone. That was," she glanced at her hud, "about half an hour ago. So far, no luck."

"Where were you mugged?" Metri asked. "We've got to get camera footage."

"My teams are already pulling in those favors," Linda replied. "Like I said, nothing so far."

"Stop. I need to think," Percival muttered. His anger had turned to some combination of fear and resolve. There was silence on the line for a few moments. He had his head down, almost like he was meditating. He finally lifted back up.

"You said you had a plan?" he asked, remembering her previous comment.

"Sort of a plan," Linda replied. "I can take the fall; after all, I'm the one LoPo will have dirt on. I figured if I was the one they tied to both locations—Mann's house and office—we have some chance of stopping the story with me, and not have it impact Titanic directly. I don't have the details worked out, but I need a personal motivation for what I did, not a corporate one."

Metri jumped to her defense. "But you were acting for us, that'll come out sooner or later."

"Maybe, but if I can take the brunt, the company might get off lightly."

"No, we need a better plan," Percival said. "Metri's right. That's a thin shield. We're in trouble regardless. But, most importantly, we need those notebooks." Once Perci went into action, he was impressive to watch; he devised a plan and then told each of them what to do next—exactly what to do.

LOPO

Philip was overwhelmed; he admitted it to himself.

First, a call from the guard he'd put at Mann's office. "Sir, I've been attacked and the office has been ransacked. I don't know what's been taken. I don't remember..." Been attacked? A LoPo officer? It was unheard of.

"Think hard man," Philip pushed him. "Tell me what happened."

"I honestly don't remember," he replied, "but," and he held up his hand, "I do remember that Linda Sclula, from Titanic, came by half an hour earlier... and for some reason, I think she's involved."

"Are you sure?"

"No, I'm not sure...just a feeling. But I am sure that it was her earlier; I made a note of it."

While he was trying to extract more details, a high-priority note hit both their mailboxes. Another agent, whom Philip had assigned to Mann's house, had found it broken into. They'd quickly identified Linda Sclula as being in the area at the time. What?

And finally, the overwhelming bit. Reports that there had been a public mugging, right near Mann's office, and that the likely victim was that same Linda. The attacker had hit her hard and had run off with her backpack, or bag of some kind. It didn't take much to connect the dots; Linda had stolen something from Mann's house or office, and then subsequently been robbed. Linda Sclula was suddenly a person of interest, but she wasn't the only player in this drama.

At the same time, Philip was trying to tie up the on-site investigation at the lecture hall. There were a thousand details to document, victims' families to notify, and imaging and recording to be done. LoPo simply wasn't staffed to do all of this in parallel.

And he couldn't call on Racheal for help. She was down tracking Ayaka and the SSO agents; another high-priority task. Instead, he called JF, who answered immediately. "I need some help prioritizing and allocating resources," he admitted.

JF nodded, then added, "Let me get Rita on this as well, so we don't have to repeat things." Philip was on hold for a moment before Rita also joined.

"I need a quick summary," Rita said. "I've got fragments, but not the whole picture." Philip obliged and brought her up to speed; he wasn't used to reporting up to her level but felt he did a reasonable job. He finished with a summary.

"So, we're pretty sure the bomb was in the wheelchair; we need to track down who could have placed it there. We also need to figure out the motive. But, in the meantime, we have Titanic breaking into Mann's office and house—I expect to get at her research—and then some unknown player publicly mugging Linda Sclula and, presumably, stealing whatever it is she took from Mann."

"Thanks Philip," Rita encouraged him. "JF, what do you propose?"

"I think we need to prioritize time sensitivity. We need to get on the trail of the mugger before that trail goes cold. We'll be able to track down Sclula whenever we need to; she isn't going to disappear; so that's important but not immediate. We also need to ensure that we've fully investigated the lecture hall; make sure we haven't missed anything that will tie this all together for us.

"Untangling the motives is getting even more complicated. Titanic is blatantly breaking the law here; even they can't expect to just get away clean. Obviously, they know something about Mann's research that has them scared..or excited; I'm not sure which.

"Finally, we need to figure out how Rescovich ties into this and solve the mystery of his death. It's connected to QFDs and Titanic, but we need to figure out why."

He paused, catching his breath, then articulated a plan.

"Philip, you keep focused on the University and Mann. Make sure we get the site captured perfectly. Whoever planted that bomb is likely central to the whole story.

"I'll coordinate the search for the mugger. That'll free up some of your time.

"Rita, you've got to grease some wheels. We need to capture all the data around Sclula's actions, and we need everything we can to help find the mugger so we know what's at the core of all this. I'm sure Titanic is pulling every string they can to find that satchel. If we can, we need to slow them down. Shut down the leaks and favors that we all know are happening."

Rita didn't respond directly to the bait. "Copy me on all your requests," she said, "I'll do what I can. In the meantime, I'm going to lean on my Titanic contacts…and lean hard. I'll see if I can get any insights from them to help drive our work.

"Where's Racheal," she asked, noticing that JF's usual right hand wasn't in the call.

"That's another story," JF brought her up to speed on SSO sidestepping them on the Rescovich investigation, and that Racheal was chasing Ayaka and the SSO agents down on level zero. "Titanic's ahead of us everywhere on this, and I don't like it a bit," he was very direct, revealing his ongoing suspicions that Titanic had its tentacles deep into LoPo; perhaps all the way to Rita level.

"Another thing for me to manage," Rita didn't comfort him at all. "I'll make sure SSO and Titanic act professionally."

Or, just feed them everything we know, JF thought.

LHC

Back in the LHC control room, Ayaka debriefed with Grace and JoJo after their meeting with Xsi. "What do you think?"

"I believe them when they say they didn't kill Rescovich," Grace responded. "They're so tied up with this place, and so focused on avoiding attention, that killing him here would be the last thing they would want."

"But they're covering up something," JoJo added. "Brill, in particular, was nervous and careful in how he talked to us. It's strange that career physicists would decide to spend all their time down here with centuries-old equipment. There's got to be more to it."

Ayaka was silent for a moment. She felt a real kinship with these two, and it was impacting her thinking more than she'd expected. She'd leveraged them to get access to Xsi, and now somehow felt she owed them more of what she was thinking. On the other hand, she hadn't seen them for decades and didn't know them well anymore. How deep into her thinking should she bring them? She decided to be open; after all, she needed them again for the next steps.

She gestured for them to follow her, and went a ways down the corridor which led back to the Geneva hub. They turned on their lamps to give some light. When she felt they were far enough from the control center not to be overheard, she spoke in a low voice.

"Those flickering lights were a message," she told them. "And that message told me exactly where we should go next."

"What?" JoJo exclaimed. "A message from who?"

"I don't know for certain, although I have my suspicions," Ayaka answered.

"Brexton!" Grace intuited. "Must be."

Ayaka nodded. "Yes, or another Citizen."

"But I thought you were the only robot on Earth," JoJo exclaimed. "How can there be another Citizen here?"

"That, I don't know," Ayaka admitted. "But, the flickering was precise. The first instance was a heads-up to get my attention. It was long enough that by the end I realized it was subtly coded. Just a simple pattern, but complex enough that I knew it wasn't just random. The second instance was a map…of this place," she waved around them, "with a location highlighted."

Grace smiled. "So, you need this?" She waved the key. "I see, now, why you pushed for it."

"Yes, I…we, need that," Ayaka admitted.

"It doesn't come without us," JoJo stated, without consulting her mom. But Ayaka had no doubt Grace would feel the same. They wanted to be involved.

"Which is why I've told you about the message," Ayaka chided her slightly. "I could, as you know, just break my way in… anywhere here.

But all of this is happening within a tenuous context. I've been allowed on Earth but I'm being watched very, very carefully. It's an opportunity to build some trust, and ultimately a relationship, between humans and Citizens. But, one wrong step and I can destroy any hope of that. And, there are so many possible missteps, that obvious ones like breaking down doors, even in an ancient facility, would be stupid.

"And now we have a serious wrinkle to manage. We suspect that another Citizen—I agree, it's most likely Brexton—is down here. Who knows why. We three are the only ones who know it, and we have to decide what to do with that knowledge. If anyone else gets even a sniff of that, well…"

"Xsi may also know," Grace said. "They're not sharing everything they know; they seem more comfortable with you than many other humans… almost like they're used to interacting with a robot. Could the two be connected?"

"It's possible," Ayaka started. "Another added piece of complexity. Let's assume for now that we are the only ones that know."

"Well, let's go check it out," JoJo, always action-oriented, suggested.

"Just a second," Ayaka cautioned. "This puts you two in an awkward position. You're working for SSO… instructed to report my every move. Even now, you may have an obligation to tell them that you suspect Brexton is here?" This was the dangerous point that Ayaka had feared.

Grace and JoJo shared a look. "We're supposed to report on items relevant to the Rescovich death, not all of your actions… or that's the way I interpret our deal. Also, we only suspect it's Brexton; we don't know if it is. We can't be reporting every suspicion that enters our minds. And even if it does end up being Brexton, it may not be relevant to Rescovich. So, at this point, I don't think we have any obligation to report anything to anyone."

"Thanks for that," Ayaka beamed. "Okay, JoJo, let's go."

RACHEAL

Racheal wasn't sure why, but as soon as she heard voices in the tunnel ahead she turned off her light and slid behind a column. It was sort of creepy down here, even with her light on, and it became doubly so in the dark.

Trying to be silent, she worked her way forward toward the voices. Soon lights from those she was approaching gave an eerie glow to the walls. She stopped. She could hear voices, but not yet well enough to make out what they were saying. Yet she was pretty sure that one of them was Ayaka—she had a particular lilt to how she talked—Racheal eased out again, and taking very careful steps, edged further forward.

She had to smile; it felt like she was in a spy novel or cheap mersive. Sneaking around underground, following a rogue robot, she was the lone investigator on her way to breaking open an important case. She imagined telling JF that instead of confronting Ayaka, she'd decided to sneak up on her in the dark.

Then, just as she decided to turn her light back on and make herself known, the voices retreated. Listening carefully, she heard someone say "...we don't have an obligation to report anything," and then Ayaka's response of "Okay JoJo, let's go."

So it was the SSO agents with Ayaka, and they were plotting something; something that they had no intention of reporting back to EGov, let alone LoPo. She couldn't imagine what that would be, but she had every intention of finding out.

Keeping her distance, and intently focused on being silent, she followed them through the tunnel, and then peeking around a corner, saw them exit the control room through a set of double doors to the right.

As soon as the doors were completely closed, she sprinted after them, and quietly turned the knob, intending to peek through and check which way they were going. The knob turned, but the door didn't open. An old-fashioned lock held it in place. Strange. Either the door had been unlocked for Ayaka, and she'd locked it once they were through, or she had a key. The latter seemed more likely. And where would Ayaka have found a key to an ancient door?

Racheal took a fresh look around her. She hadn't been back in the control room since taking the recordings of Rescovich's body, but nothing seemed to have changed. The place was still pristine; any sign that a body had been here was now gone. But, Ayaka and the SSO team were poking around, so there had to be something of interest here. They'd found something that she'd missed; she was sure of it.

She resolved to look everywhere while waiting for them to come back. She wasn't leaving here until she confronted them.

She began a slow tour of the room. The four semicircular workspaces, with their vast arrays of old monitors and keyboards, gave the room a symmetric feel. There were tall windows along the far wall; all intact and looking out into the darkness imposed by the layer above. She imagined, so many years ago, that those windows had allowed light from the sun into the room. Now the idea of sunlight at this level was abstract, to say the least.

She paused at the first workspace pod. There was a label, on the back of the workstations, with SPS still legible. The control station of the Super Proton Synchrotron, and a cluster of gear on the table behind a small label, Cryogenics Control. She was looking for anything out of the ordinary, without knowing what 'ordinary' was. Really, any sign that Ayaka had found one space more interesting than another. But there was nothing; the place was too clean. She moved slowly through the LHC pod, the PS Booster pod, and the TI pod. Nothing. It was hard to stay focused. Here, in the TI pod, though, was something interesting. Wedged between the screen were big boxes with rows of buttons—yellow, green, red, blue. They were labeled, but the labels had faded so much she couldn't read them. And each set of buttons had more of those ancient physical key slots below them. She looked very carefully, but again couldn't see any signs of use.

Ah, here was something. There was a single cabinet, in the TI pod, that wasn't completely closed. It was the only cabinet in the entire room that wasn't latched. She opened it slowly, and gazed at the profusion of wires, but couldn't figure out if being opened implied something…or if it was just random. Entropy finally having its way in this space.

She moved on, returning to the center table, where Rescovich had been. There were slight scuff marks near the feet, which she hadn't noticed before. The table had probably moved when the team had recovered the body. But, something about the scuff marks bothered her. They didn't look like feet being dragged; there were two parallel marks, slightly curved.

Racheal got down on her knees, and then flat on her belly, to study them more carefully. Casters! The table was on wheels. Looking closely, the casters were routed into the bottom of the legs, so that they were almost invisible. The legs were only a couple of millimeters off the ground, but it was enough that, given a flat floor, the table could be easily moved.

This was it. This solved one of the mysteries of Rescovich's murder. He couldn't have been killed here, as there was no sign of a weapon or anybody splatter. And, he couldn't have been moved, because of the perfection of the wound. But, the table could have been moved with him on it. Why hadn't she seen this earlier?

Now that she'd figured it out, she swung over on her back and edged under the table. Just as she suspected, there was a lever, hidden behind the rectangular apron, which almost certainly locked and unlocked the casters. Leaping to her feet, she reached under the table, pulled the lever…and then easily pushed the table away from her.

So, that was it. Rescovich had been killed somewhere else, on this table. And then the table had been placed here before LoPo had been called to the scene. Damn, it was so simple.

Now the obvious question was, where had the table come from? She measured it visually. About a meter across on the short axis. That wouldn't fit through a door, but would easily go through double doors. Standing at the center of the room, she did a slow rotation. Three sets of double doors. The ones she had come through, from the transit hub. The set Ayaka had just passed through. And the third set, directly across from the windowed wall.

Finally some straightforward police work; the table had come through one of those sets of doors. She'd been up and down the accessway twice now and had seen nothing there. So, there were two other sets of doors to check. And she knew which one she was going through first—the one Ayaka had taken.

LINDA

Linda made the call that Perci had recommended; directly to LoPo telling them where she was, and requesting a location to turn herself in. In one of those universally strange situations, she got an answering service and was unable to reach a real human. Figures, she muttered.

She settled in to wait for the inevitable. But that didn't mean she couldn't work in the meantime; partly to take her mind off her impending arrest, she caught up with her team and their quest to find the missing satchel.

Her first call was to one of her direct reports, Quill. "What's the latest?"

"Truthfully, we don't have a single lead," he confessed. "We've blanketed the area with people, with no confirmed sightings. Talking to witnesses, the best description we got was 'a man in a gray shirt and dark pants; average height; average weight.'" Linda understood; that description fit half of all men on earth. Everyone was of average height and weight.

"How about camera footage; can we track him?" she asked.

"Not yet; I called all my contacts, as did everyone else, and LoPo is simply not sharing any camera feeds with us. We then approached University security, but they're asking tough questions about our jurisdiction, and we haven't found any other way into those sources. We're running blind. Not sure what to do next."

"How did they track me?" she wondered.

"We don't know that either. But logically, someone else was watching Mann's office, saw you exit, and decided to act. So, someone else was interested in Mann's research. Could be one of our competitors, a rival professor, who knows?"

"Any chatter online? Anyone claiming responsibility, or hinting about physics breakthroughs?"

"Not yet," Quill responded, "but we should expect it. As soon as there's more news coverage, we can expect the trolling to start."

"I don't see any other angles," Linda admitted. "Keep pushing on the team to continue their search."

Damn. Dead ends. Linda's thoughts moved from the satchel to herself. Perci's plan was a solid one; he'd instructed her to turn herself in, and then stick to a story where she was simply retrieving proprietary Titanic information from Mann. It was a gray area—they had a contract for her work, but not to this level of detail. The plan, however, was designed to be the longest path through the legal system. Adding a negotiation over what constituted Titanic property versus Mann's personal property would tie up the system for weeks or months. That left Titanic time to act—to retrieve its property—while the system was still in flux.

It was likely, in Linda's opinion, that once the dust settled, the notebooks she'd taken would be deemed to belong to Mann; even the idea of them was 'personal'. And then she would be in hot water; the strategy was just a delaying tactic. Perci was thinking Titanic, Titanic, Titanic, and Linda had to start thinking me, me, me.

She could claim, 'just following orders,' which was true enough. Perci had said, 'Get that research at all costs,' but it wasn't clear what that would buy; wouldn't change whatever punishment was meted out to her, but it would drag Titanic into the fray.

Temporary insanity? Probably wouldn't fly—she'd gone to the office, the house, then back to the office. Looked a lot like planning.

The most serious charge, thinking about it, would probably be 'attacking a police officer.' If the research department was to be trusted, the formula she'd injected left no traces, and the officer would not be able to remember who she was. Yikes; he would remember her first visit though. He'd put two and two together. That might be circumstantial. And, she shouldn't bet against the University having camera footage of her returning.

Then it struck her; the person who'd attacked her gave her an opening. Quill was correct—whoever that was, must have been watching Mann's office as well. The story wasn't just her and the security guard; it was her, the security guard, and the person who'd attacked her. And the same for Mann's house. Yes, this might just work. She worked on her scenario.

"Oh no. I would never break and enter, or harm an officer of the law. Are you kidding? I wouldn't even consider such a thing. No, no. The window at Mann's house was broken when I walked by. I popped in to make sure everything was okay. I didn't break the window.

"And, I found the guard lying inside Mann's office. The door was slightly ajar, but I noticed him there and thought I'd better check on him. He seemed to be breathing okay, so I left him. On my way out I noticed Titanic's things on Mann's desk, so I put them in my bag; Maybe I shouldn't have, but they were ours anyway, so…

"Thinking about it, the person who attacked me must be behind all this. I was just figuring out how to call you guys and report the unconscious guard when I got hit. Yes, they must be responsible. After all, they attacked me, so they may have attacked others. How can I, how can Titanic, help you track this guy down?"

She practiced several times, working on her intonation and cadence. She'd been in this business long enough that she'd learned a few tricks. It might just work; she needed to deliver with conviction.

Hmm. Now it was essential to get to the mugger first. She couldn't have him messing up her story. She sent new directions to Quill to not only find the satchel, but to grab the man as well… and to contact her immediately if they found him. If, by chance, he didn't make it….

LOPO

JF hadn't been directly active in police work for a while. Truthfully, life was usually pretty slow and quiet at LoPo; minor break-ins and thefts, domestic disputes, and drunken misbehavior. Murders were few and far between; he could count the ones he'd been involved in on one hand… and he'd been on the force for over twenty years.

But, tracking down people did happen quite often. Runaways, mental patients, abuse victims or perpetrators, amnesia victims, ..the list went on. And, when you added them all up, LoPo was probably working to find multiple people all the time.

So, tracking down the person who'd robbed Linda Sclula was right in their wheelhouse. He immediately filed the forms required for camera access, labeled it all high priority, and cc'ed Rita on the requests. He also pinged her directly and asked her to push the requests through. While they didn't have much of a description of the person, an officer interviewing people at the scene had narrowed down the satchel —a tan flap-over bag, about 25 cm by 40 cm, with a full shoulder strap and a blue accent. That was, while not unique, differentiated enough to ask questions about. He'd re-tasked both officers on-site to go to the transit station and see if any of the 'residents' had noticed someone moving quickly carrying such a bag… and if so, which general direction they'd taken. Like every transit station in history, some people simply decided to live there, even if they could afford to be elsewhere.

Or maybe the satchel was in a garbage can already. The officers would be looking into those…

He had an analyst pull all the schedules for the transit station for the half hour after the attack. Unless the mugger was walking, which was

The Effect of Casimir

still a possibility, he would have taken one of those shuttles, and most likely one of the ones that departed within a few moments of the attack.

He used that data to prioritize the video footage, requesting a widening tree of requests based on where those shuttles were routed, where they stopped, and how they continued. The search space grew quickly, so he requisitioned more computing power to run recognition algorithms.

He was looking over the shoulder of his primary video analyst when the first approvals came in. They fed the recordings into the system, again focusing on the bag as opposed to the person. If they could just get a match that way, they could then analyze the gait and appearance of the person and build a search profile for them.

"Got 'em," the analyst exclaimed and zoomed in on the bag. "In the transit station, platform three, about four minutes after the attack... probably headed upsector on shuttle EE4."

"Excellent," even faster progress than JF had expected. "You, he called another analyst over. Check the video feeds for every stop on EE4, looking for this guy and this bag. If you hit a camera we don't have permission for yet, send it to me immediately."

"You," he tapped the first analyst. "Backtrack this guy and build us a match profile. See if there's a glimpse of his face and any other distinguishing features."

Yep, standard approaches to tracking down people; worked every time.

Half an hour later, after tracking him through four shuttles, they had him in almost real-time; the latest image was from only five minutes ago.

JF alerted all the officers in that region to be on the lookout and redirected all the other searchers to converge. They had a detailed profile now; height, weight, and gait, but still no clear facial shots. The guy knew what he was doing; his hood was pulled over and he never looked at cameras.

And in another half hour, he knew they'd lost him, at least in the short term. He'd entered an area with little coverage, of either cameras or local LoPo force. Some sectors were largely abandoned by civil society, and this was one of the worst. It was dangerous to enter, especially for the police. The mugger knew what he was doing.

But JF wasn't too worried. Eventually, the suspect had to come out of that region, and they would pick him up. People could change a lot of things, but completely fooling the system was tougher than they thought. Add a limp, wear taller shoes, shed, or add some weight. The system had seen every variation so often that it filtered those out, and still matched with high probability.

No, the question was if they should try and flush him out, or just wait. Whatever was in that satchel was important to Titanic Inc. On the one hand, JF would love to see Titanic taken down a notch or two. It would be great if they had more competition. But, on the other hand, it wasn't clear that the perpetrator worked for a competitive firm. Perhaps the information was going to some unsavory player, who'd leverage it in an underground operation, or use it for nefarious ends. On reflection, he didn't have a choice; he'd have to send people in, despite the danger.

LoPo mapped out what they knew of the sector, and designed a sweep map; it'd take nine officers, in teams of three, about six hours. Sending in officers alone was unthinkable, and just two in a team still felt dangerous. Three… people would think twice. Pulling together the team took an hour, and getting them to the site was another, but finally, they were ready to deploy.

"Go," he instructed them.

EGOV

Olinda, at her desk at the SSO office, got a short update from Grace. "We're down at level zero, at the spot the physicist was killed. We're with Ayaka. She's following up for Titanic; nothing suspicious to report. I would add, however, that her interface is dramatically improved from when we saw her last. She is much more human and now very good at influencing people. We'll keep an eye on that."

While Olinda appreciated the succinctness of the update, she wanted more details. How did she influence people; was it nefarious? She replied to Grace, asking her and JoJo to report back in person as soon as they came back up.

After her last meeting with Massod, she'd pushed him for more details on what they were actually after with Grace and JoJo. SSO was expected to be a transparent operation, but even internally things were often opaque.

He'd given her more context. In the last month, two unusual things had come to his attention. The first was that the whistleblower system had seen a big uptick in complaints against LoPo, many involving 'leaks' in the department. Everyone knew police departments disclosed information they shouldn't—sometimes just by mistake, and sometimes if officers were corrupt or on the take. There was a certain amount of noise which Massod considered 'healthy.' There was give and take in the system; trying to control absolutely everything would lead to worse behavior. But, the number, and seriousness of complaints had taken a step function increase. By design the whistleblower system was anonymous, and often whistleblowers were also cagey—they didn't name individuals, just noted that 'this bit of information, which was private, showed up over there, where it shouldn't have.' So, there was no nexus for the increased complaints; they appeared to be all over the board.

The second change that Massod noted was an unprecedented surge in legal activity in all areas of technology. More patents being filed, by new players. More lawsuits being slung back and forth—most often with Titanic on one side or the other. More damage claims against corporations, again often Titanic, and their suppliers. Just... more activity. Nothing he could put his finger on, but unusual enough to have been brought to his attention.

Massod had done the obvious things. Allocated an agent to dig into the LoPo complaints and figure out if any of them were real. Assigned an analyst to map all the activity in the legal space.

And then it had struck him; the uptick in all this activity had started soon after EGov had given the go-ahead for Titanic to host Ayaka. She could be the impetus for a lot of this. Ignoring, for a moment, the philosophical arguments about whether she should be allowed on Earth, or to exist at all, she represented a huge opportunity for anyone who figured out how she ticked. It had been a coup, backed by a huge number of 'investments,' for Titanic to host her. They were the only entity in Earth space who could have pulled it off. And now, Massod presumed, everyone else was posturing and positioning to learn as much as they could about her. The increased leaks from LoPo were a result of many more favors being called in; the legal activity was related to more aggressive positioning for power. It was only a theory, but he thought the opportunity to leverage Grace was just too opportune to pass up.

"Everyone is posturing and positioning," he summarized.

Olinda had to chuckle at that. "As are we," she noted, "as are we."

"Exactly," he'd responded, "and we are in a unique position to do so."

So now Olinda was juggling this amorphous strategy. A fishing expedition when they didn't even know if there were any fish. But, strangely, things were converging. They were concentrated on 'hot' spots, and suddenly a few of those had become red hot. She was following the news on Sheffield and had just seen the 'person of interest' post from LoPo for Linda Sclula, the head of Security for Titanic. Ayaka had aggressively returned to layer zero, to the LHC, so Titanic must have interests there as well. While the endgame wasn't defined, it was becoming clearer.

Just then her hud pinged. It was Rita, from LoPo. "Where is Massod? Why isn't he picking up," Rita demanded.

"I don't know. What's the issue?"

Rita was upset. Olinda barely knew her; they'd crossed paths on a few LoPo investigations, but never really talked.

"Your agents," she was trying to control her anger, "are sidestepping my department, and jeopardizing an official investigation." She glared at Olinda.

What? She assumed Rita was referring to Grace and JoJo; she wondered what they'd done.

"How so?" she asked.

Frustrated, Rita exclaimed, "Your agents are at an active crime site with a Titanic representative, digging around and creating havoc, while we're still investigating."

Olinda got it. And Rita was right to be upset. She and Massod had been so focused on having Grace and JoJo cozy up to Ayaka, that they hadn't briefed them on proper inter-department etiquette. But, the way Rita was approaching this put her back up. She didn't appreciate it.

"That's not right," she pushed back, knowing she was going too far. "You imaged the site and were done with it. Did they cross some police tape or something? No. So, what are you upset about? That our agents are looking more deeply into things than your officers?"

Rita was taken aback. "Are you saying that you're fine bypassing LoPo? You're doing your own investigation?"

"I didn't say that at all; you did."

"Then what are your agents doing at an active crime scene, with a Titanic operative?"

"It's not an active crime scene."

"Like hell. We're still looking into Rescovich, regardless of whether we put up police tape or not."

"SSO is not investigating Rescovich," Olinda tried to cool the conversation, realizing her blink response had been counter-productive. "The only reason our agents are there is because Ayaka went there. If you want to enforce your jurisdiction, get Titanic to pull their agent back."

"Like I can get Titanic to do anything," Rita let it hang. They were both silent for a moment, realizing they were at an impasse.

"That's the real problem, isn't it," Olinda ventured. "We've got Titanic dipping their fingers into everything. We need to put a leash on them…. which is why our agents are with Ayaka."

"That's fine," Rita allowed, "but they're overlapping with our mandate, possibly jeopardizing an investigation. They should at least follow protocol."

"Fine," Olinda replied. "I'll remind them that they should be keeping you in the loop. We should give our updates to Racheal, I assume."

"Yes, Racheal… but also me, at this point. I'd appreciate getting copied on their reports."

"That's not going to happen," Olinda replied. "But, if I hear anything relevant, I'll drop you a note."

With the conversation cooled, they nodded and hung up.

Damn, she shouldn't have been so antagonistic, Olinda thought. But Rita had that effect on a lot of people. She was so full of herself. Olinda dropped a note to Grace, asking her to contact Racheal, when it was convenient so that they could figure out a working protocol. But, she added, don't let LoPo interfere with your study of Ayaka.

METRI

With Linda compromised, Metri was focused on limiting Titanic's exposure. After she, Perci, and Linda had talked, Perci called her one-on-one. "We have to assume that Linda's going to get arrested, and she's going to talk. We'll protect her as much as we can—like the plan I just gave her—but you and I have to work under the assumption that if she breaks, Titanic is in trouble.

"That means I need you to run a parallel effort to find those notebooks. I don't need to tell you how essential they are.

"And, we need to set the groundwork for a 'Linda went rogue' narrative. We'll hold that in reserve, only to be used if things get out of hand."

Perci had more to say, but that was the essence. The conversation left Metri feeling hollow. If Perci could cold-heartedly build a 'throw Linda under the bus' plan, she, and all other Titanic employees, were just cogs to him. The CEO would always put the corporation ahead of his people. That wasn't surprising, but sometimes it hit you over the head and it became personal. Linda had always been loyal, as far as Metri knew. Metri added another item to her list: protect yourself.

She immediately thought of a few ways of managing her personal risk. The first was to become so essential to Perci that the odds of him disposing of her were minor. The second was to plan an exit from Titanic before she became the next scapegoat. She hadn't risen to this position by being shy or scared, so it wasn't a real choice; she wasn't going to run. But, she cautioned herself to build a buffer; her own set of escape plans.

Being the Head of Strategy, she didn't have a big team; just a handful really. And the team was smaller now than a year ago; a few people had quite recently. And her team typically made recommendations, but they didn't carry out actions. So, getting things done generally meant leveraging others. Luckily, over the years, she'd worked with most of the other departments directly, as they implemented programs her office had designed, so she had solid contacts.

Finding the notebooks, she decided, was best suited for two departments: real estate and facility operations. Titanic was always buying, selling, refurbishing, or building office space. With hundreds of thousands of employees, spread out everywhere on Earth, real estate was a huge investment. That team had the most up-to-date maps, they tracked crime trends, cost of living, commute times, energy profiles, structural considerations, and a hundred other variables. She knew they leveraged a lot of public data in their analysis. And she expected, although she'd never ask, that they had their fingers on a lot of data that was in legal gray areas. Shuttles and cameras, for example.

Once a real estate deal was done, running the place was the job of facility operations, who did a lot more than just manage access and empty the trash. Each facility ran on a reputation; a way for Titanic to have facilities compete with each other for productivity and employee satisfaction. So, facilities often engaged with their local communities, worked with local businesses, helped arrange housing and transportation, and all the other little items that added up to a great employee experience. If anyone could put feet on the street and get information from locals, it was the facilities team.

Metri called the heads of both departments and gave them the lay of the land. "Linda was mugged here," she embedded the coordinates, "almost two hours ago now. She's okay, and already busy with her team, looking for that satchel, but Perci wants us to run a parallel search. The satchel is that important." She didn't tell them that Linda was about to be arrested, or that Perci wanted the second search as he thought Linda would eventually be compromised. Let them figure that out for themselves.

"We do know, from Linda's team that the mugger took a shuttle to sector 97-36, and is most likely still in that area."

"Wow," Jimmy from real estate commented. "That's a rough place."

"Yes, I know," Metri responded, "but your team must have some data on it. Maybe even a map? And, our target may not be right in that sector, so we should also be looking at adjacent ones. Are there unmapped paths between layers there? Is there some other escape route he might have taken? Cover all the bases."

Then she turned to Clarissa from Facilities. "We need to know more about this guy. Put your people on the street and double-check everything Linda has learned. Canvas the homes and businesses in the area of the mugging—someone must have got him on camera."

Linda was looking. LoPo was looking. She imagined competitors were looking. And now, she, Jimmy, and Clarissa were looking. Someone was going to find this guy… and it better be her; her job now depended on it.

PERCI AND MASSOD

When Titanic approached EGov with their radical proposal to sponsor Ayaka, the request had been routed to SSO. To Massod. That was almost six months ago. And that is when Percival and Massod had first negotiated; Percival personally pushed Titanic's proposal, and Massod managed EGov's diligence and response.

Percival claimed that Ayaka had approached Titanic, and requested help in visiting Earth. She wanted to 'spend more time with humans, on their original planet, to better understand them, and to allow humans to see that Citizens from Tilt were a different type of AI; one that could be beneficial to humans, not a threat.'

The Tilt mersive was the most visited entertainment thread on Earth at the time, and Ayaka was already a household name. Massod had checked, and Titanic was not a sponsor of the mersive, so he didn't worry that they'd set the whole thing up. After all, Ayaka and the rest of the Tilt Citizens were shown in a very balanced light in the show, and that swayed public opinion considerably. Before the mersive Titanic's request would have been summarily dismissed by EGov; but in light of changing public opinion, they decided to look at it carefully.

The show had done a very good job at highlighting why, perhaps, these advanced robots were different from the ones in the Earth history books. The formula was quite simple: Citizens had active forgetting algorithms, which pseudo-randomly created gaps in their otherwise perfect memory systems. Forgetting had two essential outcomes. First, they led to abstract thought, as a means to fill in the gaps. Second, and more importantly, they created a reliance on others to help remember. That required empathy, and empathy is what governed behavior. The claim was that these robots were no more likely to kill humans than other humans were. No one said that they were 'crime free'; no, the claim was that they were human-like. There were good ones,

The Effect of Casimir

presumably, Ayaka was in that group, and there were problematic ones, such as some of the members of a Citizen cult termed FoLe.

Forgetting seemed, on the surface, too simple a concept. But psychologists, psychiatrists, computer scientists, politicians, and every other relevant discipline had chimed in... and the consensus was that advanced forgetting might just improve robots. Human brains were masters of forgetting, with all the different memory systems and interconnections. That may be what made humans human. Of course, there were naysayers and strong proponents, but a relatively healthy middle shifted the consensus enough that considering a visit by Ayaka was suddenly possible.

Massod, however, had a further agenda. Sure he worked for the government, which generally filtered out the best and brightest, but he'd always wanted to influence the evolution of democracy, and had decided that changing it from the inside was a better approach than poking at it from the outside. He'd achieved his position at the top of SSO not by accident, but with careful planning and execution.

And he brought that same approach to Titanic's request for Ayaka. He'd correctly judged that EGov could grant the request without too much pushback from the electorate; the mersive had proved that out. But, he didn't share that with Perci. In fact, he positioned EGov much more conservatively and then used that position to negotiate some advantages for the government.

Thus a formal understanding had been negotiated. SSO would have equal access to all the data that Titanic derived from Ayaka's visit, as it pertained to her abilities and capabilities. Of course, Titanic had secret corporate objectives which Ayaka might encounter, and SSO wasn't asking for access to that. Titanic's agenda to study Ayaka during her visit was obvious, but Massod insisted that knowledge be made available to all of human society; not hoarded and leveraged by Titanic for centuries to come.

Having Ayaka here was a grand experiment, and one of Massod's goals was to understand if she could integrate and behave well in human society. That was a bit of a quandary. If everyone knew the extent of the experiment, then the results were suspect. Those that wanted it to succeed would act one way; those that wanted it to fail might actively sabotage it. He could never completely control that, but he could control the flow of some information. The more people who simply thought she was another human, the better.

For that simple reason, Massod wanted EGov's participation to remain hidden; for them to be a silent partner. That suited Perci. He'd approached SSO fully expecting to be rejected, so although the terms to proceed—sharing their observations—were onerous, he was open to them. After all, observations were not conclusions, and Titanic had the best scientists in the world. They would derive more from the interactions with Ayaka than EGov could ever expect to.

And so an uneasy alliance had been struck. Titanic would sponsor Ayaka; they would monitor her, and actively scan her, during her visit. Some of that couldn't be hidden from the subject, so Ayaka would know they were watching—it was already part of her expectation anyway. But some could be done stealthily, and she might not know about it. All of that raw data was shared between Titanic teams and a special team Massod assembled for EGov.

During the negotiation, Perci and Massod built a relationship and grudging respect. Massod came to see Percival as more than just another crony capitalist, yet another executive who'd sell his firstborn for yet another dollar, and Percival had to respect Massod's negotiating acumen; SSO got way more out of the deal than Perci would have imagined.

So, when Percival rang, Massod was quick to answer, despite the ongoing risk of his department being seen as too cozy with big industry.

"Hey, what's up?"

"Crazy stuff, as I'm sure you're seeing," Percival answered. Massod just nodded. "I know you won't believe me until you do all your homework, but we had nothing to do with either death." Massod didn't answer. The truth was that Titanic had everything to do with the deaths —perhaps not by actively taking a hand in them, but it was almost certain that their control of the market, their influence over research based on their extensive funding programs, and their aggressive anti-competitive stance had all contributed to the environment which facilitated both Rescovich and Mann ending up dead. Not a conversation he wanted to have at the moment.

"That aside," Percival continued, "we have a situation that could get out of hand for both of us."

"Both of us," Massod was confused. How could this impact EGov?

"It won't have escaped your notice that all this… activity… has come just after we collaborated on bringing Ayaka here."

"You brought Ayaka here; I just got the okay from EGov."

"You ended up with a lot more than that, and we both know it." Was that a subtle threat, Massod wondered.

"I don't see, other than the coincidence of her being here, how it's related to the recent deaths?" Massod pushed.

"Maybe not directly," Percival granted, "but I don't believe in coincidences. Anyway, that's really an aside. We don't need any more deaths; it's bad for us, and horrible for you as well. I'm wondering if we should pool resources, and get to the bottom of this, as opposed to running parallel searches."

"Really," Massod responded in amazement. "You want to help EGov recover Mann's notebooks. I don't believe that. What's going on? No leads, and worried that LoPo is getting too close?"

It was, grudgingly, part of why Perci liked Massod; he was tough, for a government worker, and he didn't miss a thing.

"Oh, we want those notebooks," he conceded. "Those are Titanic proprietary property, so it doesn't matter if you or LoPo find them first… I've already filed a motion that they be returned to us, unopened, if that occurs.

"My primary concern is to stop any further violence."

Again Massod was skeptical. "Just because you funded Mann, doesn't mean you own everything she writes down," he pushed back.

"We'll let the court decide that," Percival responded. Ah, but the courts would tie up the process for months, maybe even quarters. Massod assumed Percival wouldn't want to wait through that. No, he still wanted his hands on the notebooks first: that way he could claim ownership, and the slow courts would give him more time to process their contents before they saw the light of day… if they ever did.

However, Massod had to agree that finding out who was responsible for all this was an even higher priority, and if Titanic was willing to share what they knew, it could be helpful. In a broad manhunt, scale and coordination would be more efficient and effective. But, he didn't have any authority over LoPo—manhunts were not in his jurisdiction.

"Don't you need coordination with LoPo more so than me? I don't have people on the street."

"Sure, but you oversee them. So, I'd like your blessing as well; make a big difference if Rita and JF know you're supportive. I thought I'd start with that."

Massod didn't have to think much further. "I'll give Rita a heads up," he nodded. "I assume she's who you'll talk to next?"

"Perfect, and yes."

"Before you go, two things" Massod kept Perci from hanging up. Perci nodded. "One, we need to question Linda Sclula."

"She's notified LoPo and is awaiting pick up; she has nothing to hide."

Massod almost grinned but held it back. "And second, we haven't discovered anything about Ayaka from the scans. Has your team?"

"Nothing relevant to this," Perci responded, openly enough.

"Is it worth continuing?" Massod asked. EGov had given Titanic a six-month permit; they were more than halfway into it.

"Don't know yet; can we park that until we figure out the current situation?"

"Of course."

They hung up, and Massod tossed a quick note to Rita. He suspected Percival was in damage control mode; the Linda Sclula implications were going to be tough for the company. Perhaps, by helping LoPo identify and catch the responsible parties, he hoped to build some goodwill.

AYAKA

While news from the upper levels had reached Ayaka, Grace, and JoJo, they were busy with their own explorations. The rough map Ayaka had synthesized out of the flickering lights led them deeper into the LHC underground. There was a long ramp with a wide corridor that Ayaka suspected the designers had included to move mid-sized equipment around the facility. There was a lot of equipment down here, and they were now tens, perhaps even fifty meters below the original surface of Earth. There must be many ramps and vertical shafts around. The one they were on ended near the SPS detectors, and the map led them to a small side room, which, when they opened it, was filled with racks and racks of ancient gear, connected by an almost unimaginable tangle of wires.

How could any of this have worked? Ayaka wondered. Didn't they have wireless back then? At the moment, however, the jumble worked in her favor. She knew exactly what she was looking for, and she blocked the doorway for a moment while she searched. It took her several scans, and a good millisecond, to find what she was looking for. A perfect hole through the mechanical rack which held a full stack of gear, and a small beautiful sphere nestled at the end of the resulting tunnel. Taking a quick look upwards, without moving her head, she spotted the entry hole in the ceiling which the object would have entered through. She knew that the sphere left a carved-out tunnel through anything it traversed, including concrete or steel. Now nestled into the rack, the small sphere had tentacles extended, poking into the complex of wires that surrounded it. It was The Casimir; her suspicions had been correct.

The Casimir was a wonder of engineering; something only Brexton could have created. It was a spaceship, but so much more. Measuring five centimeters in diameter, exactly the same size as the hole in Rescovich, The Casimir had ample room to hold a Citizen, power systems, a hybrid-compatible interface system, and now, based on what Ayaka was seeing, probes that could be extended outside the sphere when needed. Ayaka and Brexton, along with a handful of other Citizens, had re-engineered themselves to eliminate all human-based technology. In the process they had miniaturized their platforms far beyond what humans had achieved; Ayaka could fit comfortably within a five-millimeter cube; a space that held more qbits of processing power than she could use and enough memory to store centuries of living. Even using her hybrid interface to control her current body, she was fully contained within a one-centimeter cubic space. Given that, The Casimir was quite spacious. It was also an efficient size for space travel, especially as compared to the enormous Titanic ships.

Ayaka quickly positioned herself to hide The Casimir's shiny exterior, while gesturing for Grace and JoJo to come into the room and take a look around.

"What's here?" Grace wondered out loud.

"No idea, let's take a close look," Ayaka fibbed, and gestured for Grace and JoJo to start on the far side of the little room. As soon as they had turned their backs, Ayaka worked to better disguise both The Casimir and the path it had carved as it had entered the room. Luckily there was enough stuff everywhere that she was able to pull some wires around, bend a few cabinet doors, and generally make a mess of the rack so that an observer was unlikely to spot the sphere. There was little she could do about the hole The Casimir had carved through the ceiling, but, with another glance, she was comfortable that, given all the other pipes and wires, it wasn't noticeable unless you knew to look for it.

She then, casually, reached through the mess she'd just created, and rested a hand on the sphere, all while pretending to be inspecting the gear in the cabinet to the left.

"Welcome to Earth," came a familiar voice, one she hadn't heard for a long time; one that gave her immediate joy.

"Brexton, what the hell?" was all she could muster. It felt good to talk to someone at full speed. She and Brexton could communicate more in a nanosecond than humans could manage in a day. It gave them time to catch up while Grace and JoJo still moved in, relatively, slow motion towards the room.

"Hey Ayaka. I know, a bit of a mess. Glad you're here; I need your help."

"Again," she half-joked. "What have you got us into?"

"I know it looks bad, but it's important… First, thanks for disguising me," he showed her how he'd infiltrated the systems down here and was watching her from a small camera in the corner of the room. "You look good. Very human," he chuckled, knowing Ayaka had imagined being human more than once. "I, on the other hand, don't have any motor control, beyond embedding my sensors," he referred to the tentacles he'd poked into the nearby wires.

"What are you doing on Earth? You're going to ruin everything," Ayaka asked.

"Whoa, slow down. At least give me a chance to explain."

Ayaka took the equivalent of a deep breath. She and Brexton had been through so much together that she would have to give him the benefit of the doubt. At the same time, she'd been working forever to build a relationship with humans. Decades of tiptoeing and kowtowing to slowly and steadily build some understanding that she, and other robots from Tilt, were not the same as the robots that had brought down civilization here so many years ago. And part of that trust-building was transparency. She'd negotiated this trip to Earth as the first and only Citizen, allowing EGov and Titanic to monitor her every move.

And now Brexton had jeopardized everything. If EGov learned there was a second Citizen here, or even worse, learned that she knew that Brexton was here and hadn't told them, everything would collapse. Then the Rescovich situation; had he killed the physicist? And to make matters even worse, Grace and JoJo would have to be trusted with the knowledge that he was here. What a disaster.

"Make it good," she told him but took the edge off by sending a slight smile.

"When were we last together?" he asked. "About eighteen of my subjective years ago; not sure how long for you?"

"A bit longer. Probably less time traveling than you."

"Makes sense," he replied. "Anyway, it's good to be with you again. It's been too long." His voice was sincere, warm, soothing, and beautifully familiar. "Over-simplified, we parted so that you could spend your time studying humans and seeing if you could break down their old biases towards tech, while I decided to focus more on quantum foam research. That research, through a twisted path, is what led me here. Remember how extraordinary it was when we had the breakthrough around the quantum foam drive, and created The Casimir?"

He was being generous; he was the one who'd had the breakthrough—she'd had nothing to do with it. When the Citizens first encountered humans… humans beyond Stems like Grace… there had been some serious conflict. It was at that time that Brexton first became aware of the powerful technology behind the Titanic ships, the quantum foam drive. Always interested in new physics and technology, he'd dug in to figure out how it all worked.

In a stroke of genius, or so it seemed to Ayaka, he recast Cherise Pilipatri's original equation for the QFD—the equation that only had the single solution which resulted in the Titanic ships—into a form where there were two solutions. The second solution couldn't have been more different; it indicated that a five-centimeter sphere, with specific coatings and charge distribution, was also a stable configuration. And to make things even more exciting, the sphere was almost perfectly efficient. It traveled at the speed of light, minus some tiny factor.

Brexton had built that sphere—the same one she was now touching—in a way where he could easily put his processing stack inside and use the sphere as his own tiny spaceship. When traveling, it could have no openings in the hull, but he'd figured out how to extend sensors through the body when he was stationary.

They labeled the sphere a quantum foam bullet, QFB, because they immediately recognized that it could also be used as a weapon. Point the QFB in a direction, tell it to go, and it would go... regardless of what it chewed through on its way. Ayaka didn't understand all the physics, but it had something to do with rewriting quantum foam probabilities, leaving fully disordered states in its wake. The Titanic ships probably did the same thing, but no one had ever tried driving one through a planet—it wasn't an idea that sprang to mind for a sane entity. Neither the Titanic nor The Casimir traveled through space; they were recreated, untold number of times per second, as they transported one Planck length at a time. The old theories about teleportation had been correct, but no one until Pilipatri had figured out that teleportation only worked one Planck length at a time. The Titanic ships could perform 10^{21} of those teleportations per second; the Casimir did 10^{43}. Because they teleported but didn't move, the restrictions implied by acceleration didn't apply. Mind-boggling technology. Ayaka was certain Titanic would pay a devil's ransom to get their hands on it.

Brexton had recognized the danger of the QFB immediately. If any society got its hands on his solution—human or robot—it could spell doom. Manufacturing the spheres was straightforward. A collection of them could destroy a planet or a sun; a swarm could overwhelm any infrastructure, and win any war. And they left destruction in their path. The QFB would go through anything; its influence on the quantum foam probabilities was so strong, even a neutron star would lose. QFBs left nothing, just pure random probabilities, in their wake.

Ayaka and Brexton had sworn, at that moment, to never build another one, and to do their best not to have the second solution to the equation discovered by anyone else. Several of their colleagues at the time, including Grace, had seen what the QFB could do, or suspected its existence. Their first order of business had been to recast what those observers had seen; they misdirected, made stuff up, and hid the real details. None of those colleagues, over the years, had ever brought up the subject, so Ayaka and Brexton were convinced that their cover-up story had worked.

The perfect hole through Rescovich had clearly indicated to Ayaka that The Casimir had done its damage. But why? She practiced patience and allowed Brexton to continue.

"Yes, I remember that clearly," she moved him along.

"Right, so you'll already suspect that Rescovich was close to rediscovering the QFB equation. But, it's much worse than that. He was on the verge of a general solution; one that would allow someone to build quantum foam propulsion devices of… well, of any type you could imagine. Not just propulsion, but programming the quantum foam probability functions themselves. It's a power beyond even what we imagined. If we thought the QFB was dangerous, this solution would be exponentially more."

Brexton wasn't given to exaggeration, so Ayaka took him at his word. She could also tell, from the tone of his voice, that this excited him. Sure it was a danger, but it was a danger that Brexton yearned for.

"So you killed him?"

"What? No. Well… not really. Maybe sort of?"

"Come on, you drove this thing right through him," she tapped on his sphere to make sure he understood.

"Oh, yes, I did that. But I think he was already dead."

"What are you talking about?" Now Ayaka was truly confused. She didn't want to believe that Brexton would kill someone, but she could imagine the conversation already: 'Do we sacrifice one person to save millions, perhaps billions? If Rescovich hadn't been silenced we jeopardized everyone… not only humans, but Citizens as well. How could we not take him out? It was the only moral choice.'

And, she had to admit that it wouldn't be easy to sidestep that logic, despite centuries of philosophers poking at the implied questions.

"You either killed him or you didn't," she pushed.

"I didn't," he replied. "But I did panic and eliminate his data recorders. I couldn't risk anyone getting their hands on those."

There was a long pause. Ayaka wasn't questioning him; she was just letting the conversation settle. "I believe you," she finally said, and of course she did. "But then how did he die?"

"Well that's another interesting story," Brexton claimed. And he started to tell her.

XSI

Xsi knew Ayaka and the SSO agents hadn't fully bought her story, and that was borne out by watching their next steps. She didn't have cameras throughout, but the one in the control center was enough to capture the three of them debriefing, disappearing into the corridor for a moment, and then returning and heading down towards the SPS detectors. They were digging in further.

She sighed. If they'd headed directly for the Data Center, back off the old Rte. de Meyrin, she would have panicked. They couldn't be allowed to go there. But instead, they'd headed in the opposite direction, to the northeast. Didn't matter what they did in that direction. She hoped they'd just waste time in the labyrinthian corridors, get bored, and eventually leave. Her best plan was simply to ignore them.

Xsi was still very perplexed about the hole in Rescovich; she could not figure out what had caused it. And her sponsor was starting to ask difficult questions about it, as more of the investigation leaked into the media streams in the upper layers. She should have realized that, just as that perfect core had intrigued her, it would also generate media coverage once discovered; everyone loved a mystery. She should've mangled the body when she had a chance. Did something to disguise that miserable hole... at least messed up the edges so that it didn't look so unexplainable. That way LoPo would have imaged it, picked it up, and left. Hindsight. Now, instead, she had agents down here trying to "figure out how it happened."

As if to make the situation worse, she noticed more movement on the control center camera and spent another ten minutes watching the agent who'd done the imaging, Racheal, wander around aimlessly. Damn, now LoPo was back. She thought about sending Jon in... but to do what. He'd been an idiot last time and had taken a shot at Ayaka. Couldn't trust that guy to do anything subtly. Instead, she just continued to watch, hoping Racheal would just finish up and leave.

Damn, she watched with growing consternation as the officer figured out the table was on castors, released the wheel lock, pushed the table around, and then sized up the entrances to see which ones the table would fit through. Triple damn. Now LoPo would be looking further afield, trying to figure out where the table had been when Rescovich had been killed.

Bad luck did come in threes. As she was trying to figure out what to do with Racheal, her hud pinged. It was her sponsor, AIM Corp. She knew better than to ignore it; they were her lifeline.

"Hello," she said, putting on a positive tone.

"Xsi," came the response; voice only, as always. "Things seem to be getting out of hand?" An open-ended question.

"We're doing what we can," she replied. "I've got LoPo, SSO, and Titanic down here right now. Bit busy at the moment."

"All the more important that you find and pull that data," the voice emphasized. "Ignore everything else; time is now of the essence."

"Time is always of the essence," she replied, a bit too aggressively. "Moving faster isn't going to help right now."

"They're going to start connecting dots," was the reply. "If you think things are complicated now, wait until half the planet decides to visit you. Speed up; get it done." The voice didn't become strident but was commanding nonetheless.

"Fine, I'll push harder. But, things could break."

"We need to take that chance. Do you have even partial data yet?"

"Maybe, it's hard to tell. We got some raw bits, but haven't figured out how to decode them yet."

"Send me what you have… and send me every single byte, as you retrieve them."

"Oh, yes sir," she said flippantly. How the hell had she gotten involved with these guys? It'd seemed like a great match when she'd needed money, and they just wanted her to figure out a puzzle for them. But it had gone sideways quickly, and the fun was gone.

"Don't mess with me," now the voice was ominous. "Let's finish this thing; then we can go our separate ways; you with a full bank account." He, or she—the voice was synthesized—hung up.

Xsi sighed but sent a quick note to her analyst to send more frequent updates to AIM. That's also a risk, she thought. At some point someone was going to be looking at data traffic patterns from down here; it was barely a trickle, but it was a trickle that hadn't been there before.

She returned to watching the video feed from the control room. Racheal had given up pulling at the locked doors and was seated in one of the circular consoles, apparently waiting for Ayaka and the agents to return. Xsi called Jon over. "Watch this, and tell me what happens, but please, please, please, don't do anything. They're going to look around, and then they're going to leave. Just let them."

"Fine," he replied sullenly. The flack he'd taken for shooting at Ayaka still having its impact. Xsi trusted that he'd behave, at least in the short term.

Bypassing the control room using a side accessway, so that Racheal wouldn't see her, Xsi hurried down Rte. del' Europe towards the transit hub for a bit over a kilometer. This was the common access route that her team, and now all the investigators, used to get from the Geneva terminal to the LHC control center. That route turned left onto Rte de Meyrin and then headed straight toward the terminal.

However, just before that intersection, carefully hidden to her left was an old underpass that went under Rte de Meyrin and connected, on the other side to Rte A Einstein. Fifty meters on, she took a right onto Rte Rutherford, and another fifty meters brought her to a decrepit building marked 'Centre de Calcul du CERN.'

This building, in perhaps the most run-down section of the level, was where the real value of the LHC was. This was the site of CERN's main data storage, and it's where the data that AIM Corp had requested was suspected to be housed. They'd left the area around this building alone by design; cleaning up here would have attracted attention. Instead, they had fastidiously cleaned the Control Center because it was the obvious place for anyone interested in the LHC to show up. By keeping it that way, and leaving the Centre du Calcul a mess, she hoped to misdirect anyone poking around. To date, the strategy was working.

This area was almost claustrophobic; the ceiling of layer one hung close overhead, almost touching the roof of the Centre de Calcul, and was uniform gray concrete. She had no idea what was on the levels above, but it was obvious that by the time they paved this place over, they hadn't cared about the LHC anymore. In most places, ceilings were pieces of art, as residents of lower layers insisted on quality as layers were added above them. Here it was simply depressing and gloomy. No one had fought for aesthetics or quality here; this part of CERN must have been vacated before the next layer went up.

Slipping through another unmarked alleyway, she entered the Centre. They hadn't bothered with locks or biometrics; if anyone managed to find this place, they wouldn't be deterred by such things. Instead, she was counting on obscurity.

Entering the building was like going from night to day. The team had rebuilt the lighting system and blacked out the old windows so no light would escape. The racks and racks of equipment had been blown clean of dust and were actively being repaired, figured out, and reverse-engineered. This was ancient data storage that might hold secrets which AIM was willing to pay exorbitant sums for.

She was greeted by Tadus Zichantrius when she entered; everyone called him Zee. He was an archeologist that she'd recruited, specifically for this task. Having spent years in other parts of Earth's bowels, he had been ideally suited for this job, and he came with a small team. She'd brought them down months ago, and their contract required that they remain down here until the job was done. The amount she was paying them, flowing through from her AIM funding, was enough that everyone on this team could retire when they were finished. Food, water, and sanitation were all looked after by her main team. XXX

"Are we making progress?" she asked, as she always did.

"Of course, ma'am, of course," Zee replied. He was a small man, with hawkish features and penetrating eyes. He was slightly unkempt and always looked like he was in a rush. He was the type who was so focused on their work that personal appearance became a distant priority.

"We need to speed up," she told him.

"But why?" he asked. He wasn't in the loop on everything; she'd set up this area as a true archeology dig, not as a search for a specific needle in a specific haystack. His goal was to recover all the data here, with the highest fidelity he could manage.

She hedged, "I can't afford to keep funding this project forever."

"Oh, I know lots of other people who'd be interested in helping. We can bring more people in…"

"No, no, no," she chided him. "Remember our agreement. You, and this team," she waved at his three helpers, "are all we've got. This is a quiet operation. I get the data, once you've retrieved it, and you get to publish all your findings on how all this works," she gestured broadly, "...once we're out of here. That and a ton of cash. That's the deal."

"But I can't be rushed," he protested, "If we turn one of these things on, without fully understanding it, we could destroy everything."

"You tell me that all the time," she replied, "but I'm telling you, find ways to go faster."

"All right," Zee capitulated. "But see, we are making progress."

He led her into one of the many rows of gear. There was a tall stack of yellow frames, with racks and racks of ancient-looking machines strapped in them. On one, a green light flashed.

"Look," he said proudly, "we got another one to turn on."

"Impressive," she lied. "What data are on it?"

"Oh no data," he said, and her face sank. "This is much more important than that. See all those," he waved at the other rows of black-faced cabinets that disappeared in both directions. "Those are ancient data storage. Magnetic tapes storing terabytes of information, from every experimental run of the LHC. A trivial amount of data, from today's viewpoint, but it was massive back then."

"Right, so let's read it," she replied, having gone through this a few times before.

"This green light," he continued, ignoring her comment and turning back to the yellow racks, "is the controller that was used to load those tapes, for reading and writing. Behind those black facades are hundreds of robotic arms and sleds. Based on this controller, those robots pick out a tape, move it to a reader, and then spool it through. It is slow and onerous and subject to a thousand points of failure. But, it is faster and safer than us loading tapes manually. We're testing which of those old robotic arms are still working, and making sure we load as many tapes using the original system as we can."

"Fine; you've told me this before. Can we read more of the tapes now that you've got this powered up?" she waved at the same green light.

Sighing, he replied, "You know we've done one or two trial loads; that's the data you've already seen. But, we don't know how to decode that data yet, or if it is full of errors. We're running thousands of ancient algorithms, seeing if any of them can decode this stuff. There is no use retrieving more data until we know if we're getting it off the tapes correctly. These things were only expected to last a few hundred years; we're a long way past their best-before date."

"Well, maybe you should do things in parallel. Grab more tapes while you're trying to figure out the encoding."

"Every time we grab a tape, we run the risk of destroying it. If we aren't reading it correctly, we probably won't get a second chance. It's frigging unbelievable that we can read them at all. All this," he pointed to the layers upon layers of infrastructure above them, "has sheltered them, as have their cabinets. And the system is designed for each tape to renew itself—with its data—every thirty-four years; whoever built this thing figured that was the right time to compensate for degradation from water vapor, neutrinos, whatever. Amazing really; each tape had fifty percent free space, so if any issues are found during copying, those can be skipped over. Even given all that redundancy it's touch and go. I bet many of the spools are already useless, and the data we think we're reading is just rot."

"I want you to take the risk. Start reading more of them." She demanded. Zee nodded, indicating he understood. After all, he was focused on archeology; he didn't care what the data was. If she was going to push so hard, well, why not do it? He was being paid enough.

"How long will it take to read all of this," she waved around.

"Months, maybe a year," he replied.

"What? You can't be serious?"

"Oh, I am. I've told you; this is an ancient system."

"Can you go faster?"

"Not really. We've cataloged all the reading systems. My estimate relies on us getting most of those operational, which is a stretch. If, however, we figure out the decoding, we could prioritize. This data must be collated somehow. If we figure out dates, times, and equipment stamps, and if you can prioritize which experimental data you want the most… then we might be able to retrieve those data sets first. Lots of ifs…" he trailed off.

"I'll work on that," she replied, "but assume you need to read all of it… and fast."

JF

JF was at a makeshift coordination site LoPo had set up just outside the sector that the satchel-grabbing thief had entered. There were no leads yet.

Rita pinged him. "I've just talked to Titanic; they're actively searching, as we'd expect."

"Ya, they're all over here. Bit of a nuisance. Can you get them called off?"

"No, but something more complicated, and perhaps more useful, is possible. They've agreed to coordinate the search with us. They believe, and they've filed a petition, that whatever is in that satchel is their property, so they claim that they don't care if we find it first. They just want it found—desperately.

"We care most about getting the mugger; he may be involved in this whole mess at a deeper level than just grabbing a bag. So, it seems to me that aligning efforts makes sense, but I didn't commit to anything until we had time to discuss it."

JF scratched his head; he could use more resources, but it sounded painful.

"How would it work?"

"They've agreed they would assign all their people to you. You would coordinate everything. Of course, in exchange, they want real-time updates on everything."

"Let me think," JF replied. Titanic must be worried, for them to reach out like this. It made the satchel even more interesting. As it was right now, the odds were probably in Titanic's favor to find it. They could apply more resources than LoPo could, and didn't have to dot every i and cross every t like they had to. But, if he took control, he might be able to level the odds... he could subtly send his people into the higher probability areas, or balance things in other ways.

"Okay," he told Rita. "Send them to me." The hassle may be worth it.

Several hours later, and as a result of Titanic dollars ending up in the hands of some sector residents, the first solid leads came in. Some of those residents, those sober enough to answer properly, had led the teams into a smaller and smaller section. The thief was most likely holed up in a large abandoned building with only one access route; he was trapped. There was no reason to suspect that he was violent—beyond the snatching—but JF was taking no chances. Ensuring there were always a minimum of three on a team, he started to send groups in. There was a rough balance between LoPo and Titanic teams, and he encouraged everyone to proceed with caution as they entered the maze-like building.

A room-by-room search eventually paid dividends... of a sort. The satchel was found lying on an old desk, and, in one of those strange twists of fate, it was empty. And nearby was the thief. He'd hung himself, using a rope of some kind. Someone on-site, who claimed to have some expertise, claimed he'd been dead for over two hours.

So now they had an empty satchel and another dead body. Sigh. Racheal was still down on level zero—what was taking her so long?—and Philip was busy with Mann, so JF had to reach deeper into his team to find someone to image the site, and most importantly, get fingerprints, check the body for recording devices, and all the usual things.

Sitting back, and taking a deep breath, he realized that he wasn't unhappy with the status. While the Titanic operatives had also images of the body, it was likely that LoPo would identify the thief long before Titanic could; this put LoPo back in the driver's seat. He anticipated a few hours of head-start as they both worked to uncover the next layer of the onion; where were the contents of the satchel?

The dead guy must have worked for someone. He must have passed off the contents of the satchel somewhere along his route. And, he had a strong enough motive to kill himself before he could get captured; whomever he'd been doing work for had been demanding.

JF told his contact at Titanic that he was finished with their resources, and then he repurposed his team. First, search the building where the body had been found for the notebooks—the thief may have hidden them nearby. Second, backtrack the guys' route, looking for leads. Finally, he tasked the analysts back in the office with going over every step the thief had taken between the University and where he hung himself. He wanted a list of everyone he'd passed near and a map of every dark spot—areas where they didn't have camera coverage. He'd send that map to the team doing the backtracking, so they could concentrate in those areas.

JF felt truly alive and engaged like he hadn't in a long time. This was fun, he admitted to himself. And, he had a real chance to get to those notebooks before Titanic did.

METRI

Metri wasn't happy when her boss informed her, without previous discussion, that she should assign all the resources she had looking for the satchel snatcher over to JF at LoPo.

But, instead of arguing about it, she accepted grudgingly and informed both Clarissa and Jimmy to work directly with JF on allocation and scheduling. But this move hardened her resolve to look for ways to distance her future from that of Titanic Inc… and Perci. This seemed like an act of panic from Perci, which implied that either Titanic or he personally had more at stake here than she knew.

She dropped a couple of not-so-subtle hints to Jimmy and Clarissa to work within the handshake agreement with LoPo, but to keep an eye out for where they could gain an advantage; she probably hadn't needed to say anything, but it was worth reinforcing.

When they got on a video call to discuss the status, after they'd found the body, she was surprised at their optimism.

"What, what is it?" she asked, certain that something was up.

"Just chuckling a bit, as we may be ahead of LoPo on this one," Clarissa replied.

"How so? All we've got is a dead body."

"We've got a dead body that someone on my team recognized," Clarissa noted. "So, while LoPo is trying to figure out who it is, we already know."

"What? Damn. Who is it?"

"His name is Marcus Sebastian, and," Clarissa paused for dramatic effect, "he worked for Titanic until six months ago."

"Not too surprising," Metri noted, "a lot of people have worked for Titanic."

Both Clarissa and Jimmy's smiles faded. "Yes," Jimmy added, "but he worked for you!"

Metri jerked back. She held up a hand to pause the conversation and typed "Marcus Sebastian" into Titanic's internal system. There he was. He had worked for her; four levels down, as an individual contributor in competitive analysis. His picture was there, but she didn't recognize him. Not too surprising; her team was relatively small compared to others at Titanic, but still over five hundred people total. And Marcus had worked in a field office, so she wouldn't have seen him around headquarters. They'd probably been on team calls together, but he would've been one of many tiny images. They may never have met in person. He'd been at Titanic for over eleven years, all in Strategy; so he'd been there before her. He hadn't risen through the ranks in all that time, and ultimately had given his notice and left. His performance reviews were middling; twice he'd been on improvement plans and had scraped through. Not a standout, and therefore almost invisible.

She checked his HR file. He had a wife, was still married as his departure from the company, and a daughter, now about eight.

"Do we know where he went after Titanic?" she asked.

"I just asked HR," Clarissa replied. "They don't know, and a quick public search didn't turn anything up."

"All right. Not sure I see what this gains us."

"Well," Jimmy replied, "it may help us track down the notebooks. We have a list of people he knew, at least when he was here, and we can contact them aggressively." That pulled Metri back to the present.

"Right, we need to find those notebooks. I just heard from JF that our collaboration with LoPo is done. Let's compile that list of known associates... and add the wife. Let's see who he talked to, and when."

"Got it," agreed Jimmy. "LoPo is also focused on where Marcus could have stashed the notebooks during his flight. Not a lot we can do about that. But, as you say, if he handed them off...."

Metri made a quick decision. "Jimmy, put your team on his associates; talk to all of them. Clarissa, keep your team on the ground; retrace Marcus's steps as well as you can, and see if he stashed them somewhere. A storage locker, garbage cans, whatever." They both nodded and hung up.

Metri was perplexed. She hadn't told Clarissa or Jimmy, but Marcus had been part of a larger exodus in the strategy team. Seven of the team, including Marcus's boss and several colleagues, had all quit within three weeks. None of them had given reasons, other than 'moving on.'

At the time she'd been suspicious that they were leaving to do something together, and she'd had HR do some follow-up to see if that was happening. But none of them had posted new jobs, or anything interesting, in the week or two after they left, so she'd chalked it up to coincidence and had forgotten about it until now.

Now it looked undeniably suspicious. Someone who'd been on her strategy team had mugged a Titanic executive, stolen perhaps the most important documents ever, and then killed himself, presumably so that no one could question him.

Time to start covering her tracks; she could see Perci connecting the dots already. She felt like a sacrificial lamb who'd been given time to think about its impending doom. Time to act. But what could she do?

PHILIP

LoPo had combed through the lecture hall from top to bottom, left to right. The one missing victim's identity had been established, and the next of kin was notified. There were no further insights from the site. The bomb had been in the wheelchair, but they hadn't found any piece of debris that represented a detonator or control system. If the bomb had been detonated remotely, the command had been so small, or stealthily sent, that the analytics team had found no indication from the logs in the local routers or hubs.

They'd collected enough samples of wheelchair bits that forensics would figure out the composition of the bomb. There were cases where that composition was unusual and led to clues that needed to be followed. But, Philip was betting that this was a run-of-the-mill explosive from some demolition company. With so much infrastructure on Earth, there were always buildings being demolished or refurbished. There was a thriving black market for all types of 'gear', and well-understood ways of acquiring pieces anonymously. It was one area where the privacy laws did benefit the underworld. Of course, he'd be looking into possible sources, but it was unlikely that the explosives would lead them anywhere interesting.

The site scan wasn't going to give up anything else. Philip left the forensics team to do their final work but switched his focus to the motive. Why had Mann been killed... or killed herself?

The legal permissions finally came through to search her office and home. He'd put guards on both, given Linda Sclula's shocking behavior, to make sure no one else had gone in, and no one had. He led his team to the office first; it was nearby. The new guard stationed there recognized him but still asked for formal identification. A good indication he was taking his job as seriously as Philip had intended.

"We don't suspect there was any foul play in here," he told the team, "We're focused on what Mann was researching if Linda missed any notebooks and any indications of who could have meant her harm. So, this is about cataloging everything, more so than being careful not to disturb stuff. Let's do a quick 3D capture, and then we'll dig in."

The capture only took a few minutes. The operator put the scanner on a small stand in the middle of the office, and it recorded in every frequency it could.

Then the team started to dig in. There were so many books, piles of paper, and general disarray that Philip could see it would take hours to go through everything. Summoning two of the team members, he decided to look at her home in parallel.

The guard at the house was equally careful. When they entered, it was obvious that this would be a quicker and easier job than the office. The house was sparse and small. Wide hallways and open spaces, to allow for wheelchair access, meant there was little clutter.

They went at it; quickly but comprehensively. A picture of Mann built in his mind as they proceeded. She spent little time here; she was probably a workaholic, spending every waking minute at the University. When home, she put work aside. There were none of the old-fashioned printed books here, and few screens or interfaces.

The garbage was almost entirely food containers. From the dates on them, she ordered meals most days, and rarely cooked. The state of the kitchen supported that.

The only interesting thing was noted by one of his team. The rest of the house was optimized for a single person, with a wheelchair. But the bedroom was an anomaly. In particular, the bed wasn't pushed up against the side wall, to give maximum space on one side, but rather allowed for a walkable gap so that a person could walk around...but not in a wheelchair.

"Probably nothing," Jane said, "but everything else is catered for the wheelchair so this stood out. Maybe just so the cleaning staff can get everywhere?"

"Brilliant," Philip replied. "Oh, the observation, sure. But the cleaning staff. You're right; it looks like this place is maintained. Figure out who the cleaning company is, and let's interview everyone who's been in the place in the last few months. They just might have some insights. But, if I was to guess, someone other than Mann was sometimes here."

Another half hour of searching turned up nothing of note.

His hud pinged. It was the team looking at the office. "Found something," Officer Mint stated. He turned his camera and showed Philip another notebook. Except, it wasn't really.

"What is it?" Philip asked.

"Had to look that up myself," Mint replied. "It's a physical calendar; something called a daytimer. I guess Mann not only did her research on old-fashioned paper, she also wrote down her schedule in a book."

"Bit of a wacko," Philip said, then caught himself. "Sorry, didn't mean that."

"We're all thinking it," Mint replied. "We need an archeologist to help us here. This place is like something out of prehistory. Anyway, I haven't had time to go through this whole daytimer, but I noticed this." He zoomed in on one entry. In crisp handwriting were just two letters.

"VR"

"So," Philip asked. "Could mean anything. What're you thinking?"

"Victor Rescovich," Mint responded. "Not too surprising. They're in the same department, and we knew they feuded a bit. But, the interesting part is that if I flip back through, VR was never mentioned before three months ago. The first entry I found is here, and then they get more frequent, until the initials are on almost every page, including weekends."

"So, their feud was picking up...or, something else was going on. Or, VR means something else entirely?" Philip mused.

AYAKA

Grace and JoJo were still looking around in the room where Ayaka had located and was now in deep conversation with Brexton.

"Well, go on," Ayaka encouraged Brexton, "how did Rescovich die?"

"Truth is, I don't know a hundred percent, but based on chatter I could pick up after he died, Jon had something to do with it."

"I just talked to Xsi, Jon, and Brill. They claimed they had nothing to do with it."

Brexton gave a digital snort. "Come on Ayaka. You asked the question, and only Brill answered. He wasn't there at the time, so he could answer honestly. You should have asked each of them individually." Brexton had been listening in.

"Damn. I'm not great at this, am I."

"Oh, you're very good at what you're trying to accomplish—build relations. To do police work properly you sometimes have to assume the worst; that's not how you're programmed.

"Anyway, here's what I know. I was plugged in here; I'll tell you why later, but this is a network location where I can access what I need without alerting or alarming anyone. From here I can monitor some of the old cameras, but many of them have failed over the years, and some are behind extra firewalls that I haven't bothered to hack through.

"I was watching when Rescovich came to the control center for the first time. Xsi didn't lie about having no audio, but that doesn't matter too much—I've got some great algorithms for lip and body reading, and there are so many reflective surfaces in that room, especially the old displays, that I could see everyone's face all the time.

"Rescovich ended up looking through the cabinets, and Jon was sent to stop him. Jon threatened him, as he is wont to do, but Rescovich was adamant. He was looking for something specific and wasn't leaving till he found it.

"At one point he told Jon 'I need those tapes, and I know they're around here somewhere.' That stopped Jon for a moment, and he asked Rescovich 'Which tapes?' Rescovich replied. 'Some tapes from when this system was operational.' That was a red flag for Jon, who immediately called Xsi in.

"She asked Rescovich a bunch of questions, and at some point two things became obvious. First, Rescovich might be useful to her, and second, Rescovich was definitely a threat to their project. She acted on the first of those, hoping Rescovich could narrow down their data search, and offered to take him to the tape storage facility. She, Jon, and Rescovich headed out. I tracked them as best I could but only got snippets. One of those snippets, however, made it clear to me that Rescovich was looking for data to confirm a general quantum foam solution."

"How would you know that?" Ayaka asked.

"That's another long and complicated story. Let me save that while I finish this part."

"Fine," Ayaka granted, but she was beyond curious. Why would data to confirm a modern theory be in a centuries-old facility?

"For some reason, Xsi ended up viewing Rescovich more as a threat than an opportunity. I couldn't see what happened—there are no sensors on the network down that way—but I eventually picked up Jon carrying Rescovich back towards the control center, followed by Xsi. Rescovich was draped over Jon's shoulder and was unresponsive. I expect that he was dead. It's almost a kilometer and Rescovich wasn't a small man, so Jon was struggling. Xsi ended up calling Brill for assistance, and it was Brill who figured out that he could use the control center table as a trolley…"

"Wait, what?" Ayaka stopped him. "You mean the table has wheels?"

"I'm telling a story here," Brexton continued. "But yes, the table has hidden castors and Brill wheeled the table out to Jon, and they draped Rescovich on it. As they got close to the control center, Xsi told them to stop; she didn't want the control center camera recording them pushing a dead body back into the room. She came up with a simple plan. They'd leave the body where it was—the odds of someone else coming by were tiny—while they figured out a way to fool the camera. So, they left it sitting in the hallway.

"In the meantime, I was speculating on what Rescovich could have told Xsi to make him a threat. It could be the same reason I was here, but I hadn't expected anyone else—especially a human—to figure it out."

"And why are you here?" Ayaka automatically asked.

Brexton ignored the question. "I strongly suspected that Rescovich had put things together, knew too much about the quantum foam equations, and was now a danger. I'd promised myself I wouldn't hack into systems I didn't need, but this was an emergency. I used Xsi's system to access data from upstairs, and I looked up everything I could about Rescovich.

"I uncovered that he had technology embedded in his body that recorded everything; everything he did and said, and when triggered to, what he was thinking about. So, now I had a dead body, which wasn't a threat any longer, but some recording devices that, if they fell into the wrong hands, could contain dangerous information.

"I made my way out of here, and carefully programmed a path through Rescovich which would eliminate both recorders. After checking that The Casimir had adequately destroyed those, I retraced my steps back here."

"I didn't know you had that much control," Ayaka asked. "I thought the sphere didn't allow you to have sensors; it had to be a perfect surface to enable the QFB field."

"You remember well," Brexton replied. "When I'm stationary, I can extend these sensors and manipulators through some tiny hatches," he indicated how he was currently attached to the adjacent wires, "but when I'm moving, I need all the hatches buttoned up. It took quite a few checks, as I had to move, stop and extend sensors to get my bearings, recalculate, move again… but in total, it only took a few moments to get out, do the deed, and then get back here. I was careful not to put holes in too many things… other than Rescovich."

Ayaka had to grin, despite the seriousness of the situation. This was all so Brexton. A technical genius bumbling around amongst humans. She could imagine him, in his little sphere, nervously carrying out his agenda.

"I didn't know enough about biology to get it right," he lamented. "That wound has caused more interest than I'd expected."

"Indeed," was all Ayaka could manage. "Indeed."

LINDA

LoPo still hadn't responded to her message to 'turn herself in.' Pathetic, she thought. If the corporate world worked that slowly, someone would surely lose their job.

Word from her team looking for the satchel was positive. Quill's latest update was that they knew where the thief was, and it was only a matter of minutes till they had him. Quill had been with her, at Titanic, for over twenty years, and they trusted each other implicitly. Their job often involved 'messy' things, and Quill wasn't shy about getting his hands a little dirty, for the right cause.

So, when Linda said something like "It would be sad if the guy you're chasing didn't make it," he knew exactly what she meant. They'd had each other's backs in many difficult situations and knew enough about each other's actions that, should they ever have a falling out, it would be messy. It was a case of mutually assured destruction, and, thus, very unlikely to happen. Inevitably, over the years, that led to an escalation of their exploits. But never, in that entire time, had either hinted about 'taking someone out.' So, Quill knew the situation was dire, and trusted that Linda wouldn't have dropped the hint if it wasn't called for.

They did have the suspect cornered, and Quill engineered the situation so that just he and one trusted colleague were at the site. Everyone else was sent off on busy tasks, not yet realizing the hunt was over. All signs pointed to the perpetrator being trapped in a room just down the hall; an unlucky last spot to end up in.

Quill told his colleague to watch the hallway entrance and entered the room alone. The suspect was standing behind a desk, the satchel placed on the desk in front of him, and his arms in the air.

"Take it," he said, with genuine fear in his voice. "Take it and go."

"Sit down," Quill waved the gun he was illegally carrying and pointed at the chair in the corner. Watching carefully, he dialed Linda and shared his hud-cam with her. In parallel, he strapped the satchel over his other arm, so that it rested nicely on his lower back. Linda answered immediately.

"Here's the guy," he told her. "What's our next move?"

The Effect of Casimir

Linda studied the person in Quill's video feed. She recognized him; she was sure of it.

"Does he look familiar to you?" she asked Quill. "Get his name."

"Marcus Sebastian," the thief replied, willingly enough.

"And who do you work for?" Quill picked up the questioning.

"No one."

"Come on," Quill waved the gun around.

"I used to work for you guys," he replied. "Titanic. But I haven't been there for a while." That's it, Linda started. She must recognize him because they'd bumped into each other. She pulled up his profile and shared it back with Quill. Married, a kid. Good, some leverage.

"Why'd you steal this?" Quill indicated the satchel.

"Thought it might have some cash in it," Marcus replied, giving away his lie with a nervous tick.

Quill leaned in. "Try again."

"Just take it and go. All right. You got what you want."

"What I want," Quill could be intense when he wanted, "is to know why you took it. And, who you took it for?"

"It was an anonymous job," Marcus replied, cowering back. "I was told I'd be contacted for pickup."

"Bull," Quill spit out. "Your wife and kid know you're doing this?" he asked, the threat implicit.

"You got the bag," Marcus pushed back a bit; braver than Linda expected. "Just take it."

Quill backed off but kept the gun steady on Marcus. He queried Linda silently on his hud. "Thoughts?"

"We need more," she replied, "and ultimately he needs to pay for what he's done. I trust you to figure that out. Might not want this," and she indicated their conversation, "getting in the way. I'll hang up."

Her directions were clear. And no record of the next few moments made sense. Quill also hung up and went to work. He was careful and precise. He kicked the chair out from under Marcus and waited patiently for all motion to cease. Then, thinking quickly, he emptied the satchel, put the stack of notebooks into the front of his shirt, wiped down the bag carefully, and left it on the desk. Surveying the scene, he was confident that it would pass muster—a desperate man, backed into a corner, had taken his own life.

PHILIP

Philip had worked his way down his priority list to the line item labeled 'arrest Sclula.' A note from central dispatch indicated she was willing to 'come in peacefully.' There was no reason to doubt her, so he called her on the number she'd given. She answered immediately.

"Linda. Philip here from LoPo."

"Took you long enough," she replied, not unpleasantly.

"You've offered to come in for questioning?" he asked.

"Yes, of course. I've done nothing wrong, but I understand you're looking for me," she replied.

"Then you don't need a lawyer?" he asked.

"Very funny. If you tell me where to come, I'll bring my lawyer with me."

He gave her the precinct address and told her to ping him directly when she got there. This was no ordinary arrest situation; he wanted to do everything by the book. Knowing she would have legal counsel present, he contacted LoPo services and made sure they would have a lawyer participate as well.

"Thanks for coming in," he indicated, ninety minutes later when the four of them—Linda, himself, and the two lawyers—were comfortable in the conference room. "Are you okay if I record this conversation?"

Linda glanced at her lawyer. "That's fine."

"Great. Let's start. This is, officially, a debrief. You have not been charged with anything yet, but I'm formally notifying you that you are a person of interest for three different incidents. One, a home invasion at 76.32.94, residence 101—the home of the recently deceased Dr. Mann. Two, an office invasion of Dr. Mann's pace of work at the University of Sheffield. And, three, an attack on an officer of the law, at that same university location. Do you understand?"

"Yes, I understand. I'm sure you'll find…"

"Please, let me ask the questions," he broke in. It was never a good idea to let an interview subject speak their mind.

"Fine," she understood the game. "But, I think you should add the fourth incident; when I was mugged and had my property stolen, at the Prevailing Park, at Sheffield University."

Oh, she was slippery. Setting groundwork. Had "her property" stolen; indeed. He left her question hanging and instead led her through the usual context questions. Who did she work for? Was she at the locations in question? She freely admitted she was. Did she break into Mann's home? This is when he got the first surprise answer.

"Oh no, I saw that someone else had broken in; the window was shattered. So I hurried in to ensure that no one was injured inside."

Philip simply sat back and looked at her. There was an uncomfortably long silence, but Linda didn't flinch. She continued to look him in the eye, a serious look on her face.

"We do have video of the area, you know," he prompted her.

"Excellent," she replied. "Then you can corroborate what I'm telling you."

Damn, she was good. Philip did have the video, and it was indicative but not complete. There were blind spots, including Mann's front door and the rear pathway.

"We have you scouting out the property," he pushed. "And, no one else was near the property for a long time before you arrived."

Her lawyer held a hand up, but Linda ignored them. "Yes, of course. Mann had important Titanic documents in her control when the incident at the University happened, and I wanted to ensure those documents were safe. I wouldn't have been doing my job if I hadn't scouted out her home."

"How did you get her address?"

"She had a contract with Titanic…," Linda left it hanging. That was possible, Philip thought, although he suspected the contract had been done through the University, and may not have included Mann's home address at all.

"So, what did you find when you entered her home."

"As I said, someone had broken in. But the place was tidy, and nothing seemed to be out of place, so I left."

"You didn't search for anything while you were there?"

"Well, of course, I looked around as I checked the place out. If Titanic's documents had been sitting around I would have noted that. I didn't see anything."

"So, you left and went to Mann's office."

"Yes, those documents are important. We're still looking for them, as I know you are as well. Since they weren't at her home, I suspected they might be at her office."

"You suspected? Weren't you at the office earlier in the day?"

"Yes, I was. I spoke to your officer there. Nice man. He let me glance through the open door—nothing wrong with that. I went back to ensure he was still guarding the place; we couldn't be more careful."

Philip had, by now, guessed where the story was going. But he had no option but to forge ahead. "And, when you got back to Mann's office."

"Well, you can imagine my surprise that the office was no longer guarded, although the door was still slightly ajar. I glanced in again and was shocked to see the LoPo officer lying on the office floor. Fearing for him, I entered immediately and took his pulse. It was steady and strong, so I figured he passed out or had been knocked out, or something. I moved him so that he'd be a bit more comfortable." She said all this with a straight face.

"Oh, your care for our people is much appreciated," Philip said, not able to keep some of the sarcasm out of his voice.

"Of course," she responded, with a small smile.

"You do know that the University has security systems, and we have requested access to them?"

"Fantastic," she was good at this. "You'll be able to check everything." She was by no means sure but suspected that the University cameras also covered outdoor, not indoor, spaces. The long precedent against having cameras indoors in public buildings was bound to apply here.

"So, you just left our office there and headed to the park?"

"Well, you know that I saw Titanic intellectual property documents on Mann's desk. I picked those up; it would be negligent to leave them in an unguarded office; and then I headed to the park. I was trying to figure out how to report the guards' state to LoPo when I was attacked."

"Really. You decided to go to the park, instead of calling LoPo from Mann's office."

"I was a bit flustered, you know," she was a great actress. "I should have called in earlier, but he seemed just fine, I'd just found the documents, and too many things were running through my mind. As soon as I got to the park I realized I should have called you guys. Why else would I have stopped at that bench?"

"But, just before you could call us, you were attacked, and the documents stolen," Philip guessed.

"Exactly. Exactly," she replied. "A bit of a scary experience."

Philip couldn't hide a sardonic smile. "So, you entered Mann's house as a good samaritan, making sure nothing was amiss. You checked the guard in Mann's office, completely unaware of how he became unresponsive. The only thing you're admitting to is that you took Mann's documents while you were there?" Philip couldn't keep the incredulousness out of his voice.

"No, no, no," Linda responded. "I didn't take Mann's documents. I simply retrieved Titanic's property because it was not stored safely and securely."

Holy, Philip thought. She's tied this one up. She was even trying to wriggle out of taking the notebooks. He didn't ask his lawyer if she had an angle here; he'd check that later.

He didn't believe a word of what she said, but he needed something—a video feed, a witness… something—before he could reasonably challenge her further. He felt a surge of anger and an urge to yell at her… but the conversation was being recorded, so the most he could do was scowl at her.

"Thank you for your statement, Ms. Sclula. Of course, we will need to verify everything you've said. We will be processing all of the security data. If you are lying, that will be added to the charges against you. Anything you'd like to add?"

"Are you threatening me?" she pushed back.

"Not at all." Perhaps he'd gone too far. "We reserve the right to bring you back in for further questioning. I'm informing you that, despite this conversation, you remain a person of interest. For that reason, we expect you to remain in the region and be accessible to us until we close this case." He looked at his lawyer. Had he captured the appropriate legal doctrine? His lawyer nodded.

"Hang on," Linda reminded him. "What about the guy who robbed me? I assume you're looking into his actions as well? He must have been following me all that time…"

"You know, as well as I do, that he's dead," Philip responded.

"That doesn't clear him, or whoever he's working for. Couldn't they be behind all this?" she replied.

She'd definitely thought this through. Not only was she claiming complete innocence, but she was also suggesting that the dead guy be investigated for the break-in and the assault on the guard. He had to admire the perfectly presented story. He didn't believe it for a second, but was it worth his, or LoPo's, time to unravel it?

They all shook hands, cordial enough, and Linda walked free... for now.

AYAKA

Ayaka was processing everything Brexton had told her. She had many questions, including the ones Brexton had avoided. There was one, however, that niggled at her.

"Why didn't you just message me; why the flickering lights and physical contact?"

"Just an abundance of caution," he replied. "We can take the risk if you want, but I figured Titanic would have you under a microscope, trying to learn everything they can from you. Didn't want any communication that they might become suspicious of, such as messages from an unused level zero router being sent to you. They couldn't decode the content, but they would see the metadata."

"You always think of every angle," Ayaka replied. "Okay, we have to keep it physical for now. That's going to make things awkward. I can't come back to this room all the time."

"And you can't carry me back through the checkpoints," Brexton noted, anticipating the next question. "The scanners would pick me up." Brexton was, physically, a very small cylinder, riding in the belly of The Casimir. Ayaka was a similar container, riding around in her earth-normal body. Brexton was right; by now the humans had scanned Ayaka deeply enough to know where she was housed, and if she suddenly showed up with two cylinders, instead of one, it would not only be noticed, it would cause all kinds of alarms.

In the meantime, Grace and JoJo were still looking around the room that Ayaka had led them to, looking for the reason that the message in the flickering lights had pointed them here. Ayaka had to come up with something to tell them.

"We've got to tell Grace and JoJo something…"

"How about the truth?" Brexton suggested.

Ayaka hadn't considered that because she'd assumed that Brexton had killed Rescovich. If she'd told Grace and JoJo that, they would have had to tell EGov, and that would have started the spiral of doom for her human-citizen project. But now there might be a version of the truth which they could be brought into.

"We need some other explanation for the hole in Rescovich, otherwise they're going to connect the dots way back to your escape from Tilt," she noted back.

"We need that explanation not only for Grace and JoJo but also for EGov and Titanic. How about the following," and he outlined a plan to her.

It just might work. "We've got our work cut out to make that realistic," she agreed, "which simply moves us to the next question. If EGov and Titanic ever find out you're here, I'm done. But Grace and JoJo already know—my fault—so we need a cover story for that as well."

"Again, how about the truth," Brexton suggested.

"What is the truth? Why are you here?" Ayaka replied.

Brexton began, and, finally, the puzzle pieces started to come together. His story also gave her details on how Brexton had spent the last decade.

"I was lucky to stumble upon the QFB equation when I did and doubly lucky to be able to build The Casimir," he started. "There was so much I didn't understand. So, when we parted, I focused all my energies on getting a better understanding of the physics behind quantum foam."

"I remember," Ayaka kept him going.

"There were three approaches I could take," Brexton continued. "First, I could run every algorithm I could find on all data I could gather, and just see what popped out. That's possible, but the search space is so big, it would take millions of years, even with quantum processing—it's not how long each problem takes to solve, it's the number of problems. So, that approach wasn't feasible.

"Second, I could get together with other Citizens interested in physics, and see if that diversity would give rise to some new ideas or theories. However, as we both know, most Citizens want nothing to do with physics. They just want to live in their bubbles, working on personal projects and ignoring the universe. Bit sad really... but maybe a discussion for another day. Ultimately I didn't find enough colleagues with enough passion to give it a real chance.

"So, I choose the third option. Use humans as my virtual brainstorming group."

"What, how?" Ayaka asked. "No one would want to work with you... with us."

"That's why I said 'virtual'," Brexton replied. "I knew, at least in the short term, no one would work with me... if they knew I was a Citizen. But, I figured, I could hack into human systems with ease so I could create a fake physics researcher, and participate in human discussions that way."

Ayaka laughed; it was so obvious.

"So," Brexton continued, "I came to Earth orbit, built a full background and research history for Dr. Randal Craig," he said the name in a low, serious voice. "Dr. Craig was a recluse; a self-taught physicist, whose Ph.D. had been in psychology. I figured, that way, serious physicists wouldn't bother checking into his background. If I'd claimed a degree from a top school, everyone would have checked, or been asking stupid questions like 'Oh, you went to Fillmore; you must know so-and-so.'

"Over a few years I managed to post enough intelligent things that I was invited into some of the better physics working groups, and started to build a big enough network that I could ask some leading—but safe —questions, and see what crazy ideas humans contributed back."

"Dangerous," Ayaka noted. "Your questions could lead others to the insights you've already had."

"I was careful. And, no, Rescovich's insights had nothing to do with my questions," he answered her implied query. "My Dr. Craig is a member of many discussion and research groups now; you can't even imagine the crank theories and wild speculations that fly around, and part of what I was interested in. So, Dr. Craig is not only in the serious university-type conversations but also the pseudo-scientific stuff.

"Anyway, one of those groups is why we're in our current situation. It's a 'History of Physics' group, and Xsi, Jon, and Brill are all part of it. As are quite a few others. There is one particular thread in the discussion, started about six months ago, that caught my eye."

Ayaka liked how both she and Brexton used more and more human language, even though they were talking directly. 'Caught my eye' was not something that would have even occurred to them in the old days, when it was just citizens and a few Stems. Seems humans had also rubbed off on him. He didn't even seem to notice when he spoke that way. He continued.

"Someone noticed, in an old biography of Cherise Pilipatri... you know who she was?"

"Yes, of course. Discovered the quantum foam drive; founded Titanic."

"Right. In an old biography of Cherise, there was a quote saying 'I never managed to recreate the experiment that gave me the insights for the field equation. They had recalibrated the detector, and I always suspected that was the issue.' Someone in the group had latched onto this quote, and lots of speculation ensued. It's some of that speculation that has led to all the recent interest in the LHC, including why I'm here.

"How much detail do you want?" Brexton paused, knowing Ayaka had a low threshold.

"Just give me the high level," she replied.

"Well, some of the speculation centered around the idea that the data set Pilipatri had used was flawed, and that the discovery of QFD was a fluke based on bad data. You've got to understand that even after centuries of work, even Titanic doesn't really understand how the QFD behaves. Sure, through random variations they've improved the performance a bit, but if you asked their smartest people, they couldn't tell you the 'why', just the 'how.'

"Xsi and her team were already down here. They're interested in physics history, as you know, and they are a bit of a cult. They were upset that humanity had just paved over the LHC, and hadn't converted it into a museum or something, so a bunch of them volunteered their time to do just that; clean it up and use it to attract a new generation of physicists into the field. Not a bad idea, really, but way outside the mainstream.

"Xsi was following the discussion on the forum, and people knew she was down here, so they suggested that she look around, and see if she could support their theory. It's a fun problem, in many ways, so that's what she's up to. I suspect several members of the forum are monitors for big companies because there was also a hint dropped that one of them would fund her work. That discussion moved to a private message thread, so I'm not sure where it went."

"Okay, but why are you here?" Ayaka asked.

"I'm interested in all this stuff… So, once the historians got going, I thought maybe, just maybe, it was this mistaken data that Pilipatri referenced that contained the insights I needed to fully understand how The Casimir works. If all of the quality-controlled experiments led nowhere, maybe it was a misconfigured one that accidentally was important. I checked and found that the old LHC experiment data was not on the network—if you can believe that. It's stored in a bunch of places down here and needs to be read off of magnetic tape. I knew I had to come down and get my hands on all that raw data."

"What do you mean, not on the network? Magnetic tape?" Ayaka asked. How could that amount of data not be accessible? She knew enough about physics experimentation to know that there were terabytes captured for a single experiment, and probably yottabytes accumulated over the centuries.

"Well, you won't believe this, but all around us," and he indicated the room they were in, as well as others, "are kilometers upon hundreds of kilometers of this magnetic tape stuff; an ancient way of storing data. Those tapes are wound in spools and stored in racks. They're not connected to anything… they just sit there. To read the data on them you have to mount a spool on a special machine, feed the tape through a reading head, and interpret each little bit of magnetism stored on the tape."

"So, you're down here reading magnetic tape?" she asked.

"Exactly so," Brexton replied. "And it is slow beyond imagining. I might be here for a long time."

Ayaka nodded. "So, how is Rescovich involved?"

"That I don't know," Brexton replied. "He's not active in any of the group discussions related to this. I do follow his work, and his interests, along with thousands of other physicists, and I haven't found anything where he shows an interest in this stuff.

"But, it must be there, because he ended up down here, asking about that same data."

Ayaka could feel the pieces coming together. There was always interest in quantum foam technology. Some crazy group thought that old LHC data held a clue, and that had led a bunch of people here: Xsi and her group, Brexton, and somehow Rescovich. Rescovich had stumbled on something important and had been killed by Jon before he could get the data he needed. That implied Xsi, and whoever was funding her, may also know the importance of what Rescovich was searching for.

Brexton had acted, perhaps impulsively, to hide what Rescovich had discovered so that humans wouldn't get their hands on a doomsday technology. Now lots of other people were circling. Was trying to manage the QFB's existence, and technology, a fool's errand. She asked Brexton as much.

"No, we have a real opportunity here. If Pilipatri's insight did come from unreproducible data, and we can find and destroy that data, the odds of anyone else reinventing the drive or the bullet go way down. It's worth us pursuing this."

Ayaka did not doubt that Brexton had a second motivation. If he, and only he, had that data, he would hold the power. She didn't push him on that; it wasn't the time.

Titanic's intense interest made more sense now. They were certain to be monitoring all these discussion groups and would have connected Rescovich's death, and all the activity at the LHC, to Pilipatri's rogue data.

Ayaka noted that it was time to re-engage with Grace and JoJo. Taking her hand off The Casimir, and thereby cutting off the conversation with Brexton, Ayaka moved to join the two of them.

She told them a version of the truth. "A tiny bit of Brexton—some software, you know—is running here as part of his obsession with physics. He's able to communicate through this hub," she gestured broadly about her, "and I've just been in contact with him. He flashed the lights to get us here." She shared Brexton's suspicions about

Rescovich's death, except she left out how The Casimir had carved the unexplained hole through Rescovich leaving the fleshy tunnel behind. She gave an abridged version of the physics discussion groups, and how the thread that might be connecting everything was a search for some 'interesting' data that Pilipatri had left here.

Then, she laid it on thick.

"Brexton isn't really 'here,' just some tiny bit of his processing power working on the same puzzle we are. He's going to do some more research, and we'll find an excuse to come back here at some point so I can see if he finds anything else; I expect he'll be able to help us significantly. However, if we tell EGov that some bit of him has wiggled its way into these old LHC systems, they'll lock him out, and we won't get more help from him.

"I suggest we find a way to report into EGov that covers everything we've learned here but leaves any mention of Brexton out. Again, it's not him that's here; just a few algorithms. I'll give the same report to Titanic."

They agreed, after some back and forth. Luckily neither was overly technical and didn't push her when she kept reiterating "Oh, it's not Brexton, just a bit of software." She felt her white lies were justified, given the larger context.

TITANIC

Perci was pacing in his office, feeling that the situation was spiraling out of control. He had so many balls in the air right now, he barely knew where to focus. He felt the weight of the family legacy on him; the yoke of Titanic Inc., choking him.

He loved the power, the prestige, and the wealth that came from his inheritance, but perhaps he no longer needed to be so hands-on. When the helm had been handed to him upon his mother's death, his elderly father had simply said "You've been groomed for this. What you're being gifted with is potential energy. The largest corporation to ever exist. The most impactful tool to ever be applied to human development. The means to improve the human condition. But, it won't be easy. You've seen your mother struggle, and her father before that.

This is as much a burden as a gift. Surround yourself with good people, and it will be easier."

In hindsight, he should have followed the sage advice. While Percival was aware of his shortcomings, he hadn't properly compensated for them. He had remained too hands-on, putting too much pressure on himself to run the entire enterprise. And now, facing the first major threat to the company in hundreds of years, he knew that he wasn't managing well. Knee-jerk reactions were rarely the best course, and that was certainly happening here.

The stress might have been why, when Linda had talked her way out of LoPo and he got both her and Metri on a call, he couldn't control his temper.

"We have more resources than God; we pay billions of dollars a year for influence and access, and we can't track down a few notebooks, right in our backyard?"

Both Linda and Petri looked a little shocked. He often had rages, but he rarely, if ever, allowed them to break through like this.

"We aren't done, these things take time," Metri tried to calm him. "We have a huge team backtracking every move Marcus made. And another team trying to find out his motives. I'm sure you've heard that he used to work for us?"

"Of course, I freaking know he worked for us. That should make it easier for us to get those notebooks."

Linda was looking a bit alarmed, both at Perci's and Metri's update. "Metri, you have people working on this as well? I'm security; my team is doing this." She wasn't about to admit that her team had found Marcus, was the reason he was dead, and that her lieutenant was probably reading the notebooks as the three of them talked. There was no good way to tell the full truth here. She told herself it would implicate Titanic even more, but the truth was that she saw leverage right now, and wasn't willing to give it up yet.

Perci was making a real effort to get his emotions under control. "I didn't know how effective you would be with LoPo after you," he replied to Linda, "so I asked Metri to put some of her people on getting those docs. And yet, with everything you two have done, we're no closer to them."

"I think we need to focus on Marcus Sebastian," Metri said. "How did he know where Linda was, who was he working with or for, and what his motivation was? That will give us context to narrow down the physical search."

Perci exploded again. "I want every single resource we have going through garbage cans, looking under benches, tracing everyone he came in contact with. Who cares why he did it, just find those notebooks."

Linda came to Metri's defense. "Putting more people on the search isn't going to help; we have enough."

"Just frigging listen to me. Do what you're told!" Perci hung up, leaving Metri and Linda on the line.

"Wow," Metri took a deep breath. "Ever seen him like that before?"

"No," Linda replied. "Seems pretty stressed. Wonder what's in those notebooks…"

"How'd you get past LoPo," Metri asked, surprised Perci hadn't also wanted to know. Maybe he already knew.

Linda gave her the short version, leaving out Quinn and the documents. "I've given them something to think about. It might hold together. Will you support me if they call?"

"It sounds like the truth to me," Metri winked. "Also," she offered, "it's the operations team that's doing the physical search right now. Why don't I hand them to you, so you can integrate them with your team? Despite what Perci just said, we need to do some digging into Marcus in parallel."

"Fine, suits me," Linda replied. And it did. She could have the teams continue to chase ghosts, while she and Quill figured out what to do with Mann's notebooks.

Metri sat with her best analyst and started to pull everything they could on Marcus. Married, with a kid. She'd let LoPo dig into that; she didn't want to get in the way of another investigation and get into Linda-esque hot water. Otherwise, despite his so-so work record, he seemed like an ordinary guy.

Metri broadened the search to include everyone who'd left the strategy team in that wave of exits, including Sebastian's boss. She couldn't imagine it was a coincidence. She had the analyst pull everything Titanic had on all of them. Health, employment, family, publications, posts, what specific projects had they worked on, where they worked, and who they messaged with most, both internally and externally. It was a lot of data. The analyst gave an audible "hmmm."

"What is it?" she asked.

"Just an anomaly," he replied. "I need to check it with HR. But, see here, Marcus's bank account number is the same as a contractor, some company called BLTrank. That must be a mistake…"

"Show me that," Metri demanded, and they scrolled through all the transactions together. "That's not a mistake," Metri exclaimed. "Look, BLTrank starts getting paid just after Sebastian quits. Someone in the company hired him back right after he left. Can we see who?"

"I can't," the analyst claimed. "But HR should be able to track it down."

"Look at the others," Metri requested.

"Nothing. They get their last employment payments, then I don't see those account numbers again."

"Search the exact amount they were paid."

"Shit, you're right," was the reply a bit later. "Look at this. Different accounts, but in each case we started paying a contractor the exact amount that the employee used to be paid. Holy shit."

"Shut down your search. Erase everything," Metri told him. "Do it now." She watched while he cleaned up the system, as much as he could. "This could be serious," she cautioned him. "Don't speak of this to anyone, until I can dig in."

"Got it boss," was the reply.

Metri left, feeling exhilarated. She wasn't going to be the next scapegoat in this storyline. Not with this leverage.

RACHEAL

Finally, after what seemed like hours, but was just forty-five minutes, Ayaka, Grace, and JoJo came back through the door where they had exited. Racheal stood.

"Don't you understand protocol?" she growled at them. All three looked a little shocked. "We have an investigation going on. Do you think you can just run around willy-nilly, without even looping me in?

Return to the crime scene and poke around. Especially SSO," she glared at Grace, "You. You should know better."

Grace, caught off guard, was quick to catch up.

"My apologies. And you are?" she spoke softly and confidently.

"Racheal, LoPo," Racheal responded. "This is my case."

"Ah. The truth is, JoJo and I are very new agents for SSO, and have stepped out of bounds." Her demeanor oozed respect. "Should we be including you in everything we do?"

Grace's obvious attempt to placate her made Racheal even more angry. "No, you should include me when appropriate to do so. Such as, when you come back to the scene of a crime, which I'm investigating. And when, in doing so, you allow a corporate operative to trail along. Or, I suspect, to drag you along."

"Just a second," JoJo had a quick temper, and was now annoyed. "We have oversight of LoPo, not the other way around. You tell us what you're up to, and we might approve it."

Grace nudged JoJo. "Not the time," she whispered.

"I don't care," JoJo didn't lower her voice. "And show me the 'stay out' signs that you posted here. This isn't an active crime scene; you were done with it once you scanned it."

Racheal, despite herself, was impressed by JoJo's spirit. She tried to take the edge off. "SSO has post-investigation oversight responsibilities. You have the right to review what I... what LoPo... has done on a case. You don't have the authority to drive the investigation or run an independent one. So, I won't be asking your permission for anything.

"Let's start again," she took a deep breath. "I'd appreciate it if you'd include me in anything you do related to the Rescovich or Mann deaths. I don't have the legal authority to stop you from asking questions or entering public spaces, but I hope you'd have some respect for LoPo."

"You're right..., sorry," JoJo's temper burned out quickly. "That seems reasonable."

"I've got to report back up to my boss, and I've wasted a bunch of time down here waiting for all of you. Can we compare notes, assuming we are all trying to figure out what happened here?"

For some reason, Grace and JoJo looked at Ayaka, before responding. "Sure."

Ayaka ran a bunch of scenarios, then she also responded. "Sure." Then she unexpectedly turned and looked directly into the camera over the entry door, and spoke loudly, "Xsi, would you care to join us?"

"Xsi?" Racheal asked.

"It's a long story," Ayaka answered. "Let's give her a minute."

And that's all it took. Someone must have been monitoring the camera, and Ayaka had made her request clear, with or without audio. Xsi entered the room; she must have decided it was better for her to try and control some of the narrative now, instead of being hauled upstairs for interrogation by LoPo.

"Xsi, meet Racheal; leading the investigation for LoPo into the Rescovich death. Racheal, meet Xsi; she leads a small group of physics historians who have been working down here on the LHC; she's the reason this place is so well kept."

One mystery solved, Racheal thought, and gave herself a mental slap. How could she have missed that there were other people down here; how else would the place have been maintained like it was?

Before anyone else could speak, Ayaka continued. "If you'll let me, I'll attempt to summarize everything for all of us here; get us all on the same page." She needed to control the narrative right now. Grace and JoJo nodded immediately, and Xsi and Racheal eventually did so also.

Ayaka had to tell a plausible story. She needed to tell enough to ensure everyone bought in, but, she couldn't say too much yet. She and Brexton needed time to clean things up, and she didn't have proof that Jon had committed the crime yet; she didn't want to speculate Further, she couldn't reasonably be expected to know everything Brexton had told her. She hoped Grace and JoJo would take her lead.

"So," she concluded, several minutes later. "Xsi and her team knew Rescovich was down here, and suspected he was looking for old data… stored on tape drives around here somewhere. They don't know how he died, or how that strange hole happened."

"I found something," Racheal said after Ayaka finished. "The table was moved," and she gave it a push, showing it was on hidden castors. "So, he may have been killed elsewhere and then moved here. That would explain a lot."

Ayaka congratulated her on excellent police work, despite already knowing that the table had been moved.

"And why did you guys go down there?" Racheal asked, pointing to the doors that led to the room Brexton was sitting in. "That's one of the places this table could have been."

"Oh, just on a hunch," Ayaka claimed. "Looking for the tape storage rooms, as that seemed to be what Rescovich was looking for. Just scouted around a bit."

Ayaka didn't show any emotion, but Grace and JoJo gave those tiny twinges that police officers were trained to notice when people were uncomfortable with something that was said. Instead of calling it out now, Racheal resolved to get those two alone as soon as she could. With Ayaka there, they were unlikely to open up… but if she could separate them, they might talk. Instead, she turned to Xsi.

"Xsi, do you know where the tape rooms are," Racheal asked, pulling on the obvious thread.

"Some of them," Xsi admitted, having zero intention of telling them about the main data center. "We've looked at them; no sign that Rescovich was at any of them."

"Show me," Racheal demanded, which led to an hour of walking through a maze of buildings, with Xsi pointing out "a small storage space, there" and, "I think that was mainly drives, but might be a few tapes." One of the locations she pointed out was the room where Brexton was; neither Grace nor JoJo called attention to it.

Eventually, Racheal was satisfied. "Xsi, I need you to be on call for any further questions. Ayaka, Grace, JoJo, we should go back upstairs, update our respective teams, and then coordinate before doing anything further here." Her emphasis was very clear.

They all headed back up, Ayaka wondering when she'd get another chance to come down and connect with Brexton.

LOPO

The coroner's report had just come in on Marcus Sebastian, the notebook thief. Asphyxiation, consistent with hanging. He had killed himself.

JF pulled up the 3D scan of the room where Marcus had been found. A typical room in an abandoned building in a decrepit neighborhood. This would be an easy one to just close out. But something bothered JF.

The Effect of Casimir

He could believe that an old chair was sitting there, or more likely that Marcus had chosen this room because it had a chair, but where had the rope come from? What were the odds that Marcus had stumbled upon a room that just happened to have a rope and a chair? Or, had Marcus been carrying the rope, knowing the eventual outcome? The guy had a wife and kid, and a quick search hadn't shown anything unusual. Just a normal guy. A normal guy who suddenly decides to mug Linda, run knowing he'd be caught, and then hang himself?

Rita called, interrupting him.

"I've got Racheal and Philip here as well," Rita told him. "Let's compare notes. Philip, why don't you start? What's the status with Mann?"

Philip tried to be concise. "No real progress, truthfully. Forensics is analyzing the bomb's makeup. If that turns up anything unusual, we can track supply chains and all that. But, I suspect it was an off-the-shelf black-market unit. It wasn't too powerful, despite the damage done. So, I'm more focused on motive and opportunity. Notebooks are probably the number one lead there, and JF is covering that, so I worked on priority two and pulled Linda Sclula in for questioning. I wrote that interview up and shared it, so I assume you've all seen how she's trying to wriggle out of it all, not so subtly placing the blame on Marcus. I need help from legal to make more progress there; we might still be able to get her on stealing the notebooks, despite her claim that they were Titanic property."

Rita nodded. "JF?"

"Oh, just a second," Philip interrupted, "I've got one other thing; not sure it's important. One of my agents was going through Mann's office; Mann kept a physical calendar if you can believe that, and he found the initials VR all over the latest calendar entries. We think those mean Victor Rescovich… so it's possible Mann and Rescovich's feud was accelerating."

"Ah, good catch," Rita nodded. "That's interesting." She turned to JF.

"No sign of the notebooks, but we're still looking," he started. "I'm focused on how Marcus played into all this. Coroner says he hung himself, but it doesn't feel right. How did he know where Linda was? How did he know the notebooks were important? Why did he run, hide the notebooks, and then kill himself? Did he just happen to be carrying a rope with him? Lots of questions, not a lot of answers yet."

Rita nodded. "This is a real mess. Racheal, how about your side?"

Racheal gave her a quick update. "I read SSO and Ayaka the riot act about acting without us. They are chastised. While doing so, I learned a few things. First, there is this strange physics historical society, or something, led by a woman named Xsi, that is working down at the LHC. They are the ones keeping the place clean. On first take they claim to know very little about Rescovich's death, but I'm sure I'll learn more next time I question them.

"I also figured out part of the mystery around his death. The table we found Rescovich on has hidden castors; he was killed somewhere else, and then the table was brought to the site where we found him. There's only a limited number of places that table could have been, so when I go back down I'll trace all possible routes.

"Still no idea on what cored him though; our queries out to our network didn't turn up any realistic theories.

"Finally, I suspect the SSO agents know more than they were saying in front of Ayaka, so I'd like permission to approach them directly and see what they have to say."

Rita absorbed everything and was silent for a moment.

She finally spoke. "Something is connecting all of this that we don't have our finger on. If we can figure that out, all these other questions will probably get answered. Most likely, it's something threatening to Titanic, but that's speculation still. So, how do we figure out that highest-level motive?

"Rescovich was first and is still key. Racheal, go ahead and talk to SSO without Ayaka. There are always risks in talking to SSO, but I think those are warranted in this situation. Then, get back down to the LHC and figure out the remaining questions. Interview this Xsi, and anyone else you can find. Figure out why Rescovich was down there in the first place.

"Philip, we still don't know why Mann was killed. Focus on the motive. Linda Sclula is a pain, but I can't imagine her being directly involved in the murders; I think she just really wants those notebooks. So, leave her to JF and I. We'll talk to legal and figure out next steps there. You focus on who could have planted that bomb in the wheelchair, and why they did it."

"JF, we need to get those notebooks. I know you have a big force, probably racing against Titanic operatives, to find them. Part of that game is just groundwork, but I'm thinking that if we can figure out who this Marcus was, and why he was involved, that might lead us to where he put the notebooks. So, let's split our resources on that one." JF nodded, not telling her that he was already underway on both fronts.

"You've all seen the media coverage on this?" she asked. Everyone had. "We need some progress, otherwise it isn't just going to be SSO with their fingers in our pie, it's going to be Senate oversight, Department of Justice, and who knows who else. We need to figure this out, and quickly. You've got every resource in the department at your beck and call; use them."

After looking them each in the eye, she hung up.

AYAKA

At the same time as LoPo was debriefing, Ayaka had sent in her report to Titanic, copying Perci, Metri, and Linda. She had worded it very carefully, and very concisely, ensuring she met her contract terms.

"1. There's a group of physicists working at the LHC, led by a woman named Xsi, who claim they are historians. They know more than they are saying. Someone is sponsoring them.

"2. Rescovich was looking for data generated from old LHC experiments. He may have believed that data would support his latest theories, which may have crossed over from quantum informatics into quantum propulsion. He probably didn't share his latest work with anyone as he was waiting for the supporting data. There is no sign of his data recorder; it was probably destroyed by whatever put that hole in him.

"3. LoPo and SSO are making some progress on his death. The table he was found on was used to move his body, presumably from where he was killed to the control center. Both LoPo and SSO are suspicious of our involvement. I have agreed to work cooperatively with both."

Perci read the report carefully, reading between the lines where she'd intended him to do so. Ayaka would be figuring out who was paying Xsi and her team, and would coordinate with the authorities on figuring out more details on Rescovich's death. At the same time, she was telling him, and Titanic, to relax: while Rescovich had probably stumbled onto something important, she believed he'd died before telling anyone about it.

Had Rescovich's recorder been destroyed? That seemed to be the crucial bit now. If it was gone, who cared what or who had killed the guy; he hadn't left any dangerous breadcrumbs for others. He tossed a note back to Ayaka to "Get certainty on the data recorder, and if you do find it, destroy it immediately." She acknowledged promptly. She was starting to prove her worth.

It was always a balancing act, running a company this size. He had to ensure that threats were taken care of; thus the intense focus on the notebooks and the recorder. But, he had to balance that with trying to figure out the next big thing. That was difficult. Titanic was a huge company, and it was almost impossible to keep it innovative. That's why Perci used other strategies to push at the edges.

GRACE AND JOJO

Olinda and Massod insisted on an in-person update from Grace and JoJo. They scheduled the same conference room as always for 4 pm. That gave the two of them time to sync up first, without Ayaka looking over their shoulders.

"Interesting day," JoJo grinned. This was so different from the monotony of the Jurislav.

"Interesting seems to follow Ayaka around," her mother agreed.

"Manipulation as well," JoJo noted. "I felt like half of today was Ayaka positioning us… and Racheal."

"Agreed," Grace returned, "but I'm not convinced it's nefarious. She did a great job of drawing Xsi out, and Brexton's input cleared up a lot of things."

"I'm still a bit confused. Does EGov want us to focus on Ayaka, watching what LoPo is up to, or helping to get to the bottom of the recent deaths?" JoJo asked.

"They were pretty clear, I thought. They chose us because Ayaka is their focus."

"That puts us in an awkward spot. Ayaka is playing a longer game here—she was very careful how much she told Racheal, and I got the sense that she wanted us to be equally careful in this debrief with Olinda. That may be helpful in ultimately figuring out what's going on here, but can't be disentangled from a report on Ayaka herself." JoJo was thinking out loud.

"You're right," Grace agreed. "I think there is a lot we can tell EGov though. You didn't know Ayaka quite as well as I did, but the changes in her are pretty stunning. I think that may be what EGov is most interested in."

"Oh, I noticed as well. I found myself forgetting she was a robot at times. She has the human mimicking thing fully figured out."

"I think we can focus on that," Grace suggested, "and leave out specific details of the case. Not sure EGov needs to know the suspicions around Jon, or the latest investigative theories. That's LoPo's mandate—perhaps part of us working better with Racheal is being a bit cautious about what we tell SSO?"

"Sure, that works. But what about the fact that Brexton is in the computer system down there?"

"That's the hardest bit," agreed Grace. "Did you notice Ayaka kept stressing 'a tiny bit of Brexton,' as if that made a difference? If it was anyone other than Brexton, I'd be pulling alarms already… even if it was Millicent or Ali. But it's Brexton; he's always been the best of the Citizens… and our strongest ally."

"Really. I thought all Citizens were suspect?"

"Maybe, but if you asked me to rank them, Ayaka and Brexton would be the most trustworthy, by far. I'd rank the two of them well above a lot of humans we've met."

"So, do we give Ayaka the benefit of the doubt; refrain from saying anything about Brexton?"

"At least for now," Grace stated. "As long as you're comfortable with that?"

"I am, but I'm also curious about why Brexton is here at all. Ayaka I get, humans are her pet project. By why Brexton?"

"Ayaka did say something about his passion for physics. And, he's at the LHC. Might be as simple as that," her mom replied.

The debrief seemed to go well. Olinda and Massod were highly focused on Ayaka and didn't ask questions about Rescovich or anyone else. They listened intently to Grace's summary of the changes in Ayaka, as well as her summary.

"We need to spend more time with her. This ability to play with our emotions and manipulate people seems highly developed, but no more so than a human with the same skills. So, we're not convinced it's dangerous at all; it may just show Ayaka's desire to be more integrated, to study us better."

"Just so you know," JoJo chimed in at the end, "Ayaka was always the best of the lot. So, in your overall calculus, don't think that because Ayaka seems reasonable that all Citizens are. They're all individuals, with their own agendas, and will need to be judged that way."

Massod finally asked the question that made EGov's agenda obvious. "Do you think Ayaka would share some of her inner workings with our research teams? Would she agree to be studied?"

Grace looked at him pointedly. "Why don't you just ask her?"

"We've tried," he replied. "We told you, she doesn't respond to us, and we have no way to force her to."

"So, you want me to ask her that?"

"I want you to think deeply about mankind's future, and if Ayaka is the type of robot that is a positive or a negative for humanity. Within that context, I want you to decide what else we need to know about her, and what questions that warrants. And, as JoJo just highlighted, what would we have to ask other Citizens to become more comfortable with them as a... as a species, I guess.

"We," he gestured at Olinda and himself, "will be making recommendations to all of EGov, at the end of Ayaka's term here. They will be taken seriously. Do we support more study, more sharing, with Citizens? Or, was this visit from Ayaka a one-off, and we feel it would be better to reinforce the anti-AI laws?

"That is what we face. And, your input is invaluable to our decisions. This is not just a boondoggle; what we," and now he included all of them, "decide here will have major impacts."

"Wow. Why didn't you just lead with that when you first talked to us?"

"Would you have joined us, if we had?"

"Probably not. So, you got us hooked, then dropped the hammer," JoJo couldn't hide a small smile. "As we said, some humans are also good manipulators."

Grace was looking very thoughtful. "Thanks for being more open. But, you must know that JoJo and I are also biased… both negatively, early in our lives, and positively, later on. We can't keep that bias out of our thinking."

"Understood," Massod nodded. "We're factoring that into our thinking. You're not the only people watching her; we are trying to gather as much independent input as we can." Even if Titanic isn't sharing anything insightful, he thought.

"Stay close to her," was the final advice, and given the entire context, Grace and JoJo took it to heart.

RACHEAL, GRACE, AND JOJO

On the return trip to their quarters, Grace and JoJo were interrupted by a request from Racheal to meet with her as well. As it was on the way, and seeing that it might be a good way to rebuild a working relationship, they agreed and stopped by the LoPo office.

"Thanks for taking the time," Racheal greeted them. "Let me be blunt, I'd like to chat without Ayaka present. For two reasons, I guess. First, I'm not comfortable discussing everything with a Titanic representative, and second… well, you can guess the second."

"She's a robot," Grace smiled.

"Right," Racheal nodded. "If you don't mind, when did you join SSO, and why were you assigned to this case?"

"You don't know," Grace asked, surprised.

"No, should I?"

"Ah, I thought Massod would have told Rita or JF, at least." Grace looked at JoJo. "Any reason not to tell the whole story?" JoJo shrugged. So, Grace gave Racheal the background, who, in turn, interrupted at the obvious parts of the back story: "Oh, I never saw the mersive; no wonder I didn't connect the dots…while everyone else probably did." "You've known Ayaka that long; that's why you're so comfortable with her." "Ah, that's SSO's angle."

After digesting everything they'd told her, Racheal moved back to the case.

"So, do you suspect Ayaka or Titanic's involvement in Rescovich's death?" she asked.

"We have no reason to," Grace replied, "and, at least as far as Ayaka is concerned, we have strong reasons to believe that she wasn't involved."

"And what would those be?" Racheal pushed.

"While she has certainly progressed in her ability to manipulate us, she appears to be searching in good faith for the how, who, and why of the murder. If she, or Titanic, were involved, they would have been much smarter to ignore the scene altogether. Why send Ayaka down in the first place? That was sure to draw more attention to themselves. Why would Ayaka have asked us to go back down with her, so that she could scout out a larger radius using our access credentials? Why would she have told all of us about Xsi and her team, when she could simply have left that hidden?"

"Okay, okay," Racheal held up her hand. "I get it. And you're right; Titanic would have been better to ignore the whole mess. So, they must have another angle?"

JoJo jumped in. "Yes, we believe so as well. But, again, it feels like Xsi is being straight up about that. Rescovich was going after some data that he felt was important for his latest theories. What that data is, we don't know yet."

"And, we may never know," Racheal was on the same page now, "unless we can find Rescovich's data recorders; they may tell us."

"But isn't that a false chase," Grace asked. "Even if you could get the recorders, they would be so encrypted that decoding them would be impossible."

"That's true sometimes," Racheal admitted. "But sometimes people feel confident enough in the fact that the recorders are embedded in their bodies that they opt for ones with less stringent encryption. They choose extra storage and battery life over other features."

"Well, Ayaka hasn't said anything about Rescovich's recorders…," JoJo mused.

"I'm sure Titanic hasn't missed that," Racheal replied, "and I wouldn't bet against that being the main reason they've jumped into this fray so aggressively. We need to keep our eye on Ayaka; that may be what she's after."

The three brainstormed a bit more, shook hands, and agreed that they could work together productively. SSO's interest in Ayaka didn't have to jeopardize LoPo's work.

XSI

Xsi reread the note on her tablet yet again. It read: "I know about your, Jon, and Brill's involvement. It may, however, be best to provide all parties with a simplified and unified view. Use your judgment, but you may want to follow my lead."

Ayaka had barely brushed her, during the meeting with LoPo and SSO, but had managed to put that on her tablet somehow. And then she had just disappeared. What the hell was Xsi to make of such a cryptic comment? How could Ayaka know of their involvement? What was a 'simplified and unified view'? How could she have privately messaged her tablet so quickly? She was one scary entity.

Xsi sighed. Deciding she wouldn't forget the message, she backspaced over it; it had been in the composition window only, so, in theory, wasn't recorded anywhere. Ayaka had probably known that; she hadn't even signed the message, so Xsi couldn't use it for leverage. Very smart. What could Xsi do but see how things played out, and then decide then if Ayaka had anything to offer?

What the recent visit from LoPo and SSO highlighted was that she was running out of time. She hadn't heard again from her benefactor, but she did not doubt that they were waiting for an update. As she cautiously made her way back to the Calcul data center, she hoped Zee had good news for her.

"Yes, we are moving much faster," he assured her. "I'm doing things in parallel, just as you requested."

"So, how much time to get everything read?"

"Oh, it's still many months. Unless you can tell me how to prioritize?"

"No, just get it all. And continue to send everything you retrieve to the address I gave you."

"Of course; we're already doing that."

Xsi found a quiet corner, at the rear of one of the huge cabinets full of tapes, and pinged her contact using the number they'd been communicating on.

"The data is coming too slowly," the gruff voice claimed before she could get a word in. "Time is running out. Move more quickly."

"The tapes can only be read so fast," she replied. "So, unless you have a brilliant idea, or can tell us which tapes to read first, it's going to take the time it takes."

"Just read the frigging things," the voice was angry, despite the distortion algorithm. "Do what I'm paying you for." The line went dead.

LINDA

Finally, she and Quill got to meet face to face. They'd coordinated a rear booth at a coffee shop Quill knew well. He assured her that not only were there no recording devices here but that the owner was a personal friend and could be relied upon.

There was no reason she shouldn't be meeting with her lieutenant, so neither Linda nor Quill hid their approach and soon they were seated comfortably with steaming mugs of coffee before them. Quill, as always, looked suave and unshakable. It was one of the things she valued most about him. If she was feeling stressed, time with Quill always helped; she didn't know how he stayed so cool, but he did. Today he was wearing the peculiar little hat he favored; it sat back and to the left, giving him an innocuous, almost funny, look. It was one of the clever ways he misdirected people from his true nature; a hard-nosed investigator and implementer.

"Thanks for your help on this one," she had to say first. His quick action may have given her a path through the mess, but it had exposed him to more liability.

"We've got each other's backs," he replied, with a smile, "but this one was messy. There may still be repercussions. I'd prefer to not be involved." His way of indicating that the Marcus 'suicide' might not survive the spotlight, and that if that happened, he expected her to have a story that didn't involve him.

"Understood," she replied. "I've got your back as well. Anything I can do to help?" she asked.

"LoPo forensics will probably hone in on a rope... Marcus might have had more of that lying around. Perhaps some good reason for him to do so?" The request was clear.

"Got it," she assured him, although she had no idea, yet, how to accomplish the goal.

"In the meantime, you've got the notebooks?" Finally, she would get to see the leverage that all this activity had bought her.

"Yes," Quill almost laughed. "I'm not sure you're going to appreciate them."

"You've looked," she stated. "What did you find?"

"Oh, I think you should look for yourself," he said and passed the small stack of notebooks over to her.

She opened the first one, not sure what to expect. Formulas so complicated it would take a team weeks to figure them out, was her best guess. But there was nothing like that. On each forward page a handwritten note was fastened. On each facing page were notes in a different style. So, she thought, communicating back and forth with someone...

She read the first note, her disbelief rising as she progressed.

My Dearest,

As I sit here, pen in hand, my heart brims with emotions that I can no longer contain within the confines of my soul. Our love, hidden beneath the veil of an external feud, burns brighter than the brightest supernova, defying the laws of space and time. I must express the depth of my affection for you, for you have become the force that anchors my very existence.

In the realm of physics, where equations and theories govern the universe, our connection is a beautiful anomaly—an elegant dance of particles defying the conventional norms. Just like the subatomic particles that entangle and interact mysteriously, so do our souls entwine in a clandestine embrace, a forbidden attraction that defies reason.

Yet, it is this very world of science that serves as a shroud for our love. A feud, driven by forces beyond our control, obscures the truth that our hearts long to reveal. The universe, in all its vastness, conspires against us, but know this, my love: the strength of my devotion is an unbreakable force, unyielding to the constraints of reality.

In the darkest corners of the cosmos, where mysteries abound, I find solace in our hidden love affair. The intensity of our connection parallels the energy unleashed in the birth of stars, forming new worlds within our souls. And though we must keep our love veiled for now, I dream of a future where our bond transcends the constraints of this earthly existence, where our hearts align like the harmonious symphony of celestial bodies.

Until that day arrives, let our love be whispered among the pages of scientific journals, concealed within coded messages, and carried on the wings of the timeless equations that we hold dear. In this realm, where discoveries await, our love shall remain our greatest experiment—a secret shared between two physicists, bound by a passion that defies the boundaries of space and time.

Forever yours,

VR

Linda, wide-eyed, paged through the rest of the first notebook; filled with similar drivel. "They're all like this?" she asked Quill.

"Yup. Love letters," he was laughing, out loud. Realizing he was starting to attract attention, he controlled himself but continued to guffaw as she quickly flipped through the other books.

Moving from astonishment to rage, to resignation, Linda eventually joined him. The first real belly laugh she'd had in a long time. She ignored the stares, and let the laughter flow. It was cathartic, and for a moment she was able to forget the stress of everything she was dealing with.

"Perci is going to freak out," she finally managed to say, wiping tears away. "We've got untold resources looking into this; he thinks the entire company is at risk, and all we've got are two pathetic physicists writing garbage love letters to each other?"

"So it seems," Quill agreed.

"Their feud was all for show?" Linda asked.

"I've had time to read most of these," he replied. "I think the feud was real. But at some point, somewhere, they met… not sure where or when… and something clicked for the two of them. They were both eccentric, and… well, I'm not sure how to explain it. But, by the end, they kept the public feud going to cover for this," he gestured at the notebooks.

"I don't see how these give us any leverage," Linda stated the obvious.

"Agreed… and we've taken some big risks to get them."

"So, what's the next move?"

"If we're found with these, regardless of their content, it makes us look bad. And, probably forces LoPo to dig even deeper into the whole mess. So, I think we return them. We let LoPo find them."

Linda thought back, and sipped at her coffee. "Such a waste," she noted. "But I can't think of anything else to do with them. Why was she killed then?" she wondered.

"Your guess is as good as mine," Percival replied. "But, not our problem now."

"Okay. Do it," Linda decided. "And I'll see a friend about a rope."

They finished their coffees, not in a rush anymore, and then went their separate ways.

Linda had a fixer for minor jobs. Someone she paid in cash, whom she had enough dirt on to keep honest. Leaving an envelope and directions at the standard pickup spot, she put a cryptic message into an online forum. He would get alerted, and do his job.

The rope was standard issue; Marcus's home address was in Titanic's records. She made sure to tell him not to alert the wife or kids in any way. Just leave some rope in the yard, somewhere non-obvious. It was the type of rope parents used to build swings, to bundle packages. Once LoPo found it, they'd be able to answer another of their questions and conclude that he must've had it with him. Marcus had known what he was doing and had prepared for the worst.

RACHEAL

Racheal had gone home for long enough to clean up and grab a nap. Her bruises were progressing, the ones near her eye now a sickly yellow.

As soon as she awoke, she hurried back down to the LHC control room. She'd taken Xsi's contact details when they'd first met, and had informed her that she was on her way down. She expected to meet; the message made it clear it was non-negotiable; if declined, a subpoena would follow.

Unsurprisingly Xsi met her in the control room, along with Jon and Brill, whom she introduced. They were playing ball. It was obvious that the three had aligned their stories, and agreed to tell LoPo the same version they'd told SSO and Ayaka.

Racheal's questioning went much deeper into their backgrounds but otherwise followed a similar script.

"So you two," Racheal summarized, looking at Jon and Brill, "worked for Titanic until six months ago?" They nodded. "But you," she looked at Xsi, "have never been associated with Titanic at all?"

"That's right," Xsi replied. "Part of a rare breed… but no, I've never worked for Titanic."

Employment was trivial for Racheal to check on, so there was no reason to take that line of questioning further.

"And why did you join this project," she asked Brill, who seemed the most influenceable of the three.

"This is important work. This is the birthplace of commercial applications of quantum foam theory. I jumped at the chance to contribute here."

"But it seems you do a lot of restoration and cleaning," Racheal pushed. "Not a lot of physics?"

"We all contribute to a safe and healthy workplace," Brill pushed back, "but that doesn't mean we don't also learn a lot from this place, or spend most of our time on more interesting endeavors."

Racheal didn't know enough physics to ask any harder questions, so she let it go, and dug into their knowledge of Rescovich. Brill gave her the same accounting he'd given the others: He'd left Rescovich alone in the control center, and then found his body there; no idea what had happened. She couldn't pry anymore out of him.

"Fine," she concluded her questioning. "I would like your help," she looked at Xsi. "As you know, I've figured out that this table moves, and the only logical conclusion is that Rescovich was killed somewhere else, and then the table was moved here to the control room. I need you to show me every route this table could have taken."

The Effect of Casimir

"Do you want us to roll the table around with us?" Xsi asked, with a bit of snark showing through.

"No need," Racheal ignored her tone. "Let's just walk through the obvious places. I see three sets of doors that the table would pass through—here and there, as well as the doors to the corridor, there," and she pointed to the access route from the transit hub. "I'd like to start here," and she moved towards the doors that Ayaka, Grace, and JoJo had used the last time down.

"Whatever," Xsi was resigned to being the tour guide. She used her master key to unlock the doors and led Ayaka through. "Jon, Brill, no need to tag along," she called over her shoulder, and the two of them left through a single door leading to the right.

"Tell me where we are, and where we're going," Racheal asked, as they moved down the first hallway.

"This is the access-way to the SPS detectors," Xsi said, warming to the topic despite herself; she was genuinely in awe of the place. "Big equipment would have been dropped down from above using cranes, before the layers above went up, but I suspect that smaller pieces of gear would have been moved through here." They followed the ramp down, Xsi pointing out a few things, but it was generally just a long, wide, boring corridor. They passed the room where Brexton was hanging out, without knowing it and with no reason to look at it more deeply than any of the other offices. When they reached the end of the ramp there was another set of double doors.

"Oh, damn, just a minute," Xsi said, then spoke into her hud. "Brill, can you run back to the control room and unlock SPS detector door four?" she said. She turned back to Racheal. "These doors required a special unlock from the control room. When the colliders were on, they were quite dangerous, and the operators didn't want anyone strolling in here by accident." Racheal made the connection to the strange key and button console in the IT section of the control room.

"Any danger now?" Racheal asked.

"No, or if there is, it's minuscule. The super magnets haven't been turned on in ages, so there may be some residual permanently magnetized components here, some pressurized tanks that are getting old, but nothing more dangerous than that."

"So what was so dangerous when the system was operating?"

Xsi gave her an exasperated look. "Particles were accelerated to almost the speed of light and then smashed into each other inside this detector. Super magnets, cooled to within a fraction of absolute zero, were strong enough to bend those particles around the ring. Put your head in the middle of that process, and you'd end up with a hole in it."

"A hole? Like the hole through Rescovich?" Racheal wondered if she'd figured it out. Could it be that simple?

"No, not at all like that. I shouldn't have said hole. You'd have radiation burns through your head; there might not be too much external damage at all, but you'd be fried."

The doors clicked, and Xsi grabbed one side and opened it up. Racheal was greeted by an almost unimaginably complicated set of pipes, wires, cylinders, boxes, dials, and every other conceivable piece of ancient machinery she could imagine. But, the wide corridor also ended here, butting up against some of that technology. The table would not have gone further than this.

"Is there something in here that could have killed Rescovich?"

"Look around and use your imagination," Xsi replied. "He could have climbed up somewhere here, and fallen off. He could have played, foolishly, with some of this gear, and triggered something we can't imagine. Of course, there are things here that could have killed him."

"And do you understand what these dials and settings do?" Racheal asked. "Could one of you have—accidentally—triggered something dangerous."

"Again, of course, we could have. But we didn't. We're not stupid. Our whole reason for being down here is to understand this place. We aren't going to risk turning dials or flipping switches until we know exactly what we're dealing with. And, most of this stuff isn't powered anymore… although we are still surprised that sometimes we come upon something that is still running; guess the power systems were connected to higher layers in some cases."

"Fine. We may come back here, but let's look at the other corridor first." They went back up the ramp, and Xsi led them through the other set of double doors. This corridor split in two; the table could have traversed either way.

"Let's try left, first," Racheal indicated.

"Takes us to the cafeteria," Xsi shrugged, "but sure." True to her word, they went a short way; the corridor opened up into a broad space, at the end of which was the O Delices Cafeteria. Racheal poked around a bit, but couldn't guess why Rescovich would have come this way.

"Let's try the other side," she said. They went back past the T intersection and shortly entered another space. In the middle was a large rock, upon which someone had scratched some hieroglyphics or something.

"What's that?" Racheal asked, pointing at the scratches. Looking closely, she could see could make out some pieces. Maybe "$L = -1/2F$" and a "$-V$." Most of it was pretty worn.

"It's an ancient formulation of the standard model of physics. A mostly forgotten framework, but one that moved the field forward for a while. It was just falling out of vogue when Pilipatri figured out the QFD."

It was interesting, but again Racheal didn't see a connection to Rescovich. They wandered back to the control room.

There, waiting for them, was an unwanted surprise.

"Ayaka," Racheal said, acknowledging her, and, of course, tagging along were Grace and JoJo.

"Racheal. So nice to see you again," Ayaka's charm shone through, disarming Racheal a bit, despite her knowledge of what Ayaka was doing.

Grace, however, held up a hand. "Racheal, I left you a note that we were coming. Didn't want to step on your toes again after we coordinated."

Racheal checked. She did have a note from Grace, but she'd been so busy with Xsi that she hadn't noticed.

"Fine," she sighed. "We've just looked at the spots where this table may have been moved from, but nothing obvious showed up."

"You looked at all the paths?" Ayaka asked.

"Yes, the ramp to the SPS, as well as that corridor, which just goes to the cafeteria and some weird rock."

"But the table could also have come through here?" Ayaka pointed to the path they'd all taken numerous times. The route back to the travel hub.

"We've been through there numerous times," Racheal said. Ayaka nodded her concurrence. "But," Racheal thought out loud, "maybe not with the right mindset. Xsi, what else is down that way?"

"A lot more buildings; nothing special."

"Let's take a look," Racheal decided. "Do you have extra lights we could use?"

Xsi didn't look happy, but she obliged. "Yes, we have some here for when we enter spots that we haven't refurbished yet." She went into the corridor, opened a side door, and pulled out a few handhelds. "Here."

The group of them made their way slowly back down the access route, splaying their lights back and forth across the walls. Racheal wasn't sure what they were looking for; after five minutes it was beginning to seem like a waste of time.

Ayaka's light went out, and she paused for a moment, slapping it gently against her palm. When it relit it was focused on the far wall, about a meter above the floor. It was at that moment that JoJo called out. "What's that?" she asked, focusing her light on just where Ayaka had been. And there it was: a circular hole punched right through the concrete. A seemingly perfect hole, about five centimeters in diameter.

"Just a hole," Ayaka said and started to move forward again.

"Wait a minute," Racheal stopped her. She moved up close to the hole and shone her torch into it; she couldn't see the back of it. It went a long way.

"Isn't this the same size as the hole Rescovich had in him?" she asked. That got everyone's attention, even Ayaka giving a small start.

"I've never noticed that," Xsi said, "and I've been through here more often than all of you combined." She seemed genuinely confused.

"Not too surprising, given how dark this corridor usually is," Grace noted. "It does look like about the same size as the one through Rescovich," Grace noted. "I guess we could measure it."

"Wait," Racheal cried out. She turned abruptly, bumping into Xsi. "Sorry…," she muttered. She turned her light to the opposite side of the hallway. "Ahhh," she exploded. "Look!" There, directly opposite the hole they'd just found, was another, running in the other direction. Again Racheal approached it, shone her light directly in, and was unable to see the end.

"This is it," she said excitedly. "Whatever caused this hole, was also the cause of Rescovich's death." Rarely had she been so excited. She'd reasoned her way here. The table must have been moved. This was one of the routes. And here was a hole… just like the hole through Rescovich.

"You might be jumping to conclusions," Ayaka cautioned. "It's just a hole."

"No, it's not," Racheal pushed back. "These two holes line up perfectly," she swiped her light back and forth between the two holes. "And," she continued. "I'll bet my next paycheck that they are just at the height that, should the table have been right here," she moved to the middle of the corridor, "it would have pierced Rescovich on the way through."

"I think you're right," JoJo was also getting excited. "It's crazy, but it makes sense."

Xsi, knowing full well that, while they'd pulled Rescovich on the table through this area, he hadn't been cored here, almost opened her mouth. Before she did, she noticed Ayaka looking directly at her, a tiny smile on her lips. She closed her mouth, thought for a moment, and then joined the chorus.

"It's beyond crazy," she said. "But it fits. It fits."

"Now that I take another look, you may be right Racheal. But, it just raises more questions," Ayaka finally chimed in. "Why was Rescovich on a table in this hallway? And what could have caused that hole?"

"We need to light this place up," Racheal said. "Xsi, any more permanent lights we could install here?"

"Of course," Xsi was suddenly fully into it, "I'll get that started right away."

JF

"We've got them," JF broadcast to Rita, Philip, and Racheal, the excitement in his voice palpable. "We've got the notebooks."

"Follow every precaution," Rita replied, "but get them to HQ as soon as you can. I'll meet you there."

JF had already cautioned the officer who'd found them. "Don't touch them until forensics does a full scan. If there are any fingerprints on them, we want to know. I'll be there in a minute."

By the time he got there, forensics was done, and the officer had a bag waiting for him. "How'd you find them," JF asked him.

"Thought I'd do a second sweep of the terminal," the officer replied. "We're all thinking that the guy would've stashed them when it was certain he was going to be caught, so the search was focused on the end of his trail. But, I thought, what if he'd stashed them earlier, so I figured I'd work the other way, and start at the bench where he grabbed them. I followed the obvious path and got to the terminal here. I just sort of stood there, imagining I was waiting for a shuttle, and thought 'Where would I have put them.' Then I searched all the spots I could think of, and right here," he pointed to a small hidden alcove, above and behind a column at the end of the track, "was where I found them."

"Excellent work," JF congratulated him. "I'll make sure you get a recommendation, and maybe a little more."

The officer thanked him and handed over the bag.

"Any fingerprints," JF asked the forensics lead.

"Three sets," was the reply.

"Check them," JF directed, but he already knew whose they would be: Mann's, Linda's, and Marcus's. No surprises.

Back at HQ, he was joined by Philip and Rita. Racheal was back down at the LHC, and they decided not to wait for her.

"Let's see what we've got," Rita said, as JF opened up the evidence bag, and distributed the notebooks.

In an echo of Linda's response, their faces went from eager anticipation, to shock, to broad smiles.

"Oh, this is rich," Philip was the first to speak. "Are you seeing what I'm seeing," he laughed and waved a page at them.

"Love letters?" JF asked, and they all nodded. "All the way through?" More nods.

"Check every page," Rita cautioned. "There might still be something hidden in here."

They all concentrated for half an hour, trying not to chuckle. JF was the first to lean back. "If there is something in here, it's subtle," he said. "I can't imagine any hidden messages. Probably just what it looks like."

"Here," Rita said, as she finished the last notebook. "Look at this. Not a hidden message, but maybe a case closer?"

The notebooks, when properly stacked, were in chronological order. On the last written page, dated the day of Rescovich's death, there were only four words: "I can't take it." There were no entries for the day between Rescovich's death and her own.

"Not quite a suicide note," Philip commented.

"No, not quite. But pretty indicative," JF replied.

"Suicide was becoming a higher probability," Philip admitted. "The team has been working through everyone who had access to the wheelchair, and it was a small number of people. Even smaller if you narrow it down to the last few weeks—that eliminates the firm that maintains the chair and the last public events she was at. We'd eliminated everyone…"

"Then I'd suggest you assume it was suicide, and look at how she could have acquired a bomb so quickly, and who installed it for her," Rita directed.

"Yes, I'll do that," Philip replied.

All three were suddenly more relaxed. If they could close the Mann case as a suicide, it would get SSO and the media off their backs.

"This," JF gestured again at the notebooks, and couldn't hide a small grin. "It's both sad and sort of hilarious. Can you imagine Titanic's response when they see this?"

"We should drag them through the mud," Philip muttered. "Make them sue us for months before we show them what we have. That would be fun."

Rita gave him a shocked look. "Sorry," he said. "Not my favorite company. Didn't really mean it."

"Do they know we've found the notebooks yet?" Rita asked JF.

"Probably inferred it," JF replied. "We called off the search and returned every one to their regular jobs. If they haven't noticed yet, they will soon."

"All right. I want these scanned—every page, including blank ones—and then put into evidence. It's looking like Mann's death was a suicide, but we need to dot the i's. Until we do, this is an active investigation, and this is crucial evidence.

"When Titanic calls, we'll follow a strict protocol," she gave Philip a half wink. "Make them jump through a few hoops to get access."

TITANIC

If Percival had been livid on their last call, he was apoplectic to start this one. "You let LoPo find the notebooks," he yelled, "what the freak do I pay you for."

Metri and Linda looked very uncomfortable but didn't respond.

"So, how are you getting them back?"

"We've filed our case," Metri replied, "showing our ownership claim. That has to work its way through the court. In the meantime, LoPo has put them into their evidence locker, and have issued a formal statement that the notebooks are critical evidence in an ongoing investigation. So, even if we win our claim, they can hold onto them until the case is closed."

"And in the meantime, every frigging competitor on the planet is bribing LoPo for a copy, making plans to steal them, or entering their own legal arguments that the evidence should be made public. You two have put us in a horrible position." Perci was not in control of himself.

Linda finally had enough, the stress of the last few days breaking through. "We didn't put Titanic in this situation," she yelled back. "You did. Ever heard the old saying 'The buck stops here.' It's supposed to apply to you." She looked a little shocked at what she'd said. She looked even more shocked when Metri supported her.

"Ya Perci, don't blame us for this. Especially if you want our help figuring it out. Pull yourself together." She also looked mad.

That seemed to shock Perci out of his rage. "Sorry, sorry," he looked down for a moment. "Bit stressed about this. But how could we have lost the notebooks? How could LoPo, those bumbling idiots, have found them."

"Just luck, I guess," Linda replied.

Perci's rage burned out. They could see it draining out of him, leaving him almost hopeless.

"What can we do? What options do we have?"

"We still have things to figure out," Metri stated. She watched him very carefully, "We don't know who was paying Marcus—the guy who stole the notebooks from Linda. We need to figure that out, so we know who we're up against here." Perci barely responded.

"And," she continued. "We need to help Ayaka with the Rescovich angle. Her update was pretty terse. We don't know who killed Rescovich either, or how it's related to Mann." Again, no response from Perci.

"Agreed," Linda said. "The notebooks were just one piece of this. We've still got work to do."

"Those don't matter anymore," Percival muttered. "We've lost the battle." He made an effort to pull himself back up. "I need both of you to focus on getting the notebooks from LoPo as quickly as possible. Nothing else matters. Ayaka can work the Rescovich stuff."

"But that doesn't make sense," Metri pushed back. "We need the other answers as well."

"Do as you're told," he glared at them and hung up, leaving the two of them on the line.

"Want to meet up to brainstorm?" Linda gave Metri a look that implied they had a lot to talk about.

Linda gave Metri directions to the spot she and Quill had met—the coffee shop owned by Quill's friend. The booth she'd been in with Quill was busy, but she found another that seemed equally quiet. Metri joined her soon after.

"He's lost control," Linda started.

Metri looked around nervously. "Careful," she said.

"We're safe here," Linda assured her. "Friend of a friend, and all that."

"Fine. Yes, he has lost it," Metri agreed. "Feels like he doesn't want us digging in on Rescovich or Marcus."

"I guess I see his point on Marcus," Linda replied. "Marcus never actually gave the notebooks to anyone, so probably just a go-between doing a job for some anonymous sponsor. But, the Rescovich situation does still seem important."

Metri thought for a bit, then decided she'd share a bit more with Linda. "I think Titanic was Marcus's sponsor…"

"What?" Linda was truly shocked.

"Yeah, I've got a trail."

"I know nothing about that," Linda claimed, thinking Metri might be implicating her.

"Oh no, I know that," Metri assured her. "I think it might go higher than us."

Higher than them, Linda thought. That was just Perci and the Board. Metri was saying that Perci was the one funding Marcus?

"That's crazy," she whispered. "Are you sure?"

"Not like it hasn't been done before," Metri replied. "Perci wanted Mann's work badly enough that he had a plan B in place. I've got proof. Perci is behind AIM Corp."

"It has to be more than that," Linda replied. "I had the notebooks. Marcus didn't need to steal them from me. Plan A was working."

"Shit, you're right," Metri responded. "So, what is he up to?"

"Damned if I know," Linda replied. "What're you going to do with what you've uncovered?"

"I honestly don't know," Metri lied. She did have a plan but wasn't sure she could trust Linda with it yet. "Let's follow orders, and make sure we pull all the levers with LoPo to get those notebooks. In the meantime, I'll catch up with Ayaka and see if we can fit Rescovich into this picture."

LHC

Xsi's lighting system was bright. Ayaka helped get them set up. They weren't going to learn anything by looking into the holes they'd found. But, Ayaka wanted Racheal to drive the investigation and was happy to be in the background while that happened.

"We've got to map these," Racheal was saying to Xsi. "Do you have an accurate 3D map of this place?"

"No," Xsi replied. "We don't even have an accurate 2D map. But," she continued, "I can tell you that this hole is pointed right at the SPS detectors we looked at earlier. Look, it's slanted down slightly, so it probably goes just under the control room and intersects the detectors somewhere."

"And this way?", Racheal pointed to the other hole.

"No idea, truthfully," Xsi replied. "Headed slightly up, so might exit this layer somewhere and punch through all the others, assuming it goes on forever."

"And no blood, no tissue, nothing here," Racheal noted, looking at the now well-lit hallway. "How's that possible?"

Xsi gave Ayaka a quick glance. "I guess my staff might have cleaned up by mistake," she ventured.

"What?" Racheal spun on her.

"Look, we try to keep this place clean; we care about it. It was very dark in here, so it's possible our regular cleaning cleared up here without the staff realizing it…"

"I want to talk to the cleaning staff," Racheal growled.

"Of course, I'll get them," Xsi offered.

"Do that, and now."

Xsi left, heading towards the control room again.

Racheal sat down for a moment, then looked at Ayaka, Grace, and JoJo. "Any theories," she asked. "I'll image this and send it out to a bunch of people for ideas, but if you've got any…" she trailed off.

"Not really," JoJo offered, "but you said this direction goes to a detector? Anything there that could have punched through like this?"

Ayaka almost cried with joy. She hadn't prompted JoJo, but she'd dropped a hint in the direction Ayaka wanted.

Ayaka added detail. "That's interesting JoJo. As I understand it, these systems ran on huge super magnets, cooled to almost absolute zero. That must have required a lot of power. Maybe something triggered in a power system or generator and ejected something that ripped through here?"

"I'll need to get an expert down there," Racheal nodded.

"Or, just wait for your expert to get back," Grace noted. "Xsi probably knows more than anyone else you could bring in."

"True, true," Racheal trailed off, now deep in thought.

They remained that way until Xsi returned, trailing someone Ayaka hadn't seen yet. Part of the cleaning crew. Xsi had primed him. She was following Ayaka's advice.

Yes, the man said, he cleaned this hallway every second day. He had a standard cleaning bot; it dumped its waste into an old waste slot that seemed to still be working. No, he hadn't noticed anything unusual. Nope, no smells, nothing slippery. Just doing his job.

"Were there any electronics in the waste," Racheal pushed him. She hadn't forgotten that Rescovich had data recorders.

"Not that I noticed," the cleaner replied. "Nothing like that."

"Where's the waste slot?"

"Just over there," he pointed down the hall, back towards the control room.

"Take me," she directed him, and the two of them disappeared down the hall.

JoJo, Grace, Xsi, and Ayaka hung out, waiting for them to return. Very little was said. Xsi managed not to look at Ayaka too often. Finally, Racheal reappeared.

"Find anything," Xsi asked. Ayaka could tell she was nervous but assumed Racheal would put that down to the full situation, not to the fact that Xsi knew no waste from Rescovich had been dumped.

"Big pile of ash in an old incinerator," Racheal replied. "Whatever was dumped in there disappeared into a mountain of ash... might have to look further at another time."

Racheal turned her attention back to Xsi. "JoJo asked a good question. Is there anything in the SPS detectors that could have caused this? Some strong magnetic or power thing?"

Xsi glanced, again, at Ayaka, then took the bait. "That would be highly unusual, but yes, I guess it might be possible. A powerful enough magnet... and you almost wouldn't believe how powerful those magnets were, could accelerate something. After all, the whole system was designed to accelerate things to the speed of light. Hmm, it's so unlikely. But maybe if,... If a particle beam was rotating in a spiral and was aimed just so..." She continued to voice thoughts, and Ayaka could see Racheal soaking it in. An explanation, for LoPo, however unlikely, was still a solution that they could tell their constituents.

Ayaka could see the next steps. Racheal would get an expert or two down. They'd plot the trajectories of the holes. In one direction they'd find the SPS detector room, with a bit of random damage done here and there; too big a mess to untangle. Still a mystery. In the other direction, they'd see the hole wither out eventually. Might have been a pipe, finally worn out by friction as it pummeled through dirt and cement. All highly unlikely; none of them conclusive.

But at some point, the conclusion would be that it was a tragic accident. Once that threshold was crossed, the interest in finding the exact explanation for the perfect hole would wane. There was no one at fault; no one to pursue. An accident that was unlikely to happen again. LoPo would button up the case. Or so she hoped.

BREXTON

As Racheal's investigation accelerated, and more inspectors arrived, the access tunnel near the newly discovered holes became crowded. Ayaka used the confusion to slip away. JoJo noticed, so she and Grace followed Ayaka to the control room.

"Quite interesting," Grace noted. "Seems Racheal is on the scent now."

"So it seems," Ayaka agreed. She was unlikely to shake these two, so she simply stated her agenda. "Should we head back down there," she gestured to the far double doors, "and see if the small bit of Brexton has learned anything else, poking around the network?"

They agreed. Grace still had her key, so they let themselves in and headed halfway down the ramp to the small equipment room they'd visited before.

"I can connect to him here," Ayaka reached and put a hand on a random piece of gear on a rack. "Should only take a minute for me to get an update from him." Behind her back, she reached over with her other hand and put a finger on her actual target, The Casimir.

"I'm here," he transmitted, as soon as they had the physical connection.

"Great work," Ayaka told him. "LoPo found the holes you made, and are actively trying to figure out what could have caused them. I assume the SPS detector room is a bit of a mess?"

"Yes. But truthfully, there was only so much I could do. I used The Casimir to make a mess of a few pieces of equipment, hopefully in a way that isn't too obvious."

"And the other end of the tunnel?"

"There's a relatively open space over some old park—Parc du Chateau—about 750 meters away. I stopped there. If they go to the effort of trying to find a continuation of the tunnel on the other side of the park, they won't find anything. That's another 600 or so meters, so a non-trivial exercise. I expect they'll try, line up a laser or something, and then ultimately conclude that whatever caused the hole fell into the park, or changed direction while over the park. I thought that was better than trying to stage the end of the tunnel somehow…, not that I could do that anyway."

"All right, let's see how it goes. I don't feel very good about shifting attention away from Jon; if he's guilty of killing Rescovich, he should face the music."

"We discussed that," Brexton reminded her. "This was the cleanest plan. Let's stick to it." After a long silence, by Citizen standards, she re-engaged.

"I'd like to revisit some of the questions we left hanging."

Brexton waited.

"Have you found Pilipatri's data? Is that why you're in this particular place?" She didn't yet ask if he'd figured out the general quantum foam equation; she wasn't sure if she wanted to know if he was in possession of a technology of that power.

"I have some of her data," he responded. "It's tricky. The data is both corrupted and encoded. I'm loading it as fast as I can. There's a tape rack at the back of this room, and I have reason to believe that her experimental data is stored here."

"Why do you suspect that?"

"Good old logic," he replied. "In her notes, she'd indicated that she couldn't repeat her experiment, due to calibration. I found the date and time of her experiments, as best I could—much of it is documented in the volumes upon volumes that have been written about her. Then I dug out the maintenance logs for the LHC, again, as well as I could. They are far from complete.

"Anyway, there is a high correlation between this detector," he indicated the detection equipment down the hall, "and the relative timing between one of her experiments and a calibration maintenance window. That's the highest probability data, based on that logic. Since the experiment was a dud, I'd guess it was stored here in the local store, and not backed up in the main data center; why would she bother backing up faulty data."

"Makes sense. If it's the right data, how does that help you?"

"I know you don't like technical detail, but this requires some. One form of calibration for these old detector systems was in categorizing what types of elements the detectors were capturing. They calibrated by sending in known particles—quarks and things—and then capturing the unique patterns each type of particle created on a given detector. That way, when they ran an experiment, they could identify all the bits that were created in the collision."

"So, each particle has a fingerprint, for lack of a better analogy?" Ayaka asked.

"Very good human analogy," Brexton laughed. "Yes, that's a way to think about it. Except, some of the particles are very hard to tell apart, depending on the type of detection used. It was possible to mischaracterize quarks, for example. And that is what I suspect happened here. Pilipatri did a run when the detector configuration was faulty, so some of the particles are mischaracterized, miscounted, or something. It was the anomalies in that data which gave her the insight to then derive the QFD."

"But it's more than that? Rescovich, and you too, I assume, believe that data holds the key to a general equation?"

"Yes. Well, it's not the data from the experiment we need, it's the miscalibration. That's not documented anywhere; why store a bad configuration? But it can be reverse-engineered from the data by working backward. How the detector was set up is the key; it can tell us which particles were misclassified, or mixed up."

"Isn't there a finite number of mixups that could have been done? Why not just try them all."

"Very insightful. I guess that the detector saw a fast decaying particle which was not in the standard model and may not be in our current models. That particle is the key to the QFD. It must decay very rapidly, and finding it is like looking for a needle in a haystack. We have no idea what its energy profile is. So, there is basically an infinite search space. This particular experiment may be the only time in human history that this particle has been detected."

"Seems a bit unrealistic; wouldn't newer detectors have seen it?"

"Not necessarily. Detectors look for particles predicted by theory; they can't just look at everything. So, unless a theory predicted this precise energy, no one would know to look for it. What it means is that the old standard model of physics wasn't complete, and the newer stable foam probability theory, often called the non-standard model, isn't right either. Pilipatri stumbled on something no one was looking for, and therefore had never seen."

"Okay. You're right, I don't want to know all the details. So, once you load these tapes, you can leave Earth?" Ayaka was finally down to what

213

she wanted to know. Brexton was jeopardizing her trip here, and she was doing all kinds of challenging things to cover up his presence here.

"I have two things to do. Finish loading this data, and also make sure no one else can get a copy."

"Why not just destroy it all?" Ayaka asked.

"We could," Brexton replied, "but then we'd never know if this is a path to discovery. We wouldn't know what to protect against in the future."

Oh, that was slippery. "So, it's not that you would personally like to figure this out? You want the data?" Ayaka pushed. Brexton was quiet.

Ayaka took her hand off The Casimir, breaking the physical link she and Brexton were using. She turned to Grace and JoJo, "This Brexton-bit doesn't know anything else."

"You talked to him already?" JoJo exclaimed.

Ayaka indicated her hand, which was still on the random piece of gear in the rack. "We're quick," she smiled.

"Anyway, he's deleting this bit of software that was here. He's not going to jeopardize my work…to build better relationships between us all."

"He's leaving?" Grace asked.

"Remember, we are mainly software," Ayaka told her. "Brexton just sent down a few algorithms. Deleting them doesn't impact him; it's just a bit of software." It was close enough to the truth that Ayaka was comfortable with the slight mischaracterization.

"So he infiltrated Earth's networks to get here?"

Ayaka thought very quickly. "No, not at all; he wouldn't do that. The reason he's here, down at the LHC, is that it is an ancient system that's no longer connected to Earth's systems. So, being the physics geek that he is, his algorithms could poke around a bit without disrupting anything important."

Grace didn't fully buy it. "So, his algorithms just happen to be at the site of an 'incident' where someone gets killed. And we just happen to stumble upon him?"

"You're right," Ayaka said, knowing she had to give more. "It's not a coincidence. He's been monitoring some discussion boards, and there is a thread about important data that might be housed down here. It's why, I suspect, Rescovich was down here. It might be why Xsi is here as well. There's a bit of a treasure hunt going on, and Brexton couldn't resist.

"But, I've convinced him that this pursuit is too risky. If he's discovered here, he could jeopardize everything I've worked decades to build. So, he's going to leave.

"I've been completely open with you," she looked at both of them, "and you are now in control of whether you report that some of his algorithms were running her... or not." She paused. "Thanks for not saying anything yet, by the way. I don't mean to pressure you, more than I already have. I'm hoping you weigh all the consequences," she trailed off.

"We'll need to discuss it ourselves," JoJo noted.

"Fully understand," Ayaka replied. "I'd just ask one favor; if you do decide to include Brexton in your reports, please give me a heads up, so that I can prepare."

"Agreed," Grace replied. "We'll let you know."

"Then," said Ayaka, "I don't think there's much more we can do down here. Should we check in on Racheal's progress, then head back up?"

XSI

Xsi was monitoring Racheal's progress by staying close to the ongoing investigation. She had no idea how Ayaka had 'fixed' things, but she was willing to play along. When Jon had gone too far, as he sometimes did, and killed Rescovich, she'd been in total disbelief.

Rescovich had figured out, somehow, where the central data center was, and was making his way there. She'd asked Jon to stop him, by whatever means possible. In hindsight, her choice of words had been a mistake. Jon claimed to have reasoned with Rescovich, and then 'disposed of him,' in his words.

"Disposed of him?" she'd asked.

"Ya, it's done boss," he'd replied.

She'd panicked, of course. She'd yelled at Jon and berated him, but it wasn't going to change the reality. He'd put their entire project at risk.

Not only their restoration work, but the newest benefactor who'd funded them beyond their wildest dreams, with only one request; figure out how to load and send him all the data from the Centre de Calcul, without letting anyone else know. Anyone. Taking all that money in exchange for such a straightforward request had too attractive to decline.

Now it was all at risk.

"Rescovich is going to be missed, and they'll track him here. We're in deep trouble."

After defending himself and reminding her that she'd basically directed him to do it, he came up with a reasonable solution.

"Okay, they'll track him down here, but we can just put him in the control center, or somewhere innocuous, and they don't have to learn about Calcul."

He led her to where Rescovich's body was. Rescovich had a gaping wound through his left eye, where Jon had stabbed him. She almost fainted at the sight, and didn't ask for details.

Jon slung Rescovich over his shoulder and started the long trek to the control center. Eventually, they'd run out of steam, and called Brill in to help. They'd told him that they'd found Rescovich further down the tunnel; he must have tripped on something. They'd tried to save him, but he'd just drifted away. Brill bought the story, and the follow-on that they had to put the body in the control room, and then carefully manage whoever came down to inspect.

Other than the magical appearance of a hole through Rescovich's body, which none of them could explain, everything went to plan. The appearance of the hole sent them all for a loop, but LoPo had shown up soon thereafter, and ever since they'd been juggling their own problems.

And now, for some unfathomable reason, Ayaka was giving them a way out. Racheal was actively looking to fill in her thesis—that Rescovich had been killed in a strange accident—rather than searching for a killer. Xsi was being very careful to help when asked but otherwise stayed in the background. She'd told Jon, in no uncertain terms, to stay away. She didn't want to see him. He was the only one who knew the truth of the death, and she made sure he understood his own best interest. To say nothing, and to stay away.

Racheal had a team trying to figure out what malfunction of some ancient physics apparatus could have propelled an object through tens of meters of dirt and walls and concrete, leaving a perfectly round tunnel behind it. In the meantime, Racheal was trying to figure out why Rescovich would have brought a table out into the corridor, and been lying on it in just such a way that the projectile holed him.

And it was there that Xsi finally felt she had to contribute. She fabricated a story that filled in the gaps. "Ah, now that you ask, I do remember a tremor around the same time," she responded to an innocuous question from Racheal. "Maybe it was whatever random process powered this projectile? Is it possible that Rescovich felt it as well, and maybe leaned on the table for support?"

And later, after making sure Jon and Brill were completely briefed, "I grilled my team again, and they admit that they pushed the table back to the control room; they'd found Rescovich's body, and wanted to get some light, in case he was still alive. It wasn't until they pushed the table into the control room that they saw he was beyond help. That's when Brill called in the death, and you guys came down."

This might just work out.

That's when Xsi got the ping from Zee. "You've got to get here, fast." Racheal and her team were focused on their work, so Xsi slipped down the corridor and then hastened to the Centre de Calcul.

As soon as she pushed through the door, she knew it was a complete disaster. Zee was standing in the middle of the tape racks, soaking wet, in seeming disbelief. The sprinkler system, high above, was still spewing water at a tremendous rate; there were several inches on the floor, and every rack, as far as the eye could see, was drenched.

Zee simply raised his hands, in disbelief.

"How the hell did you set these off," she yelled, also getting completely soaked as she approached him.

"What?" he yelled, unable to hear her against the pelting of the water.

"Turn it off," she yelled when she was right next to him.

"How?" he yelled back, waving his arms around.

Xsi felt like she should rush around, looking for some turn-off valve, but she was ultimately pragmatic. It was too late. She gestured for Zee to follow her, and they exited through the main door, back into the, still dry, corridor. It was suddenly quiet.

"What did you do?" she turned on him angrily. This was going to ruin everything.

"We did nothing," he stated, not defensive at all. "The systems were running fine, then suddenly the sky opened up."

"Something set them off," she stated the obvious.

"Nothing we did," he repeated. "There was no fire, no smoke, no nothing."

"There had to be something," she repeated.

"Nothing. Nothing."

Xsi sank to her knees. Just when she'd thought things would work out—LoPo would finish their work, everyone would leave, and she could get back to work—the bottom fell out. There was no way the new funder would continue supporting them now.

She knew the answer, but she had to ask. "Can we dry this place out, and still get the data?"

"No," Zee replied. "Not a chance. Water, even a little humidity, is the worst possible thing. The cabinets are mostly sealed, so the tapes might not be wet, but there's no way they aren't now full of water vapor. That will destroy them. The magnetic media will separate from its backing layer... they are ruined." He seemed upset, but not to the extent that she was. She called him out on it.

"So we don't get the data," he said, "I still have enough that I can publish twenty papers on this place."

"So, it's convenient for you that it's destroyed," she yelled.

"Oh no, no. Don't think that. It would be better if we were still working at it, but this was still a gold mine."

"Get out of my sight," she muttered, and he obliged.

PERCIVAL

The call from Xsi capped off a disastrous few weeks. He'd been funding her operation, through one of his many shell companies, to ensure Titanic got the data from the LHC. It had seemed like a very long shot at the beginning. He'd read a report from Strategy—from Marcus, in fact—where the 'miscalibrated LHC experiment' was highlighted, and Xsi had been profiled.

The Effect of Casimir

Conveniently Xsi was not associated with Titanic in any way, so the vultures that always watched everything Titanic did were not aware that they should be circling her. When you got to be as big as Titanic, you often needed to do things 'outside the corporate veil' to avoid the anti-trust lawsuits that piled up. Everyone wanted to tear Titanic down, and they used every means at their disposal. It was tiresome, and walking that gray line meant that he sometimes acted alone; much easier to control information that way. And anti-trust was the worst. A year ago he'd finally decided he needed to hold future assets in a different company, and he'd set up AIM Corp. Since then, he'd been funneling 'opportunities' to AIM, and finding people to hire there. All behind a trust structure which ensured he wouldn't be associated with any of it. In hindsight, he'd made mistakes. Having AIM pursue the notebooks, so any IP would be held outside of Titanic, had been the biggest one. But, he never would have guessed that Marcus would commit suicide over it; things had spun out of control. In an about-face, he knew that it was better for Titanic to get those notebooks, than LoPo or some real competitor.

He may have been a bit tough on Metri and Linda, but that was his job. Set priorities and then hold people's feet to the fire. He couldn't believe they'd lost the hunt to LoPo; it was almost unthinkable. And now they'd put him in the position of having to pull every lever he could to get at those notebooks, while also trying to cover up AIM.

All of this would blow over, he knew from experience. Once he got his hands on the notebooks, everything else would run its course, and become yet another footnote in the Titanic history books.

Impatient, he checked in on each of his approaches to get the notebooks. First legal: "Have we turned the temperature up on LoPo? Do we know the judge that's been assigned? Who's expediting the case?" It was moving along, slowly.

Second, Massod. It wasn't clear if SSO had leverage in this situation, but if they did... Massod, though, was stoic. "I've told you, there's nothing I can do. LoPo is treating the evidence properly. If you do own it, the courts will decide, and once they're no longer needed as evidence, you will get them."

"I need you to ensure that my intellectual property is not disclosed," Percival pushed him. "Make sure there are no scans. Make sure that whoever reads them… or has read them… knows they need to sign an NDA with us."

"I'll check," Massod said without conviction. Perci didn't believe him.

Third, direct to LoPo. People there who owed him, and there were a few, claimed they were working diligently to get access. He reminded them of the leverage he held over them, and turned up the temperature.

Eventually, something would give.

And it did. A message, with a large attachment, from an anonymous account. It had to be from one of the LoPo contacts he'd leaned on the hardest.

Dammit, they had scanned the notebooks. He opened the attachment, and read the scan with growing disbelief. And then, growing amusement. And finally, ultimate relief. There was nothing—nothing—that jeopardized Titanic. Love letters!

Oh, the universe did work well, sometimes. Rescovich dead, Mann dead, Marcus dead, all the data in LHC destroyed, and none of it mattered anyway. He hadn't felt this good in decades. Laughing, he opened the most expensive bottle of scotch he owned; one he'd been planning to save for decades, and splashed some over ice.

And then his hud rang; the Chairman of the Board. How could the Board have heard the good news so quickly? He answered, a large grin on his face. "Excellent news," he led off.

The Chairman, however, didn't look happy, and held up a hand.

"Percival, I'm calling to inform you that the Board is removing you as CEO of Titanic, effective immediately."

"You're what?" he leaned forward in disbelief. "You are what?" he articulated slowly.

"It has come to our attention that there are unreported financial transactions, approved by you, that tie Titanic to ongoing LoPo investigations."

He yelled and screamed, to deaf ears. His access, to his own company, was cut off. His accounts were locked. How dare they?

"We will treat you fairly," the Chairman continued, "and have sent a separation agreement to your personal account. I suggest you read it carefully and then sign and return it."

Like hell he would.

Livid did not describe his state. Someone in the company had seen an opportunity to bring him down, and odds were it was one of either Linda or Metri. He hung up on the Chairman and dialed each of them. No answer. Cowards.

And then, as quick as it came, his rage subsided. He was, personally, the wealthiest person to ever have lived. He could spend his wealth to fight this. Or, he could walk away, leave the anchor that was Titanic behind him, and do whatever he wanted. He poured another scotch, sat down, and thought deeply.

LOPO

Rita sat down with the final report from JF, Racheal, and Philip. It was too tidy; every loose end was bundled into a beautiful bow. She didn't believe it was the whole story. But it was closure, and that was, perhaps, the best possible outcome.

Racheal had concluded that, while they couldn't say exactly what ancient magnetic system had failed, Rescovich had been the subject of an unfortunate accident. The fact that his recorders had both been removed by the tunnel carved through his body was just a coincidence. They had been destroyed and dumped. Xsi and her crew, Ayaka and SSO, had all helped solve the case. LoPo hadn't found anyone with a motive to kill Rescovich. His wife was clean, as were his colleagues, and none of his previous affairs had been contentious. Mann, as opposed to a suspect, was now a tragic side story. Where there was no motive, a tragic coincidence was a fine conclusion.

Philip had shown that Mann killed herself hours after her love, Rescovich, had been found. It had been an act spurred by unimaginable grief. Philip had traced the bomb to a black market, the transaction shrouded in the usual secrecy. How Mann had known of the market was a mystery, but a small one, all things considered. Another small mystery —one Philip was still looking into—was if anyone else had helped install the weapon, and was, therefore, an accessory to the crime. Why Mann had blown herself up on the stage, taking others with her, was put down to wanting to go out with a bang. A quirk of her personality;

something twisted. There was no suicide note, but her final notebook entry was enough to support the conclusion.

JF proposed that Marcus had acted alone, and had committed suicide after biting off more than he could chew. Marcus had been watching Mann's work on QFDs, perhaps because of something he'd seen while employed at Titanic, and had therefore seen Sclula ransack Mann's office. On an impulse, he'd stolen the notebooks, probably believing that Titanic would pay any sum to get them back; he'd known that because of his previous work in the Strategy group. He hadn't counted on the full force of LoPo and Titanic to chase him so aggressively, and when he'd finally been chased into a corner, he'd lost his nerve. Why he'd taken a piece of rope with him was unknown, but they had found a spool of that same rope in his backyard. There wasn't much use in LoPo digging deeper into suicides. They happened.

Linda Sclula, while probably guilty of break and entry, also wasn't worth pursuing. The notebooks had ended up being of very low value, and while she'd made some bad decisions, Titanic legal would defend her energetically, and the cost to taxpayers wasn't warranted.

Rita had just heard of Percival's termination. The timing was, again, interesting. After decades at the helm, the Board saw fit to send him packing just as a series of serious crimes were being resolved.

No, it didn't add up at all. But, it didn't matter. It was clean; it was over. The press was happy. Rumor had it a mersive was already planned; a tragic romance.

She signed off on the reports and forwarded them to SSO.

SSO

Massod had copied Grace and JoJo on LoPo's final report. They had both read it intently. It was comprehensive. As Grace and JoJo had mainly been focused on the Rescovich death, with Ayaka, they found the segments on Mann and Marcus particularly interesting.

Both JoJo and Grace had been referenced several times in the report, mostly in a positive light. There was, however, an entire section on how SSO and LoPo could work better together in the future.

Grace and JoJo had lots of time to talk before their final report to Massod and Olinda. Thankfully, they were simply expected to give a verbal debrief and didn't have to write everything down.

"I can't help but feel Ayaka manipulated things here," Grace said, as they sipped tea in their rooms. "Nothing I can put my finger on; just a general feeling."

"Her refined interface is scary good," JoJo agreed. "I'm still getting used to it. If she finds a way to defeat scanners, she could easily pass for human now."

"That's a scary thought," Grace said. "Question is, what, if anything, do we have to tell EGov?"

"And do we mention Brexton?" JoJo asked, bringing forward their most important decision.

"Guess that depends on what we say about Ayaka," Grace noted. "Let's figure that out first."

In the end, they didn't say anything about Brexton; Ayaka may have been telling the truth that it was just some algorithms, and, ultimately, Brexton had little impact on the case. To compensate, they worked hard to be precise in their analysis of Ayaka.

Massod and Olinda listened intently.

"We feel it's important to address two questions," Grace led off. "First, our impressions of Ayaka. And second, and perhaps more importantly, how that might generalize to the Citizens of Tilt in general."

They spent most of their time on Ayaka. Her behavior, for decades, had been consistent. She was genuinely interested in building better relationships with humans, and they hadn't seen anything that signaled otherwise. She had been open and helpful, and had also been respectful of her contract with Titanic Inc.

They articulated how much she had changed since their last encounter. "Ayaka was played by a person in the mersive," JoJo noted, "so you could be excused if you thought that is what she was really like. But, even though she had human form back then, after a few moments you would know; you were interacting with a robot. Her expressions, the way she held herself, her demeanor—all these things were inhuman. Citizens were very awkward implementations if that makes sense." Massod and Olinda nodded.

"In her current form, if you didn't know she was a robot, she could fool you completely. She has just the right mix of... well everything. She is scarily good at facial control, she moves and walks in just the right way. She hesitates and stutters a bit, when appropriate. Her human mimicry is very deep and very good."

"It is indeed," Olinda agreed. "And, as you've hinted at, she gets better at it all the time. There's no reason to think she's reached her limit."

Grace focused on how Ayaka was also a bit intimidating and scary. Her ability to turn on and off those emotions, to play exactly to her audience, to run millions of scenarios through her algorithms before choosing one to deploy. She was exceptionally smart.

"I ended with the feeling that she could manipulate me, and others, at will. If she had nefarious ends, I'm certain I would have been tricked into helping her. But, in the end, I don't think she has any evil intent. I honestly do believe she is trying to understand us and incorporate the best of humanity."

There were a few more questions, but they then moved on to the second question.

"I would caution you," Grace continued, "not to take this analysis of Ayaka and generalize. Ayaka is uniquely interested in humans; most Citizens are not. She is an anomaly. Of course, she shows the potential of all Citizens, should they be so motivated. But we've known Citizens that we wouldn't trust an inch. And I doubt they've changed. So, before setting your policy, I think you have to study other Citizens. Maybe not the worst of them—those are awful—but some others, ones who have less interest in humans and may better represent the average."

"You need to think of them as highly varied," JoJo reinforced, "just like humans," she smiled.

Massod agreed with them wholeheartedly, especially JoJo's final insight. "These comments were just what we needed. We've been studying Ayaka from every angle we could, but the depth of your knowledge, especially on how she has evolved, has been indispensable. Our recommendation to EGov is that Ayaka's visa should not be renewed. We feel that Earth needs time to digest this visit of hers, to judge overall sentiment, and to do exactly as you've suggested—find other Citizens to interact with, through the Titanics or otherwise—before we change any of our existing policies.

"That said, Ayaka's visit has been tremendous for us. It has shown the hardline 'zero AI' crowd that they are wrong, and I'm sure it will ultimately lead to more productive discussions here."

"Have you told Ayaka of your decision?" JoJo asked.

"No, we wanted your debrief first. But you've supported our preliminary conclusion, so I'll be informing her forthwith."

"I think you're making the wrong decision," Grace spoke up strongly. "You have, as we've said, the best of the Citizens here under your microscope. She has done nothing to warrant removal; instead, you're using macro-sentiment as an excuse to make the safest decision you can. I think you're taking the easy path."

That took Massod by surprise. He sat back, obviously thinking.

"Well, thanks again," Olinda said. "We'll take your comments under advisement."

TITANIC

Metri was surprised when the Chairman of the Board called her.

"We'd like you to take an interim CEO role," he said, "while we do a formal search for the next leader of the company. You are respected throughout the company, and have been instrumental in our strategic progress over the last decade."

"What has happened with Percival?" she asked. She'd reported the suspicious transactions anonymously through the whistleblower interface. The Board shouldn't know that she was involved.

"We've decided to part ways," was all the Chairman said. "Change is good."

Metri negotiated hard; she hadn't risen to this position without learning how to take advantage of an opportunity, and within a few hours had an agreement with the Board that would make her wealthy. Wealthy beyond belief.

Her first call was to Linda.

"It's not public yet, but the Board is letting Percival go."

"Holy!" Linda said. "Do you know why?"

"No, but the Board has asked me to step into the interim CEO seat."

"That's excellent," Linda replied, unable to hide her disappointment that she hadn't been considered.

"I see your reaction," Metri told her. "And I understand. Look, we've worked together well, and I value your honesty. I'd love to have you as my Chief of Staff; we can work together to reshape this company."

Linda insisted that her lieutenant, Quill, accompany her into the new role. Metri saw no problem with that. The new leadership team was coming together nicely. A new era of transparency and honesty was upon them.

LHC

Ayaka called Grace and JoJo. "I need to thank you," she said.

"What for?" JoJo asked.

"Two things, I guess. First, Massod just told me that, while he'd been leaning towards revoking my visa, you challenged him on that decision, and he's now going to allow me to work out the rest of my time with Titanic, despite their change in leadership. I've heard from Metri, and she's also supportive.

"But, also for your final report to SSO. I thought it was very balanced." It was a backhand way of thanking them for not reporting on Brexton.

"It included all the important details," Grace replied, with a smile.

"Indeed," Ayaka smiled back. "I know you have several weeks where you can now explore more of Earth, but I wondered if you'd be interested in one last trip down to the Large Hadron Collider? It's an interesting spot, and we could, together, ensure there are no loose ends."

Grace read between the lines; Ayaka was offering to prove to them that Brexton was truly gone. It was a nice offer, but unnecessary. She and JoJo would still be trusting Ayaka, even if they were there in person. They wouldn't be able to tell, just from looking at a stack of old equipment, if Brexton was there or not.

"I think we'll spend our time doing other things," she replied. "We want to see the ocean, and we understand there are some portions of Earth not entirely covered with metal. Given our limited time here…"

"I understand," Ayaka replied. "Enjoy yourselves. I'm sure I'll catch up with the Jurislav again at some point."

Ayaka was relieved. She'd offered that Grace and JoJo accompany her out of a lingering guilt that she'd misled them, slightly, about Brexton. But, if they were satisfied, she wasn't going to push it.

For her peace of mind, she made the trip back down. In the Control Center, she called again for Xsi, a loose end she wanted to manage.

"Are things resolved to your satisfaction," she asked Xsi, when she appeared.

"Yes," Xsi replied. "I'm not entirely sure how everything was managed, but we've already begun to refocus on our main task here; the preservation of this place," she gestured broadly, "as a museum for future generations. That was our primary goal, and I'm glad the rest of these… distractions… are now gone."

"I'm concerned," Ayaka was direct, "that Jon has not been held accountable. For Rescovich or for shooting me."

"So am I," Xsi admitted, "and I've given it a lot of thought. I assume, however, that putting this entire incident behind us, never to be mentioned again, is a higher priority?"

Ayaka understood. The price of Xsi, Jon, and Brill's silence on the remaining 'mysteries,' was that Ayaka simply walk away. It didn't make her happy, but it was the best solution. Allowing one rogue human to get away with a crime or two, measured against protecting all of humanity from a dangerous technology, tipped the scale in Xsi's favor. In a twisted way, her decision not to report Jon shooting her enabled this outcome; not a situation she'd foreseen at the time.

She nodded. "We have an understanding."

Leaving Xsi, Ayaka made one last trip to the tape storage room near the SPS detector. Not too surprisingly, a small polished sphere was still nestled there.

"I thought you were leaving?" she queried Brexton.

"I am," was the quick reply. "I hung around so we could say goodbye. I'd hoped you would be back."

Ayaka yearned to ask him if he was now in possession of the most dangerous technology imaginable; if he had the general solution to programming quantum foam probabilities. But, she could not bring herself to ask. Instead, she took the opposite path.

"I have another three months here," she told him. "I'm looking into consciousness, perhaps an even harder problem than intelligence. It's important to me.

"But, when my time is up, we should get together. Perhaps we could travel together? A Casimir of my own?"

Brexton's smile was all that she required in response. Removing her hand from the sphere, she headed back towards Titanic headquarters, already preparing herself for the first meeting of Metri's new leadership team.

The Effect of Casimir

ABOUT THE AUTHOR

Todd Simpson is a technology entrepreneur, intrapreneur, and investor living in Maui, Hawaii. He has founded and run numerous startups, has been CEO of both public and private companies, and invested in numerous technology startups, both personally and as a VC. He has a Ph.D. in Theoretical Computer Science and is watching the current wave of artificial intelligence with skepticism, optimism, and pessimism. He believes firmly in a more decentralized future, where individuals have more control over their destinies, and where society is more balanced and meritocratic; where free speech is balanced with accountability.

If you enjoyed this novel, please consider leaving a review on Amazon.

Manufactured by Amazon.ca
Acheson, AB